DEATH ON THE PROWL

DEATH ON THE PROWL

Ann Granger

HEADLINE

First published in 2024 by
HEADLINE PUBLISHING GROUP LIMITED

1

Cataloguing in Publication Data is available from the British Library

ISBN 978 1 0354 1146 7

Typeset in Adobe Garamond by Palimpsest Book Production Limited, Falkirk, Stirlingshire

Printed and bound in Great Britain by Clays Ltd, Elcograf S.p.A.

HEADLINE PUBLISHING GROUP LIMITED
An Hachette UK Company
Carmelite House
50 Victoria Embankment
London EC4Y 0DZ

The authorised representative in the EEA is Hachette Ireland, 8 Castlecourt
Centre, Dublin 15, D15 XTP3, Ireland (email: info@hbgi.ie)

www.headline.co.uk
www.hachette.co.uk

I would like to thank my grandson, William Hulme,
who kindly read through an earlier version of the manuscript
and made several helpful comments. Hope you enjoy
the finished story, Will!

Not to forget Coco, the inspiration for the pugs!

But the cat walked by himself, and all places were alike to him.
Rudyard Kipling, *Just So Stories*

Chapter 1

Ian Carter was well aware that, as a career police officer, he'd often been absent or distracted from family matters. Perhaps that had contributed to the breakdown of his marriage. Certainly, when they had still been together, his then wife, Sophie, had been more than ready to remind him of his failings. These had included his frequent preoccupation with criminal matters and often physical absence on police business.

'You seem to spend so much time dealing with so many dreadful people!'

He had pointed out the purpose of his job was to make sure the dreadful people did the time. Mistake.

'And I don't appreciate bad jokes on the subject, Ian.'

She'd also complained that he had a policeman's suspicious mind. *And that isn't attractive, Ian, really, it's not!* The words echoed in his head. He had been tempted to reply, *Why? Have you something you'd like to hide?* And he'd known that the reason he'd never asked was because he already knew the answer. Sophie was planning her escape from their marriage; and an old admirer, Rodney, was lurking in the background. *You're not jealous of Rodney, are you, Ian? He's an old family friend. I've known him all my life.*

Eventually, he'd told her he was certainly not jealous. Definitely not of Rodney the man, who was prosperous, smug, pink-faced and a tad overweight. But that was Carter's opinion. He conceded that Rodney had a golden touch in business matters; and would be well able to support Sophie in a manner Sophie thought she deserved. But neither was Carter a fool. He wished she would just make up her mind. In the end she had done so, and left.

'Of course she did!' pointed out a worldly-wise colleague at the time. 'Telling her you *weren't* jealous, well, it was like holding open the door for her; and offering to carry her suitcases to the car.'

Still, he liked to think that, despite his failings as a husband, he'd done his best as a parent, no matter what Sophie might have suggested. Sophie, together with Rodney and the couple's young son, now lived in France. Millie, his daughter, had been packed off to boarding school in England. Time not spent at school was divided between her mother's new household and his, such as his was.

'Dad?'

This from Millie, standing in the doorway and eyeing him sternly. It was half term, and she was spending it with him. Clearly, she did not mean to waste valuable time.

'We really need to talk.'

She was propped against the frame of the open door into the kitchen, and he was struck by how much taller she seemed to have grown. She wasn't a little girl: she was a teenager. She wore leggings terminating in flower-patterned laced boots; a baggy sweater with the sleeves pushed up above her elbows, and her arms were festooned with bangles of the sort sold at craft fairs. More alarmingly, she was beginning to look and sound like her mother. That minatory gleam in the eye; the reproachful tone; ah, yes, he remembered all so well . . .

'What about?' he asked warily.

She came into the room and advanced on him ruthlessly. 'You need someone,' she said.

He knew what was coming, but still asked, 'What for?'

'Look at this place!' She gestured around her at the sitting room, with its jumble of furniture.

OK, it wasn't the former manor house not far from Lyon which Sophie, Rodney and their infant son enjoyed. But it suited him. He defended himself.

'I've got a cleaner. Her name is Katie. You've met her.'

She uttered a faint dismissive sound. 'I *know*! *Yes,* I've met Katie. And, by the way, you need to have a word with her about bleach. She's mad keen on the stuff. I've told you before about it. After she's left the kitchen and bathroom stink of it. At least get some air freshener. But that's not what I mean. Look around!'

Ian found himself looking furtively about him, but he still wasn't sure what he should be looking for. 'What?' he mumbled.

'This place is exactly the same as when you moved in here!' Seeing his puzzlement, she added crossly, 'It ought not to be! Dad, face it. It's like, like you just unpacked.' Her tone changed to the kindly but firm. 'I worry about you.'

Hang on, wasn't he the one who worried about her? When did they exchange roles? Apparently, while he wasn't paying attention.

'You need to move on! You and Jess could set up a proper home . . .'

Proper home? His house was small but warm and he liked to think it was cosy. He toyed briefly with the idea of sharing it with Jess Campbell. It was an attractive idea. But Carter heard himself say loudly and very firmly, 'No!'

'Don't say "no" like that.' She was unimpressed. 'You sound like a policeman.'

That was Sophie's voice absolutely. Carter rebelled.

'I am a policeman!'

'You are a superintendent and everyone says you've had a top-notch career . . .'

Who are these people who reckon I've had a great career? Carter wondered. *And why do they use the past tense? I'm not ready to be put out to grass!*

'But what about home life? Unless I'm here, you're on your own. Don't let chances slip by, Dad. You and Jess get on so well and—'

Time to stand up for himself. He took a deep breath and said aloud, 'Millie, take it from me, it's a great mistake to try and organise other people's relationships.'

'I'm not organising you!' she protested huffily.

'You're doing your best. Look, sweetheart, I appreciate your concern. But if there are any changes to be made in my life, I will make them. I realise you mean well, but I don't need help.' He saw her mouth open to argue and added quickly, 'Can we leave it at that, please?'

'All right,' said his child graciously. 'For now.'

He remained staring at the spot where she had been standing. She'd made a dignified retreat to her room; where she had probably turned on her computer. *It's what they all did,* he thought, *or seemed to be what they all did, youngsters. They retreated to an artificial space, probably because real space was too difficult to deal with.* That was a concept too alarming for him to deal with at the moment. But it wasn't a thought that went away. Instead, it threw up a memory of a toy bear named MacTavish which had been Millie's one-time confidant, friend and constant companion. *Where was MacTavish now?* he wondered. Why could he, her father, not offer the support a toy bear had once done? He could run a crime investigation department, with all its twists and turns, unexpected horrors and moments of success or failure, run it pretty efficiently. Now it appeared a piece of cake compared with running his own life.

He went to the window and stared out into the night scene with the streetlamps glimmering and only the occasional dog walker venturing out into the cold. *Somewhere out there,* he thought, *crime is being planned or is already underway. The weather is never discouraging enough to deter the criminal world.*

So-called white-collar crime did not have to consider the weather, of course. But criminal activity is a many-headed hydra. Somewhere out there something was about to happen. Who knew where? Or why? Or of what kind?

The light was still showing under Millie's door when he went to bed. He tapped on it and called, 'Goodnight, love!'

'Night, Dad!' came the reply, muffled by what sounded like a soundtrack from a film.

Tomorrow, he thought, *I'll suggest a game of chess, or Monopoly, or something. Why didn't I suggest that this evening?* Self-reproach filling his head, he slept very badly. That's what a guilty conscience did to you.

Or what it did to the honest citizen. Guilty conscience, in his experience, seldom troubled the career criminal. Even when heinous crimes had been committed, they rarely accepted the blame for what they'd done. Unless they were going up before the parole board, of course. Then they were quick to say they had changed.

Anger, that was what so many of them felt. Anger against a world that somehow had cut them loose from society, and from what they believed was theirs by right, whatever that might be. It was the same kind of emotion, absolving them from blame, that meant they also so seldom took the responsibility for what they had done. It was always someone else's fault, even the victim's.

He fought back, didn't he? What was I supposed to do? The aggrieved voice of one teenage mugger echoed in his ear. Useless to attempt to explain that what he ought not to do was attempt to mug an innocent pedestrian in the first place, let alone stab the victim. Such logic bounced off a wall of incomprehension. No wonder he worried about his daughter, soon to leave school and set forth into the world unprotected. *Any ideas, Sophie?* Ian snarled mentally. *Over there in France, living comfortably, washing your hands of inconvenient details?*

He didn't know it then, but he was not the only one facing tricky personal problems; and some cannot be resolved by thinking about them. Some require action.

Chapter 2

Elsewhere, the evening was clear and cold; and out in the countryside, far from the city streetlamps Carter had seen from his window, it was also very dark. The moon was a perfect sickle hanging in the indigo sky; like a giant Christmas bauble that someone had forgotten to take down on Twelfth Night. But the light it cast was limited to its immediate surrounding sky. This other watcher, in the concealed spot he'd chosen, stamped chilled feet and thrust hands deep into pockets. It didn't make any difference. At least the earlier rain had stopped, but it was still bitterly cold and the movements were an instinctive attempt to generate more warmth and fostered the illusion that toes and fingers were less chilled. Relief only lasted for a moment, though, and then reality returned. Too bad; the watcher could wait it out. It was nearly time to make his move. He felt that concentration of the senses experienced by the hunter when the prey is almost within reach. The prickle that ran along the spine. His hearing was alert for the smallest sound.

But perhaps he wasn't alone? Something else had moved first in the darkness. There was a faint rustle beneath the leylandii that stood lined up like guardsmen along the roadside edge of the property, and behind which he'd chosen to conceal himself. He raised a hand to push aside their wintery foliage and peered into the blackness, muscles tensed, ready to defend or attack as required. But he could make out no more than an indistinct

7

darker patch in the murk at the foot of the trees. Then it – if it had ever been there – was gone. The watcher pulled out a mobile phone and pressed it to read the time. Not much longer. No point in getting jumpy now, imagining things. It had probably been a cat . . . or a fox. Yes, most likely a scavenging fox. But the sounds and scents of countryside unsettled him. He had an impulse to get the business over and done with. Time to make a move, to get what he had come for. No more putting it off. He pushed open the wrought-iron gate. It creaked and he wondered whether the sound could be heard within the cottage, like a warning signal. No, that was unlikely. He was the only one whose nerves were on edge, he told himself. The other one, he was sitting comfortably indoors, imagining himself without a care in the world. Well, something will have to be done about that! It should have been done long before. Nothing is gained by putting things off.

The watcher set off down the path, the gate closing behind him with another mocking creak. It began to rain again, quite heavily, as if all nature were taking an interest in what he did; and joining forces against him. That was an uncomfortable thought and he pushed it away.

Behind him, the breeze rippled through the trees again and another shape briefly shimmered across a moonlit corner of the garden, and was lost in the tangle of shrubs. The night has its own inhabitants, each about their own business. Even the fox had paused to watch with its yellow eyes as the caller reached the door, before it slipped away.

If Jeremy Harrison felt surprise on seeing his visitor, that wasn't the emotion that registered on his face. As the unexpected caller observed, it was more in the nature of annoyance.

That encouraged the new arrival. 'Put your nose out of joint, has it? My turning up? You might try and look pleased to see me, Jerry!' He grinned, nearly laughed. But that was nerves, not humour. *Get a grip!* he ordered himself.

'Why?' retorted Harrison. His original surprise was giving way to anger. What was so damn amusing? Fellow was standing there on his doorstep, grinning like the Cheshire Cat. Pleased to see him? Of course he wasn't. He scowled out into the cold winter evening and the rain threw a handful of what felt like ice pellets striking his face. His impulse was to recoil back into the warmth of his hallway. But he couldn't do that. He had to stand his ground, rain or no rain.

The caller didn't offer a reason, only said, 'It's perishing cold out here, old son.'

'It's still winter, and it's been cold for a couple of months,' parried Harrison. 'You haven't turned up out of the blue to tell me about that, I suppose.'

He remembered the last time they'd met. It had been a very long way from here; somewhere that could hardly have been more different from the present location; and the weather had been decidedly hot. This meeting now was not only in sharp contrast weather-wise but, unlike the previous chance encounter, had evidently been planned by the caller. Yet the whole thing was wildly, what? Bizarre? Perhaps, perhaps not. Life had a way of throwing up unexpected mantraps. Perhaps, years ago, when they'd bumped into one another in that expatriate workers' club amid the desert sands, it had only been, after all, a pre-run of this encounter on a wet, near-freezing late evening in the English countryside.

The caller was speaking again, in that same maddeningly chatty tone.

'You need to get a plumber in to look at the overflow. There's water dripping off this thing you call a porch . . .'

The visitor jabbed a finger upwards to indicate the tiled shelf projecting from the cottage wall and supported by a couple of unpainted wooden posts with nails protruding from them at random intervals. This suggested climbing roses; so possibly the porch had a more eye-pleasing appearance at a different time of year. Harrison already had a plan to fix it in the spring. In the meantime, it was no damn business of anyone else's; and it was particularly annoying to be told to do something that was already planned. What was more, a glint of mockery in the caller's eye knew this. Harrison wanted to snap, 'Shut up and go away!' But he didn't.

The caller seemed intent on rabbiting on about it.

'By morning it will have frozen. You need to get up in the loft and take a look at the tank. You don't want the ceiling caving in on you later on, when you're tucked up snug in your bed. You're some sort of engineer, aren't you? I'd have thought you'd fix it straight away. You *do* fix things, don't you, Jerry?' The visitor gave a semblance of a smile, but this time there was no humour in it. 'And don't you let this place out in the summer?'

'Don't stand about under the porch, then,' said Harrison curtly, realising, even as the words left his mouth, that they might sound like an invitation to come indoors. That was certainly not what he had intended. But he was shaken at seeing the visitor; and it had thrown him off his stride. Moreover, the remark about his letting out the cottage to holiday-makers in the summer suggested the caller had been taking an interest in him for some time. To have expected that the visitor might have phoned ahead to let him know he was coming tonight was also a waste of time. Of course he wouldn't; because he knew full well that, forewarned,

Harrison would've gone to earth, like the fox that haunted his garden after dark. The caller would have knocked at the door in vain. His quarry would have long gone.

So he felt unable to do anything about it, and was seized by a paralysis that was mental, not physical, in origin. He should slam the door in the visitor's face. He still wanted to do that. But the moment for it had passed. He should have done so as soon as he saw who the new arrival was. Now he felt oddly powerless. He couldn't even contact the police. The caller wouldn't allow it. In any case, what would he tell the cops? The forces of law and order were miles away from here. Even if they took his appeal for help seriously, they still couldn't get here in time. He didn't even have the option of phoning the pub down the road and asking the landlord to do something on his behalf. He was on the point of being taken prisoner, here in his own home. Indeed, he'd already been rendered powerless by his own earlier inaction. Standing here, as he did, letting the newcomer take all the initiative, make the running . . .

Now he simply stood aside as the newcomer pushed past him, scattering moisture and leaving wet footprints on the hall tiles. Those wet marks increased Harrison's resentment. They appeared symbolic, marring the perfection of the space, his space. A fresh blast of icy wind blew through the open doorway, causing Harrison to slam it shut in an automatic gesture. Too late, he realised that he'd lost the last chance of escape.

He watched with increasing but silent fury, a small knot of fear forming inside him, as the newcomer took off his waxed coat and hung it up with others on the row of hooks, screwed into the wall for that purpose. Drops of the rain that had adhered to the outer fabric now began to trickle off the garment and form a small puddle on the floor. The puddle began to spread, eating up the footprints, underlining that, from now on in, things could only get worse.

'I'm surprised you didn't sell this place, along with everything else.'

Why shouldn't I? Harrison wanted to shout. *It was mine. I could sell it all if I wanted. Every porcelain ornament, every smoke-darkened oil portrait of forgotten Victorians, every bit of silver that made work cleaning it. And I did sell it. It's absolutely nothing to do with you. This is my life and I run it as I wish!*

But he had never been able to run it as he wanted. He'd only deluded himself into thinking that he could, seizing the reins of his own destiny. A stupid fancy, that was what it had been. Harrison said nothing . . . and as for Destiny, that had proved an unbroken horse, galloping off into the distance.

There was a small mirror on the wall beside the coatrack. The visitor had been peering into it as he spoke, back turned to his unwilling host. He gave every sign of being at ease. Not at all worried, as Harrison was. He'd soon be totally in control.

Do something! urged the voice in Harrison's head. *Don't just stand here letting it happen!* But its tone was forlorn, despairing.

The newcomer continued to chat as though this was a regular social visit. 'I called by back in the summer, but I missed you. You were away abroad somewhere. A couple with a young family were staying here. But I'm a patient man. I can wait. And lo and behold! Eventually the wanderer returned.'

'What do you expect me to say?' the goaded Harrison snapped. 'Congratulate you?'

'I could use a whisky, Jerry.' The unwished guest was smoothing down his hair as he spoke, using both palms. Satisfied at last, he turned to face Harrison.

Before the unrelenting stare, Harrison capitulated. Nothing for it but to lead the way into his warm and comfortable sitting room. Until just a few minutes ago it had been a snug little refuge. It had now been invaded by the newcomer; and he would never feel the same in here again, thought Harrison sadly. He brought out the bottle of whisky and hunted out a couple of tumblers, aware his visitor was watching him closely. But his original despair was fading, displaced by rage. How dare this wretch invade his home, his privacy, threaten him psychologically and – quite possibly – physically? That was when he remembered the knife.

It was a small implement, with a carved bone handle and a short, but sharp, blade, a souvenir of his travels. He remembered buying it from a stall in a bazaar. He had a flash of memory, not clear, but a moment of heat, dust, noise, so different from the cold, damp English winter. To peel fruit, that's why he'd bought it. Now he kept it in his drinks cupboard, to facilitate the opening of sealed bottles. It wasn't much of a weapon, but it was the only one to hand. The only chance he might have. He slid it into his sleeve.

Five minutes later, they sat either side of the fire, drinks in hand. Anyone, looking in through the window, would have thought them a couple of old friends settling down for a pleasant evening's chat and memory-sharing.

The visitor raised his glass in salute. 'Not too late to wish you a Happy New Year, Jerry, I hope.'

Harrison said nothing, burying his nose in the whisky tumbler.

'You owe me, old lad,' said the other, still speaking pleasantly.

'Do I, hell!' objected Harrison.

'And I've come to collect. Don't say you weren't expecting me, sooner or later.'

Harrison admitted, 'I thought you might turn up one day.'

'There you go, then, Jerry. And here I am. You know, you really should have scarpered while you could. Hanging around here, well, that was always asking for trouble. Just think, you could have sold this place and bought somewhere in a warmer climate. Spain, perhaps? Or Italy? Did you not think of me?'

'Why?' snapped Harrison. He felt the fury rising in him again, displacing the paralysis induced by shock. 'Why the hell should I sell the cottage? It suits me down to the ground, and, anyway, it has nothing to do with you. Nothing at all! You play no part in my life. You never have. Your opinions mean nothing to me.'

This elicited a particularly mirthless smile. 'They should, Jerry. You must know that. But perhaps you don't know me well enough, old chap. Or not as well as you thought you did.' He raised his glass in salute. 'A funeral libation! Your funeral, of course.' He drained the whisky in one draught.

Harrison knew his chance had probably gone, but rage flared up again and gave him strength, and the resolve needed. He said as carelessly as he was able, 'You can skip the humour.'

As he spoke he picked up the whisky bottle, as if to offer the visitor a top-up. He let his other his arm drop casually by the chair, and felt the little knife slide into his hand. It was like the unexpected, comforting touch of a friend. His fingers closed tightly on its handle, feeling the uneven shapes carved in the bone.

The thought flashed through his mind: *This is the way murder often happens . . . No one intends it or plans it.* Then he hurled the whisky bottle at the intruder and, as the wretch jerked aside to avoid the missile, Harrison launched himself after it, knife in hand.

Chapter 3

Jess Campbell pushed open the car's front passenger door. Immediately the warm air of the interior was dispelled, a bitingly cold breeze ruffled her short red hair and she shivered. DS Bennison, newly promoted and starting to wonder whether this was worth it, muttered resentfully from behind the driver's wheel: something about the bad luck of being called out on a morning as cold as this.

'All part of the job, Tracy,' Jess told her. 'Think of it as a trip out into the fresh air, out of the office.'

'HQ has central heating,' retorted Bennison, flicking her long black braids. Quickly, she added, 'I'm not complaining about the job! Just the – just thinking aloud, ma'am.' She reminded herself that this wasn't the moment to start whingeing. This was all part of the career she was working so determinedly to make.

It was clear what kind of event had brought them. All the other familiar vehicles parked around them told the tale. Jess, the investigating officer in charge of whatever this turned out to be, was last to arrive, that was all. She exited the car and surveyed the scene.

There was the van of the cleaning company whose scheduled visit had been booked for this morning. The company had a key to the property; and the cleaners opened the front door to find the body. Following them, in a macabre procession, had come the local police, the doctor to certify death, the crime-scene manager, the photographers and other scene-of-crime specialists.

The presence of the doctor's car signified he'd waited for CID to arrive. She recognised Tom Palmer's vehicle.

No, not only Palmer had waited. That windowless black van over there was standing by to take away the body, shrouded in its bag, once Jess and Bennison had viewed the scene of the crime. Another of the usual team was there ahead of them. Jess recognised a family-sized 4x4 parked discreetly under trees a little down the road. Sergeant Sean Stubbs was somewhere about.

Bennison scrambled from the driver's seat, slamming her door in a way that expressed her feelings perfectly. There was a rustle and flap of wings from a nearby oak tree. Crows flew up and circled overhead. They had gathered to watch, up there in the ancient branches, and the sound startled them. Jess thought: *They know death is about. Crows are always on the lookout.*

Like the crows, the contract cleaners had been watching, sitting huddled and resentful, wanting to be free of all this. But they'd been ordered to wait. They might have to answer some questions. Seeing the two plain-clothes officers' approach gave them a chance to voice their grievances. The driver opened his door and shouted, 'Are you the ones we've had to hang about waiting for?'

'That's us,' Bennison told him, cheering up now that someone else had been as inconvenienced as she was.

'We only found the ruddy body!' protested the spokesperson. 'We can't tell you what happened. We walked in and found – it. Horrible, it was.' He was certainly very pale, almost grey, and the shock was still printed on his features. 'I rang nine-nine-nine. It's what you're supposed to do, isn't it? So I did. We were told to wait here. We thought that meant until the first cops turned up. Since then, a whole load of guys has been and gone, *and we're still stuck here* . . . It's not the only place on our rota today. Our office is going spare!'

Jess left Bennison to take their statements. She picked her way around puddles towards the front door. There had been a substantial episode of rain in the early hours. The murderer, whoever it might have been, would have been pleased to see it. It must have either washed away any tracks around the cottage or masked them in the standing water. The sun had emerged now, but it was a pallid, sulky sort of sunshine and conveyed no heat.

A uniformed man was guarding the entry, and watching her approach with a sceptical eye. She didn't think she'd met him before. Perhaps he was bored, just standing here while everyone else had a specialised job to do. She didn't blame him. Seeing her, he put on a show of being alert.

'There's some of your people inside, ma'am,' he said. 'And the doc.'

She nodded. 'Are you a local man?' She gestured around them. 'I mean, do you know this part of the world?'

'I'm not from this neck of the woods, ma'am. I've been out here before, mind you. It's got a decent pub. The Waggoner's Halt, it's called, and it's given its name to the area. The food's good but pricey. Even so, quite a lot of people drive out here to eat. This cottage is normally a holiday let. That's what they said at the pub. But someone, they believe him to be the owner, seems to have been living in it over the winter. So I suppose he's the stiff – the victim,' he corrected himself hurriedly. 'But they know nothing about him. If they do, they wouldn't tell us,' he added grimly. 'They're a buttoned-up lot round here.' He indicated the front door of the cottage. 'Your crime-scene manager is in there, and one of your sergeants, with a detective-constable and the doc.'

Jess stepped into the narrow entrance hall and looked around her. Ahead she saw the lower risers of a narrow staircase that twisted to the right, so that the upstairs landing could not be seen. The treads of the staircase themselves were very narrow. It would need care to negotiate them, she thought, whether going up or coming down. Perhaps people had smaller feet in times gone by. At any rate, someone, not particularly light-footed, or perhaps more than one person, was upstairs now, moving around. She guessed it might be the crime-scene manager and an officer. A number of outdoor garments hanging from a row of hooks on her right further impeded any progress. She put out a hand and touched the coats. They were all dry. But there was still a small puddle of water on the tiled floor. *From the killer's coat,* she thought. *He must have been invited in, taken off his wet garment and made himself comfortable. Whoever he – supposing that they were talking of a male visitor – was. Had he, then, been expected?*

Straight ahead, to the right of the stairs, she saw an open door into a kitchen. It appeared to be housed in a built-on extension. She walked towards it but was halted by a shout of 'Mind the broken glass!'

She froze and looked down. The cottage windows had appeared intact on her approach. But she became aware now of a lingering smell of whisky and saw, lying almost at her feet, a broken bottle. There was other glass, too, a different type. A carved wooden frame stood upright, propped against the wall, although the mirror glass it had contained had been shattered. Jess imagined the whisky bottle flying through the air, striking the mirror and dislodging it. *Pity,* she thought, the frame looked Victorian and the glass had probably been original to it.

Stubbs, who had shouted the warning, appeared in the doorway of the sitting room to her left and said, 'Morning, ma'am.'

He was a flaxen-haired, pink-complexioned, strongly built young man, father of small children. He looked somehow out of place at the scene of a murder. But Stubbs missed very little, and also possessed the happy knack of putting witnesses at their ease. Respectable ladies of a certain age were (reputedly) anxious to feed him cake and homemade biscuits.

'Where are the glasses or tumblers they drank the whisky from? There's mainly bottle glass down there.' Jess indicated the debris.

'One whole tumbler on the draining board, by the kitchen sink, together with pieces of a broken one. Someone washed it all up.' Stubbs turned and pointed into the room behind him. 'But the whisky bottle is still there, lying on the floor. That didn't break. However, all the whisky ran out and soaked the carpet. Pity,' concluded Stubbs.

His regret appeared to be more for the whisky than the victim. Jess had known him long enough to understand that Stubbs didn't lack sympathy for the dead man. It was rather that he was thrifty by nature and didn't like to see waste.

She refused to be sidetracked and returned to the evidence.

'The assailant washed a single intact glass, and retrieved pieces of a broken one and washed those too. But he left the bottle to lie where it fell or was dropped . . .'

'The killer knew about fingerprints,' said Stubbs, still sounding peeved.

'Most people know about fingerprints, if they know nothing else. However, it suggests he knew he hadn't touched the bottle, and didn't have to bother with the broken pieces of that. Would you agree?'

'Looks like it.' Stubbs nodded. 'The way it looks to me, the killer was the guest. That poor blighter on the carpet there was the host, in charge of refreshing the drinks. Unless there was a third person present, which seems unlikely because there's no sign of a third glass, whole or broken, I reckon just the two of them sat here drinking and talking. After that, we don't know what happened. They fell out over something?' He added, 'The whisky had already soaked away completely before we got here. I'd guess that the whole incident took place in the late evening.'

'And do we know the deceased's name?'

'The cleaners say his name is Harrison, Jeremy Harrison. At any rate, that's the name on their schedule for today.'

'So, Mr Harrison received a late-night caller. I reckon,' Stubbs mused, 'he wasn't expecting him.'

'Why do you say that?'

Stubbs' logic was simple and practical. 'It was a filthy night. Who would want to be out and about? Especially in this deserted neck of the woods. If it had been me, and even if I had arranged earlier to stop by, I would have rung and suggested I come the next day instead.'

Well, thought Jess, *Stubbs was a family man, with children to consider.* He tended to select the most convenient way to tackle any situation. But some other person might have motives that made the previous evening's bad weather a positive asset. Few people out and about; and all of them concentrating on getting back home as quickly as possible.

The clatter of feet on the staircase heralded the reappearance of the crime-scene manager, a stocky dark-haired Cornishman she'd met before. They shook hands and Jess asked him, 'Well?'

'So far, we haven't found a passport, driving licence or credit cards in that name, nor any other private documents, letters, that sort of thing. His car is in the garage and the licence isn't in that either. In fact it's all rather weird.'

Stubbs, who had been listening, put in, 'Did the killer go to all the trouble to find and remove those things? If so, it's as if he wanted to make things awkward for us.'

'Most murderers, acting in a domestic setting, would be more concerned that we don't find anything to identify *them*,' Jess muttered. 'They don't try to delay us identifying the victim. He was the homeowner. The contract cleaners have already told us that.'

Stubbs nodded. 'It's an odd one, sure enough.'

He turned to lead the way back into the sitting room, stooping to avoid cracking his head on the low lintel. As he did, there was the sound of movement above their heads.

'DC Carr, still searching the bedrooms,' Stubbs told her. 'I told her to take another look. If we could have found any kind of document, it would have been helpful. But it's all been removed, as the crime-scene manager said.'

Jess nodded. 'We'll find out why eventually, I suppose.'

The room itself had been comfortably furnished, but in what struck Jess as an unoriginal way, traditional and lacking individual touches. If this was a holiday cottage for much of the year, perhaps that was to be expected. Somehow, the chintz blandness of the décor made the extent of the mayhem that had been wrought here all the more shocking. Chairs upturned; spilled volumes from a bookcase that had crashed forward to lie surrounded by the scattered hotchpotch of its former contents. They were mostly paperbacks: local history, romantic fiction, whodunnits. The last supplied a jarring contrast to the presence of a real corpse in the middle of the carpet.

The body, grotesquely curled in a foetal position, was that of a middle-aged man. The sad impression was of a circle closing. As he'd begun life curled in the womb, so the victim had ended it here, on his living-room floor.

The odour of blood permeated the air and it had left a dark stain on the carpet and a spray pattern of gore. It didn't quite obliterate the smell of the spilled whisky. Jess recalled how, early on in her career, she had been one of the officers called to the fatal result of a brawl in a bar. There had been the stench of blood, of alcohol. But also a presence, the sense of something else, not visible but felt: the uncontrollable outpouring of rage, allied to hatred. Had only two people been present here, killer and victim? Or more? There had been only two glasses, one broken, standing on the draining board in the kitchen. How big a role had the consumption of alcohol played in what had happened?

Another person was present, but so far had made no attempt to join in the discussion, probably because his interest was special-ised. Dr Tom Palmer, clad in a white paper suit over his other clothes, was standing over the corpse; staring down at it, frowning. He was a tall man and, in this low-ceilinged cottage, his head almost brushed the ceiling. Jess thought the image presented was almost spooky: the tall, straight, pale-clad figure with the critical expression seemed to be passing some eternal judgement on the corpse at his feet. He now looked up as she picked a cautious way towards him, and said, 'Hi.'

'Hullo, Tom, thanks for waiting,' Jess greeted him. 'Sorry we couldn't get here faster.'

'That's all right. I haven't been out this way for a while. Must be a nice spot in the summer.'

'Cause of death?' she asked automatically, although even from where she stood, she thought she knew the answer.

'There is a stab wound to the neck. The guy would've bled to death pretty quickly, probably.' Tom glanced at her. 'You're going to ask me if the killer got lucky or knew what he was doing.'

'All right, then. Which?'

'The wound could be targeted. Just my opinion, of course. On the other hand, the assailant could have struck out at the neck and got lucky. From my general observation, the victim was in his late fifties. He was pretty fit overall, carrying a little excess weight. I'll be able to tell you more when I've had a chance to examine the body properly. But, so far, it seems to have been just the one deep slash that did the damage, inflicted with force and clear intent. Perhaps our killer did know what he was doing and struck to kill.'

Tom paused to stare down at the victim again. Then he looked back to Jess. 'So far I've not observed any defence wounds on the victim's hands or arms. But there was clearly some sort of a tussle or fight before the knife was wielded.' Tom indicated the disarray around them.

'They fell out? One of the participants produced the knife . . .' Jess mused. 'But had he come to kill? The carrying of a knife "for self-protection" has become all too common.'

Palmer shrugged. 'All I can say now is that it was sudden. It was targeted. I'd guess there was strong emotion behind it. Just my opinion, of course, and made without a postmortem examination. Possibly the assailant was someone to whom violence came naturally.' Tom gave an awkward little laugh and hunched his shoulders. 'But don't quote me on that, or not until I've had a chance to examine our dead friend properly.'

'Thanks,' said Jess. *Palmer feels it, too,* she thought. *The personal hatred behind the attack. It lingers in the air.*

Stubbs said, 'We haven't found the weapon. The killer may have taken it with him.'

'We're looking for a man, then? A woman couldn't have done this?' Jess asked.

The two men stared at her. Palmer said, 'Nothing is impossible but she would need to have been strong, tall and athletic. The victim is fairly heavily built. I'd put my money on a man.'

Bennison had appeared behind her and was looking down at the corpse with distaste. 'Yuk!' she said. She glanced around the disordered room and took an extra minute to study the titles of the spilled paperbacks. 'My boyfriend and I rented a place like this a couple of years ago. That had a stack of books like that, too. In case it rained, or there was nothing on telly.'

'Tell them they can take the body away now,' Jess told her, and Bennison retreated with alacrity.

'I'll go now too, then,' said Palmer and took himself off.

'There's no sign of the weapon.' Stubbs spoke up now. He had been lurking in the doorway, listening. 'And no sign the victim disturbed a burglar; although these isolated properties are sitting targets for break-ins. What really puzzles us is that, so far, we haven't found a phone or a computer. These days, you expect to see both, even if the computer is only a tablet. It looks as if somebody took them, possibly just an opportunistic theft?'

Possible but there could be another reason; so why were *the electronic devices taken?* Jess thought. *For any value they had? Or because there was something on them that might identify the thief?*

Stubbs was still speaking. 'It might still turn out to be an interrupted burglary. But it looks all wrong for that, to me, anyway. What do you think, ma'am? I mean, it looks as if he sat here, drinking with the killer for a while.'

'A burglar doesn't take off his wet coat and hang it up neatly in the hall,' Jess murmured. 'Where does the broken whisky bottle come into it?'

'It was the only defensive weapon the victim had to hand? He realised what was going to happen and, I don't know, threw the bottle at the attacker? Struck out with it and the killer dodged it. Or the other way around? Either way, it flew past, through the doorway, and hit that mirror in the hall.' Stubbs hunched his shoulders. 'I reckon there was a lot of noise, not for long, perhaps, but some yelling, breaking glass, crash of furniture over-turned. Unfortunately, there are no immediate neighbours to overhear. The nearest would be at the pub. But that would be fairly noisy on its own account. It's a popular place for people to drive out to, apparently. The uniforms, who came out in answer to the cleaners' report, did ask up there if anyone had heard or noticed anything. So far, no one has come forward with any information.'

'I'll go there now with Tracy.' As she spoke she heard the engine of the cleaners' van start up as she left the cottage, and watched it rattle away, muddy water splashing up around its wheels.

On cue, Bennison reappeared, framed by the open front door. She wore Ugg boots and a quilted coat, but she still looked chilled. Her shoulders were hunched and her hands thrust deep into her pockets.

'I told them they could go. I've got their statements,' she said, 'but they didn't have much to say on the whole. Their company has had the contract to clean in here for quite a while. They come once a fortnight, out of holiday season, to clean for the owner. In the summer, when the owner moves out and the holiday renters move in, it's different. There's a regular pattern. The cleaning team come at each changeover of visitor, to get the place ready for the new lot. Back they come again when those visitors have left; to get it ready for the next visitors. This has been going on for several years. But not always the same cleaning team. It's the sort of job with a rapid turnover of employees. The lot who found the body are East European, apart from the driver. There are four of them.'

'Nasty shock for them,' murmured Jess.

'Yes, but mostly they're annoyed, especially the driver. One of the others was pretty shaken, and muttering in his own language. A workmate was consoling him. Another one, on the other hand, said, "Ah, this is what the English do, they murder one another in the country! I have read their detective stories.'"

'Perhaps our fiction writers have a lot to answer for!' remarked Jess. 'But if this same cleaning company has had the contract for so long, it begs the question: where did the owner live during the holiday season, when he was in the habit of moving out?'

'The cleaning team don't know, but their office will have a contact address or phone number for him. The whole business, the letting and the cleaning arrangements, is the responsibility of a holiday rental company. I've got an address for them.'

Jess turned back to Stubbs. 'Sean, you'd better get over there and talk to the company, then. If they did regular business with him, they should have contact details on record. In case a holiday tenant causes damage, or any sort of emergency arises. It doesn't mean they know very much about him personally. Did he have a family somewhere? For a start, when and how did he come to own this cottage? How long has he owned it? Did he always live here alone in the winter months? Where did he go in the warmer months?' She added a mental question. *And what the heck did he do all day out here?*

'It's a nice place,' Bennison said unexpectedly. 'And the council will have the owner's name on record, to know where to send the council tax demand.'

'We'll set all that in hand when we get back to base.'

A clatter on the staircase heralded the arrival of DC Vicky Carr. 'Morning, ma'am!' she greeted Jess. She looked towards Stubbs and then back to the inspector. 'I've taken another look upstairs, everywhere, but still can't find any computer or personal documents, ma'am. It's weird. Who doesn't have a computer or a mobile phone or anything like that in this day and age?'

Stubbs growled, 'It's not that the victim didn't own any of those things. The murderer searched first and took everything with him.'

'Take Vicky back to town with you and drop her off, before you go to the letting agency, Sean.' Jess turned to Bennison, who was still moodily contemplating the body.

'In the meantime, as we're here, you and I will try the pub. Come on, Tracy.'

As they prepared to set off towards the Waggoner's Halt, something disturbed the crows. There was a commotion in the branches of the ancient oak and a raucous argument broke out among the birds. The crows were shouting abuse in their harsh voices. Both Jess and Bennison stopped to look up and see what was wrong. Like a missile, a magpie, in its black-and-white plumage, shot from the tree. The magpie had been rash enough to venture alone into a den of ruffians, and now it chose retreat, though not without a last derisory croak of defiance. It would be back later, perhaps with others.

'Crows and magpies don't get along. They're like two street gangs,' Jess said. 'They guard their turf.'

Bennison looked at her in surprise and then smiled. 'Didn't know you were a twitcher, ma'am.'

'Oh, I'm not into ornithology,' Jess said. 'But at one time, when I was a kid, we lived in a house with a big old tree in the garden, very like that one over there.'

'Lucky you,' said Bennison. 'I grew up in a tower block.'

'At least you identify with childhood spent in one place. Mine was an army family. We moved house several times.' Jess pointed back towards the tree. 'You can't ignore crows. They're so noisy.

Pity they can't talk to us. Whatever happened here last night, they would have been aware of it; even roosting up there, they would have been aware of an intruder and a fight, including breaking glass.' She paused. 'One other thing I do know about crows is that a gathering of them is called a "murder" of crows.'

The sergeant glanced back towards the cottage. 'Good name for them, then!'

Chapter 4

'Where have all these people come from?' gasped Bennison. 'Is it just because they've heard about the murder? I mean, they can't all live round here surely? There's no proper village to speak of, not here, anyway. The nearest is Weston St Ambrose, just down the road.' She frowned. 'We've been called out there before, haven't we?'

'We certainly have!' agreed Jess.

The assortment of vehicles parked outside the Waggoner's Halt had been startling: cars, bicycles, and even a mobility scooter. When Jess and Bennison pushed open the door and walked into the bar, they found the place packed. All heads turned in their direction and the buzz of conversation was cut off. Eyes studied them head to toe, followed by muttering. *'Plain clothes . . .'* and in one instance, *'Murder squad . . .'*

They all watch television, at any rate, Jess thought. Behind the bar stood a burly man in a plaid shirt, presumably the landlord. He watched them approach with deep suspicion written on his face. Jess wondered whether he treated all newcomers to his pub with the same unsmiling countenance; or just the police. At his elbow lurked a young woman with a waterfall of tangled hair, falling in two wings, one either side of a central parting. One wing had been coloured scarlet and the other side peacock-blue. She had studs in her nose and ears and, disconcertingly, a pointed metal dart sticking out of the middle of her left cheek. Her slightly protuberant pale-blue eyes goggled at them, gleaming with excitement. For her, at least, the gruesome discovery at the cottage was a highlight, furnishing her with endless tales to tell her mates.

'Good morning, officers,' said the landlord as Jess reached his bar with Bennison at her elbow and before she had a chance to show him her identity. She held it up now, anyway, and indicated Tracy. 'Inspector Campbell and DS Bennison.'

An appreciative murmur ran round the assembled onlookers.

The landlord responded in kind. 'Barry Wilson, like it says over the door. This is my daughter, Jade.' His manner had thawed slightly and Jess sensed he was doing his best to sound welcoming. The problem probably was that bonhomie didn't come naturally to him, something of a drawback in his profession.

Jade, who was now practically fizzing with excitement, opened her mouth, but her father forestalled her. He leaned forward and added hoarsely, 'I can put the old barn at your disposal, for interviews and that. It's just behind the pub. You'll want to set up an incident room, I dare say?'

Yes, they did all watch television. However, as any investigating officer knew, eager witnesses were one thing – supposing they knew anything of value. Timewasters were another. But the offer of an incident room so close at hand was not to be refused. Provided, of course, the old barn was in a reasonable condition. As tactfully as she could, Jess asked, 'It's not in use for anything else?'

He shook his head. 'Not now. But it's all right. Roof doesn't leak. It's got electricity. We've hired it out in the past for club dances, local bands and so on.'

'We'll take a look and let you know,' she told him.

Bennison had a question that couldn't wait for formal interviews.

'Where do they all live?' She indicated the crowd with a jerk of her head.

The landlord squinted at her. 'It might surprise anyone coming from outside, but a fair few folk live around here, you know. Don't get the wrong idea just because there isn't a centre as such. Well, you could say we're the local centre, right here in this pub! The proper village is just down the road, Weston St Ambrose. But you've been there before, haven't you? You'll know that.'

He accompanied this last remark with what was probably intended to be a knowing look. Unfortunately, it took the form of a villainous squint.

'Yes, I've been out this way before,' agreed Jess blandly. She was not going to allow herself to be drawn into any discussion of the events that had led to her previous visits, although privately she was annoyed that she had been recognised.

'Well,' the landlord continued, 'you'll find houses down any of these lanes. And we get other visitors, too, poking about for Roman ruins.'

'I didn't know there was an archaeological site in the area,' exclaimed Jess, a little disconcerted. She should have known. She'd driven all round here on her previous visits and she should have spotted any interesting ruins.

Jade, who had been fidgeting at her father's elbow, increasingly frustrated at being excluded from the conversation, now seized her opportunity to join in, and also provided an explanation for the inspector's not having seen any ruins.

'That's because there's nuffin' to see!' she declared loudly; and tossed her multi-coloured tresses triumphantly before adding, in a disparaging tone, 'Only a hut.'

Her father scowled at her.

'Oh? That's why I don't remember it,' Jess told her.

'There was a Roman villa there once, they reckon,' argued her father, not to be deprived of anything of local interest that might bring trade to his pub. He glared at his daughter. She was clearly impervious to his displeasure. Jess thought it bounced off her as off a force field.

Jess supposed he meant the site had once been a Roman villa, not that the present hut had ever been part of a Romano-British household.

'Can you show me the barn?' she asked. There seemed no point in spending any more time on a long-gone villa.

'Mind the bar, Jade,' ordered Wilson, much to his daughter's obvious displeasure. 'This is a working pub and you're supposed to be working in it. The customers would all die of thirst if it was left up to you.'

Jade looked ready to explode with rage, but her father didn't give her the chance. He lifted the access panel in the counter and strode through it purposefully.

Despite the seriousness of the moment, Jess had to repress a grin. Family time in the Wilson household must see a lively scene or two.

The gathering fell back as Wilson, his authority re-established, led them from the bar, through the rooms at the rear and, finally, out into a large outside area where a few wooden trestle tables and benches had been set up. They looked as if they had been there some time and had not been in recent use. Perhaps that wasn't surprising. It was, after all, the wrong time of year to sit outside. But there indeed was the barn, an impressive building, larger than Jess had expected, and clearly of some antiquity.

The landlord produced a bunch of keys and found one that opened the small door that had been set into one half of a pair of large wooden doors.

'It used to be a coach house,' he explained as he led them inside. 'No call now for those.'

When they stepped inside, Jess had to repress exclaiming, 'Wow!' or something similar. The barn was tidier than she had expected, and there was more than enough room for their purpose. Perhaps it had indeed been a coach house. She wasn't sure. Modern use had led to a stage being constructed at one end. At the other, there was a bar area and stacks of plastic chairs. Otherwise, it didn't appear to have been altered much since its construction. Everywhere was dusty but in surprisingly good order. It was, Jess thought as she looked around it, ideal for use as an incident room.

Wilson had noted the look of approval on her face. 'We keep it tidy. It's still available for hire. No bookings at the moment, though.' As if by afterthought, he added, 'Rain don't get in.'

Jess nodded. 'I'll get a team out to set it up for us.'

Bennison muttered, 'We'll need to get a lot of heaters in, or we'll all freeze!'

They retreated to the public bar where the crowded room waited impatiently for the next act in the drama. As word spread that the police were to use the barn as a base for their inquiries, the excitement fairly fizzed around the audience. Jess suspected they wouldn't lack witnesses anxious to queue up outside the incident room, once established, and speak to the police. That didn't necessarily mean any of them would have anything significant to say. All it needed sometimes, however, was a small nugget of gold in a heap of disposable debris.

Bennison had however brightened considerably. 'Look at it this way,' she said to Jess, when they were alone outside the Waggoner's Halt. 'I reckon that, living in a place like this, none of them miss much of what goes on.'

Jess thought that might prove optimistic. One of the attractions that had led to the construction of some expensive properties, discreetly hidden behind high hedges or well-maintained drystone walls, was the privacy the area offered. People lived out here because they did not want to be seen or disturbed. They, in turn, had no interest in anyone living locally who was not in their social circle. They certainly hadn't reckoned on a murder inquiry being conducted under their noses. At the moment, the change in the usual routine was a novelty. It wouldn't be long before natural caution replaced the curiosity; and they would want their former tranquil existence back.

'We'll be setting up an incident room in the barn here,' she announced to her audience. 'But if anyone wants to speak to us before it's up and running, please don't hesitate.'

'And if anyone would like lunch,' added Barry Wilson loudly, 'we've got menus here. Jade! Hand them out.'

Because Millie was staying with him, Carter had booked a few days' leave. He'd told them all at work that, unless it was a murder, he didn't want anyone contacting him. So, what d'you know? It was a murder.

'Sorry about this!' Jess Campbell told him down the phone. 'We believe the victim to be named Jeremy Harrison. He owned the cottage where the body was found. It's not far from the pub, but still pretty private behind some trees. He only lived there over the winter. During the summer, it has been let out as a holiday place. We don't yet know where he spent the summer months himself.'

'So can we be sure Harrison is the name of the victim?' Carter asked.

'The cleaners knew him as that. But we'll need to find a family member, if there is one, to identify him. If not, someone who knew him well enough and is willing to look at the body. That might prove tricky, because he spent summers away from the cottage, and was something of a recluse when he was there.'

'Try the company who handled the letting for him.'

'We're on to it!' came the terse reply down the phone. 'Stubbs is on his way to see them.'

'Of course,' he replied hurriedly. 'I'll be with you once I've dropped off Millie with Monica Farrell.'

On checking the Waggoner's Halt, Carter had found that, in the manner of isolated country pubs, it shared its postal code with the nearest place of habitation. In this case, it was Weston St Ambrose. He felt a rising tide of frustration at being called out there, because it wasn't for the first time. But, on the other hand, Sophie's elderly aunt, Monica Farrell, a retired teacher, lived there. Millie and Monica got on like a house on fire and much of 'his' time with his daughter had meant, in practice, that when he'd been called into work, Millie had spent days with Monica. Once again this was going to be the case, if Monica was agreeable. So his next call had been to her.

'Of course, Ian, delighted to see Millie!' Monica's cheery voice echoed in his ear.

'I hope she won't be in your way,' he apologised. 'If you're busy, please say so.'

'Not a bit. Millie and I can catch up, and then she might like to explore a bit. You won't mind if she takes my bike out and rides round the area? The roads are fairly quiet and I'll make sure she wears a helmet.'

'Where is your murder, then?' she asked a little later, while Millie was renewing acquaintance with Monica's cats. 'I've just heard, in our local shop, that something's happened down the road at the Waggoner's Halt, the pub there.'

'Not at the pub itself, but not far away,' Carter clarified the situation. 'Ever come across or heard of a chap called Jeremy Harrison?'

'Is he the poor chap who's dead?' asked Monica. 'Can't say I knew him.'

'We believe he's the victim. He hasn't been formally identified yet. He lived at Rose Cottage, and that's where the body was found.'

'They won't like a case of murder, and all the hoo-hah, round there,' observed Monica. 'Apart from natural nervousness, there are the property values, you know.'

'Are there many expensive properties?'

'A few. Hideaways for the wealthy.'

Now that, thought Carter as he drove away, *might make investigations a little tricky to handle.* His mind was running along the same lines as Jess's. If there are well-off – and well-connected – homeowners around there, they will want any investigations to be speedily concluded to their satisfaction. That wouldn't be the same thing as willingness to help.

It was time for him to put in an appearance, and he left, promising to come back and collect Millie as soon as he could. Monica assured him there was absolutely no need to worry. Perhaps he'd like to come and have some dinner with her and Millie when he'd finished work for the day? 'Bring Jess, if she's free.'

Millie's sharp ears caught that. She looked up from the cat on her lap and beamed.

As if life wasn't complicated enough.

* * *

It might be wise, thought Ian, *to refresh my memory of the area.* Mindful of what he'd learned from Monica, he took time to drive round the narrow roads surrounding the location of the scene of the crime. He quickly saw what she had meant. Any stranger driving through en route to somewhere else would get the impression hardly anyone lived round there. But there were a number of large properties, discreetly screened by high hedges and drystone walls. One or two of them looked quite new. But a few were clearly older. Just one such place had a board outside announcing greentrees kennels. Beneath it was printed *Long Lane, Waggoner's Halt, Weston St Ambrose.*

He had decided to take a look first at the scene of the crime, before he called in at the pub and the barn behind it, where the team was busy setting up the incident room. His first thought, on getting out of his car in front of the cottage, was that this wouldn't have been an inexpensive rental, available to any takers. The company handling the arrangements would have been given strict instructions about checking the suitability of the holidaymakers showing interest; and it would not come cheap. It was much larger than he'd expected, a long, low, stone-built construction that, surely, had originally been two adjoined dwellings. Someone, with the money to make a first-class conversion, had turned the two into one. In doing so, the cramped quarters once occupied by two farm labourers' families had been transformed into the desirable country residence of someone much wealthier. The name *Rose Cottage* on the plate attached to the gate seemed to him a little overmodest. He wondered if it had always been called that or whether it was a marketing ploy, making the place sound delightful even before any prospective holiday visitors set eyes on it.

One thing was clear. Those responsible for the conversion of the original cottages had wanted not only more spacious accommodation but privacy. They had planted a row of leylandii along the roadside edge of the property to shield it from passers-by. *That species of tree,* thought Carter, *was a fast grower, and had probably been chosen with that in mind. But it doesn't know when to stop.* Although the tips had been cropped, the job had been left too late to prevent the trees growing to a height that was now far too tall. They'd also become interlinked, ensuring privacy to the property owner. He opened the gate and stepped through. Between the leylandii barrier and the cottage was a fairly large area of now-soggy lawn. That, too, needed to be maintained. Carter wondered who kept the garden in order. The cleaning company wouldn't do that. So was there also a garden maintenance firm? Ask the letting agency, he told himself. On the other hand, if anyone had been watching the cottage, it would not have been difficult to do so unobserved.

He, too, was being watched by the uniformed man left on guard outside the cottage door. He walked up the path to identify himself.

The constable adopted an attitude of enhanced alertness. But Carter had noticed the squashed cigarette butt on the ground at the man's feet.

'That yours?' he asked, pointing at it.

The man flushed. 'Yessir! Sorry, sir.'

'Well, pick it up, then. Don't you know better than to contaminate a crime scene?'

The miscreant, now pale rather than flushed, scooped up the offending stub and put it in his pocket.

'Anyone told you how much longer you have to stay on guard?'

'Until they come with the tape to cordon off the whole area, sir. They're supposed to be on their way.'

'I'll check on it,' Carter promised. He nodded a farewell and walked back to the lane to take another look at the property from the boundary.

Let's say I'm the murderer, he thought. *I'm standing here, shielded by the trees, waiting to see if the occupant has any visitors, or if he is there alone. Did the killer watch on just the one, fatal, night? Or had he planned a recce over a number of days? To do that might be prudent, but also would increase the risk that someone might see him hanging around, taking an interest.*

As if to prove the point, someone spoke a few feet behind him, by the gate. It gave him a considerable start of alarm. 'Are you part of the investigation team? Or just curious to look at the place?' It was a woman's voice, educated, pleasant and relaxed. But the tone was also firm. The speaker wanted an answer to her question.

Carter turned to find the speaker was an older woman, wearing a tweed skirt, fleece gilet and sensible shoes. She was not tall, but solidly built, and radiated energy. The sort of woman, Carter decided, who 'runs things'.

At the moment she was surrounded by pug dogs. Carter counted six of them and, at the sight of him, they'd formed up in a protective phalanx before their owner. Now they started towards him, uttering rumbles of warning by way of grunts and breathy growls. Fortunately, they were leashed. Managing them must call for considerable dexterity.

'All right, take it easy!' ordered the woman. The dogs fell silent, but remained on alert. Carter felt the hostile stare of their shiny, slightly protuberant eyes.

He held up his identity card. 'Sorry to be an annoyance,' he said mildly.

'Ah, copper!' said the woman. 'Senior one, too. Eleanor Holder. I live at the kennels.'

'I drove past your property a few minutes ago. Do you breed these little chaps?' He indicated the pugs, who were still regarding him with deep suspicion.

'Occasionally, but mostly I run the place as a boarding kennels,' she told him. 'A crowd of your lot are up at the pub, setting up some sort of HQ.' She twitched an eyebrow questioningly.

'It's important to get local feedback,' he explained. 'So an interview room is a necessity. We would like to talk to anyone who knew . . .' He gestured towards the cottage.

'Poor old Jerry Harrison?' she said. 'Well, I knew him, of course, but not that well.'

'But you knew him as "Jerry"? Not Jeremy? Jeremy is the name the contract cleaners have given us.'

'Well, his proper name is – was – Jeremy, I dare say. I knew Lucinda Harrison better. She always called him Jerry, so I did.'

'Ah! His wife?'

'Lord, no! Don't think he had one of those. Might have had one in the past, I suppose. No, Lucinda and I were school chums, back in the Dark Ages. Great times. We got up to all sorts of tricks. Mild stuff compared with what kids do now, I suppose.'

'My daughter is at boarding school,' Carter told her.

'Which one?' she demanded immediately. He told her and she said, 'Ah, decent school that, I believe.'

Carter thought, *it ought to be. It costs a small fortune to send her there.*

'Lulu Harrison – we called her Lulu at school – died nearly four years ago now,' continued Eleanor. 'I still miss her. She was Jerry's aunt and this was her home. He used to turn up from time to time to visit her, usually staying a few days. I don't know whether he really cared about her or whether he was playing the favourite nephew. If he was, it paid off for him. She left him everything, lock, stock and barrel. Including the house. He didn't deserve it. He let it out each summer to complete strangers. Lulu would have hated that.' Eleanor glowered at the luckless constable on guard at the front door.

'You knew him personally. That could be very interesting to us.' *And you didn't like him*, Carter thought. That could be important, because he thought she was probably a good judge of character and, also, because others might not have liked the victim either. Disliked enough to kill? No, murder calls for more that dislike to furnish a motive. But it's a starting point.

She'd guessed his thoughts. 'Think I might have had a motive to bump him off? Sorry, that question is tactless and bad form. I didn't murder the poor chap. I had no reason to.'

Carter felt an instinctive twinge, as if some invisible antenna had quivered. *Keep her talking . . .* he thought.

'But you did know him; and his aunt who lived there before him. You may be able to tell us a lot more than you realise.' Carter smiled encouragingly.

Her expression became thoughtful. 'I doubt it, so don't get your hopes up. I never really knew much about him, apart from who he was. As for what he did for a living, I knew only that it involved oilfields; and Lulu told me that. Perhaps she didn't know exactly, either. He did something in the engineering line, I believe, and travelled all over the world.'

She uttered a sort of growl, not unlike that of one of the pugs. 'I only know for sure that he was a ruddy philistine. After the will was settled, he could do what he liked; the first thing he did was clear the place out of anything of any value; and send it all off to a saleroom in London. Porcelain, silver, paintings, anything of that sort. I don't forgive him for that. It was his family stuff, too, after all. Lulu would have trusted him to look after it. He betrayed her trust, in my view. Sorry if that sounds harsh, but I'm old-fashioned in my views; and Lulu was my friend all my life.'

Eleanor clearly had good reason not to have liked the victim. But not, surely, enough to kill. Not just because he had sold off things cherished by the aunt who had left it all to him.

'If he was planning to let the place out as a holiday rental,' Carter said, 'I suppose that would make sense.' To himself, he was thinking, *But it also suggests he didn't have another permanent home elsewhere.*

'Dare say!' retorted Eleanor. 'It upset me, though. All those things mattered to Lulu. Family history in objects, you know, passed down – and if he was worried about the summer visitors breaking the good china, well, there are such places as storage warehouses.'

Carter thought, *family history in objects* . . . Perhaps Lucinda Harrison had seen everything in that light, and valued the items for the story all those things told. But possibly Jeremy, used to the bustle and modern working world of an oilfield, had seen the place as a kind of museum; and had had no wish to be its curator.

Eleanor's emotion had been picked up by the pugs who, restive at being sidelined, started another barrage of protests.

'Shut up, you silly beggars!' ordered their owner and they fell into a resentful silence. Carter could still feel the combined force of their gaze.

'You haven't any idea, I suppose, where he spent the summer months? If he moved out of the cottage, presumably he went somewhere else.'

'No,' retorted Eleanor. 'I was his aunt's friend, not his. I used to exchange the time of day with him if I met him when I was out with the dogs. I always found him a pleasant enough chap, don't mistake me, but not forthcoming. You know how it is when someone doesn't want to answer questions or volunteer information?'

'Only too well,' Carter assured her wryly.

Eleanor gave an unexpected grin and retorted, 'Dare say you do! Well, he was retired, but, as I said, all I ever knew about what he'd done for a living was that it was technical and something to do with oil. I could have asked Lulu more, I suppose, but I never did, and she never told me. Perhaps she wasn't sure. At any rate, I'm not the sort of person who quizzes other people about their lives. Even after she'd died, and he came to live here, I didn't ask him.'

'So you wouldn't know where he lived in the summer months, while the cottage was let out to visitors?'

She frowned. 'I think he might have liked cruises. A team of archaeologists had come down here. They turn up from time to time, because of a so-called Roman site we have just down the road. Lord knows why. There's nothing to see there that I've ever noticed. Last year when they came, Jerry said he wished them luck, but didn't expect to hear they'd found anything. He was about to leave on a cruise round the Med, so more likely to see some ancient remains than they were.'

Eleanor gave a grim smile. 'I believe the archaeologists are back in the area now, though not digging at the moment. I expect the soil is frozen. I haven't seen them myself, but I've been told they're carrying out a sort of survey. I don't know whether they're the same ones as came before or a different set.'

She added thoughtfully, 'I might fancy a cruise myself. But I can't go off and do whatever I want. I've got the pugs to consider.'

Carter thought, *Jeremy (or Jerry) Harrison on the other hand could go off and do what he liked in the summer. Did he do it all on money left to him by wealthy relatives, like his Aunt Lucinda?*

'Thank you,' he said. 'I wonder whether a colleague of mine, Inspector Jessica Campbell, might call on you for a chat?'

'Any time,' said Eleanor. 'But I can't tell her much about the poor fellow. I can tell her about Lulu. If you want to know about her?' She raised her eyebrows inquiringly.

'Believe me,' Carter told her, 'we want to know everything. One never knows what little bit of gossip will come in useful!' He smiled at her.

She uttered a short laugh that sounded remarkably like: 'Heh, heh!' 'Tell her to phone me first, in case I'm out with these chaps.'

The pugs all stopped staring at Carter and turned their gaze up to their owner's face. She was hunting in a pocket and drew out a slightly worse-for-wear card.

'Phone number,' she said. 'For the kennels.'

He thanked her and, glancing at it, saw that its address, which he'd already read on the board outside the kennels, was given as *Long Lane, Weston St Ambrose.* There was no mention of Waggoner's Halt. *That's stretching a point,* he thought. *Out here is hardly in the village. But from a postal point of view, it must share a code.* He pocketed the card, and nodded an additional farewell to the pugs, who again rumbled at him. Then he set off for the pub and the newly established incident room.

An official notice had already been tacked up to indicate that the police were interested in talking to anyone with information regarding the incident that had taken place nearby at Rose Cottage. Any such person could find the incident room in the barn to the rear of the pub. Carter drove up to the Waggoner's Halt, taking time to observe it as he cruised past in search of a parking place. It was a cool day; later it would turn chillier. But for now it was dry, and there were still plenty of people hanging about outside the building, some smoking, some with a glass in hand, talking in small groups. They were casually but, for the most part, well dressed, confirming the air of prosperity imparted by those large, half-hidden properties. He guessed there would be more inside. No one was going to leave while there was a chance of anything happening. The pub's landlord would be doing well out of all this trade. He wondered how many of those present had already spoken to the police and how many intended to. More importantly, had any one of them any information to impart? Probably very few. But, as he'd indicated to Eleanor, one never knew. Carter felt himself being scrutinised as he got out of his car and made his way round the side of the building to the barn.

Incident rooms vary, according to availability and location. *But this one,* thought Carter immediately, *was definitely 'a cut above'.* To begin with, it was huge and its ancient oak doors, now standing open, would once have allowed not only a coach but a laden wagon to enter. Its slightly sagging roof was adorned with moss. When he stepped inside, he felt he'd entered a woodland. The roof was supported on an intricate latticework of wooden beams, with supporting pillars, forming a spectacular canopy. He suspected this barn was older than the pub. This, surely, was not just a disused coach house. This had been constructed in Tudor times as a tithe barn. Now that a police investigation had taken it over, a number of interview stations had been set up; queues had already formed up at them to speak to the officers. But that, too, brought to mind its original use, when clerks would have been similarly busy, noting the deliveries of the harvest tithes and other goods to be stored here.

'Takes your breath away, doesn't it?' said a voice at his elbow.

He turned towards the speaker, and saw Jess Campbell's mop of red hair. She had a grin on her face.

'Yes,' he agreed, 'it certainly does.'

'The landlord told me they hire it out for wedding receptions, club functions and so on.'

'Shouldn't think they lack inquiries! It must be a real money-spinner.'

'Oddly enough, I get the impression they are careful about who hires it. Probably they don't want it to get a reputation for rowdiness. Looking round here, you'd think the place was deserted. But you can see, from the interest in our activities, that there are a lot of people about and they all want to talk to us. It's the novelty value, I'm afraid. It's not because they have any information. So far, we've received precious little of that. They're more curious about what we can tell them.'

'Who are they all?' asked Ian. 'They drive expensive cars and look pretty well heeled.'

'That's a fair description of them, mostly, or so far. Successful professionals, for the most part, some of them retired. Others commute to the sort of jobs for which they don't need to arrive too early, or they work from home. That's the thing now, isn't it? Working from home?'

'Not if you are investigating murder,' grumbled Carter. 'Millie is staying with me for half term, as you know, and working from home would suit me fine, given the chance.'

'Yes, very inconvenient,' she sympathised. Or he thought it was sympathy. He hoped it wasn't sarcasm. All the same, he felt his face redden and hoped Jess would put that down to the cold air.

'Although, as it coincides with Millie's visit, I would take leave . . .' he began.

'Sure,' said Jess. 'I'm really sorry we've had to call you out.'

She spoke briskly and he was sure no sarcasm was intended. It wasn't Jess's way.

Jess was continuing her previous words about the wealthier residents. 'They value the privacy and general quiet, they tell us. That doesn't mean they're not very interested in our progress. I ought to say that, so far, it's lack of progress. No one can suggest a next of kin for our victim. Perhaps he didn't have anyone. He was the previous owner's nephew, and she died, and he doesn't seem to have been either married or in any kind of a relationship. But we still need someone to identify the body officially. The neighbours are reluctant to do it, not their sort of thing, they assure us. I got the impression they didn't like him much and didn't socialise.'

'Someone had told me about his aunt,' Carter told her. 'And that he inherited the cottage from her in her will.'

Jess was nodding. 'Yes. They all knew his late aunt, and have been keen to tell us how much they liked her. She was a bridge player and some of them meet up, like a little club, to play. She was part of that scene. On the other hand, so far no one has spoken warmly of the victim. They agree how shocking the murder is; and are horrified that anyone should die that way. "Brutal" is a word used more than once. But no one, so far, has suggested he'll be a loss to the community. He seems to have been something of a recluse while he was staying here. In the summer the cottage has been let out to vacationers. They don't know where he went during those months. I'm beginning to think he might have made an excellent bridge player. Good at concealing his hand!' Jess concluded wryly.

'Ah, well, I've just been talking to a lady by the name of Eleanor Holder, who supports what you say. But she hasn't yet been to give a statement, and my impression is that she might not like to do that in the surrounds of an interview room. She is, however, willing to talk to someone privately. I, er, suggested you might like to call on her for a chat.'

Jess frowned and said, 'I'll check her out. Is she a local?'

'Yes, she lives in Long Lane and runs some boarding kennels. She also breeds pug dogs. I've got her card, here.' He fished out the even more crumpled card from his pocket and handed it to Jess, who frowned at it. 'The interesting thing about Eleanor is that she was an old school pal and lifelong friend of the late Lucinda Harrison who owned Rose Cottage; and left it to our Jeremy Harrison in her will. Lucinda was his aunt, as we've learned. She, and others who knew him through her, called the deceased Jerry, apparently, rather than Jeremy. He used to visit during his aunt's lifetime, and moved in after Lucinda's death. At least, he occupied it in the winter/early spring months. He was in the habit of letting it out for the summer, as you've also already discovered, and taking off for destinations unknown. But he liked cruises, so holiday companies specialising in those might well have a record of him.'

'Then I need to talk to her,' said Jess immediately.

'I've told her to expect you, but I should give her a ring first. She didn't like Harrison much. It seems that, as soon as he inherited the family silver and antiques, he sold everything off. Eleanor disapproved. The previous owner, the aunt, had set great store by it all. For all Eleanor declares she doesn't know much about him, she has given us the first personal details about him, not to say some indication of his character. It's something. We now know what brought him to live here. Harrison had been, for part of the year at least, her neighbour.'

Jess frowned. 'It's possible she knows more than she thinks she does. At any rate, it sounds as though she might turn out to be our only source of personal details so far. What about identifying his body, would she be up for that? If we don't find a relative or anyone else, that is. She's elderly, you say? We don't want her to collapse from shock. But so far, we do not even have his passport; and the best you can say about a passport photo is that it's how he looked at the time it was taken, supposing it to be a good likeness then.'

'He obviously had a passport. He'd been a worldwide traveller for his work and after retirement he still went on cruises, so Eleanor told me.'

'We've not found it yet but he may have kept it elsewhere for safety,' Jess mused. 'Perhaps his bank? We don't yet know where he banked, as his credit cards and chequebook are missing. It's possible the killer found all that and removed it. If so, why?'

'Straightforward theft?'

'Perhaps. A burglary gone wrong is always something to bear in mind.' Jess hesitated. 'I just have a feeling there's more to it than that. There is no sign of a break-in. The victim and his killer seem to have sat drinking whisky and talking for a while. Everything that's been taken seems to fall under the heading of personal documents – and a computer, probably. He must surely have had one.'

'I'll get Nugent on to that, as soon as I get back to HQ. As for Eleanor, I got the impression she's pretty tough. Whether she'd be willing to identify the body is something else. But you could ask.' Carter paused. 'She's the sort who might consider it her duty, owed to her old school chum.'

Jess nodded. 'Stubbs has gone to talk to the holiday let agency, by the way. If they've been doing business with the late Jeremy for the past few years, they should know something about him.'

Carter muttered in a noncommittal way. Any information about the deceased, in murder cases, was helpful. But if the dealings the firm had had with the now deceased Harrison had been business only, they might know almost nothing at all about him as a man. *A man*, he thought, *who seems to have been very little liked.*

He left the barn and set off to where he'd left his 4x4. As he did, he caught a movement from the corner of his eye; and saw a familiar form scrambling for the cover of a clump of trees.

'Millie!'

The figure stopped in its tracks, turned and faced him defiantly. 'Hullo, Dad!' she said with aplomb.

'Spare me the careless attitude! What are you doing here and how did you get here?'

'On Monica's bike, of course.'

He might have been talking to Sophie. That same defiance, challenge, the readiness to meet any criticism he might make with a countersuit.

'Where is it, the bike?'

She pointed at the clump of trees. 'I left it in there.'

'Let's hope it's still there when we take a look. Come on!'

Now she was annoyed. 'Of course it's there! I chained it up. I wouldn't just go off and leave it. Honestly, Dad!' She trotted after him as he strode towards the trees, still radiating indignation. 'I'm not stupid, you know.'

No, she wasn't and, like her mother, she'd never admit to losing an argument. The most she'd concede would be to leave it unresolved – for the time being.

The bike was there, of course, discreetly hidden and chained to a post bearing a sign ordering no fly-tipping. He noticed that the order had been rigorously enforced. No sign of black plastic rubbish sacks or old television sets. Round here, the residents made sure of that. He wondered how many of the owners of those large houses behind the hedges were or had been magistrates. *We'll have to find our murderer quickly*, he thought, *or we'll be inundated with complaints of police incompetence.* It struck him how furious, as well as deeply alarmed, the locals must be. Monica had spoken rightly. Someone murdered in such a rural setting casts a wide shadow. Nothing upsets the middle classes so much as falling property values. Plus, the holiday let company responsible for Rose Cottage wouldn't find it so easy to find takers now, he told himself. Who fancies relaxing in a place where a murdered corpse has only recently been discovered? Even if the murderer has been apprehended? What if he hasn't? Is the killer still out there, lurking in the shadow of the leylandii and watching the house, waiting for a new victim? Supposing, of course, that the new owner wants to continue letting it out. Who is the new owner? That's another question to be resolved.

'We'll discuss this tonight,' he said, sounding, to his own ears, like a Victorian papa.

His daughter was looking at him in genuine puzzlement. 'Discuss what?'

His turn to stonewall. 'Tonight, right? We're conducting an investigation into a serious crime here, and that's what I'm concentrating on now, if you don't mind.'

'Why should I mind? I know what you do.' Her expression suggested she thought his attitude strange.

'And I do it best without interference, Millie!'

'I'm not interfering. What have I done to interfere?' Righteous indignation flooded her voice and expression.

He was going to lose this argument as he'd lost all those arguments with Sophie long ago.

'Just let me load the bike in the boot of the car and I'll drop you back at Monica's—'

He realised immediately, even as he spoke, that he had made a major tactical error. Her face reddened, eyes flashed, her whole attitude and expression suggesting she was about to explode in a shower of sparks like a firework.

'I'm well able to ride back to Monica's place on my own. I don't need a police escort of any kind. I'll go right now and not hold you up any longer!'

With that, she was on the bike, and pedalling off down the road like an aspiring entrant in the Tour de France.

A voice behind him said, in an amused tone, 'Am I allowed to say that interviewee appeared uncooperative?'

He turned to see Jess behind him with a Cheshire Cat grin on her face. 'I could have conducted my side of it better,' he conceded ruefully.

'Don't worry, she'll calm down. I came out to ask if you wanted to come with me to find this kennels.' Jess waved Eleanor's crumpled business card at him. 'I thought I'll pop along there now, and see if she's back from walking the dogs.'

'You'd better go on your own,' Carter said ruefully. 'I'm not doing very well so far today. Finding the right approach, I mean.'

'Hey, come on! You've found a witness and possibly someone who'll agree to identify the body. It's more than we've done in there so far.' She indicated the barn. 'The locals all want to come in and tell us what a respectable area this is, and that no one living here could possibly have anything to do with a murder. They want to know how long do we think we might be here. But when we suggest they might have some information, no matter how trivial it might seem to them now, they rear back like startled horses. So they haven't actually told us anything, not so far, anyway.'

'You might have better luck with Eleanor. I'll drive round the area and see if I can spot anything of interest. Renew my acquaintance with the place.'

Neither of them had noticed an unimpressive but far from unfamiliar figure to the police, who had been observing the exchange between Carter and his daughter with interest. Now, on seeing Jess arrive on the scene, the watcher chose discretion, and faded away. Alfie Darrow turned to set off across the fields to his home in Weston St Ambrose, brooding on the undeniable fact that the police were always turning up and complicating things. Moreover, that bloke Carter had a 'down' on Alfie. So did the woman with the red hair. But Alfie worried more about Carter.

'I ain't murdered no one!' protested Alfie, oblivious to the pitfall of the double negative. 'But that won't stop them trying to pin something on me.'

What was more, the police presence at the barn interfered with Alfie's plans in another way. His hope, when he heard that there was a more than usual amount of activity in the area around the end of Long Lane, was that it would take Barry Wilson's attention. Normally, Barry was the obstacle between Alfie and Jade Wilson, Barry's daughter. Now there were a whole load of cops as well. This hadn't provided the distraction Alfie had hoped for. It just put more obstacles in his path. Alfie had a strong sense of life's injustice. But he wasn't going to give up. He'd just have to find some other way of contacting Jade.

Alfie stopped and looked back over his shoulder. He wasn't far from Rose Cottage, scene of the crime. There would be cops there, bound to be. They'd be swarming all over it. But, on the other hand, he could go and have a look. Then he could tell his mother, later on that day, that he'd actually seen it.

Alfie knew the surrounding fields like the back of his hand, as the saying goes. He approached Rose Cottage from the rear and concealed himself in some trees at the side of the premises. There were vehicles parked up there and a uniformed copper standing guard outside the door. He looked familiar to Alfie, whose acquaintanceship with the local police was of long standing. There was also still one car there, so someone was inside the cottage. But they wouldn't stay for ever. They would be called away to deal with something else, or just go back to base and write up their reports. That would eventually leave no one at the cottage. No one at all. A grin spread across Alfie's face and he retreated under cover of the trees and resumed his homeward trek across the fields. An empty cottage, full of stuff . . . and other possibilities.

Chapter 5

Sean Stubbs, meanwhile, was attempting to obtain information – any information – about the victim, and former owner of Rose Cottage, from the woman in charge of letting out holiday cottages at the agency concerned. He also wasn't doing very well. He did not regret having been detailed to carry out this part of the inquiry. After spending a good part of the morning watching the scene-of-crime specialists work their way methodically around the slaughtered Harrison, he'd found himself feeling oddly possessive about the victim. But he still needed some other image in his head when he went home at the end of this day, not just that lifeless form and the blood-soaked carpet. With luck, this chat with the lettings manager might help with that.

Looking at the manager now, he wondered whether he'd been over-optimistic. She was smartly suited, with a no-nonsense manner, and a gleam in her eye that told the world she was well able to see off any troublesome caller. Stubbs was momentarily so discountenanced that he stumbled over his opening questions; and that, he found, was a very big mistake.

She leaned forward over her desk. 'Are you sure you're from the police?'

'I showed you my ID,' Stubbs retorted.

'Anything can be faked,' she pointed out sharply, unrepentant.

'You can phone Inspector Campbell.'

'I dare say I could phone any number you care to give me. It doesn't mean that's any more genuine than you declare yourself to be.'

'We are investigating a murder!' argued the goaded Stubbs. 'And it took place in one of the cottages on your list of holiday lets!'

'Yes, *we have handled the letting out of this property for summer holiday use in the past.*' She spoke slowly, stressing the words. More briskly, she continued, 'I *can* assure you that it is not let out at the present time, not by us. So, I'm afraid, there is *nothing* I can tell you about any occupant living there now. You will have to contact the owner or his representative. We do not at present represent him.'

'It's a suspicious death!' snapped Stubbs. 'We have reason to believe the victim may be the owner. His name is Jeremy, otherwise he's known as Jerry, Harrison.'

'Indeed? Has the unfortunate man's body been identified beyond doubt?'

'By employees of the cleaning company you use to service the cottages.'

'But, as I have told you, Sergeant Stubbs, the property in question is not let out by us at the moment.'

'The owner used the same cleaners all the year round.'

'He may well have done. But, if they were there this morning, it was not because *we* sent them there. It was as part of a private arrangement between the owner and the cleaning company. It is an independent company and we use it as required. That's all.'

Stubbs opened his mouth to counter this argument but she was quicker.

'I should add, Sergeant Stubbs, that your hopes of the contract cleaners being able to confirm the deceased's identity may not be as well founded as you seem to think. There is often a high turnover of cleaning staff used by these companies. The same company may well have been cleaning the premises in question regularly. That does not necessarily mean the same actual cleaners. You will need a more reliable identification than their word. The present crew may have seen Mr Harrison once or twice; or even not at all.'

She made a good point, Stubbs had to admit. All the more reason not to give up his attempt to get some information, any information, from this dragon.

'But you must have some sort of contact details for Mr Harrison. We just need to verify—'

A gleam of triumph entered her eyes. 'Ah! So, you are not certain it is Mr Harrison's body.'

Stubbs clung heroically to the last of his patience. 'Please, madam, if you could just consult your computer . . .'

'We are not at liberty to divulge details about any former client of the agency to anyone else.'

'*But the poor bloke's dead!*'

She didn't exclaim 'aha!' but she might just as well have done. '*You* told me he had yet to be identified by anyone other than the cleaning company employees. I've already explained why you can't rely on that. Quite often they never see the owner of the property, or see him very rarely for a few minutes at most. You could try the company office. But if you want any details about Mr Harrison stored in *our* records, you will need a court order.'

Admitting defeat, Stubbs retreated 'in good order' and tried the cleaning company. In contrast to his previous encounter, this time he found himself facing a tearful teenager, clutching a damp paper handkerchief in her scarlet talons. Her name, improbably but aptly, was Misty.

'Are you sure that's your name?' asked Stubbs, genuinely curious.

'Yes.' Sniffle and more use of tissue. 'What's wrong with it?'

'Er, nothing. It's, um, unusual, but, er, very pretty.'

'My mum thought so!' she defended her parent's choice.

'About Rose Cottage. I understand this company employs the cleaning team who discovered the body—'

Misty whispered confidentially, 'They're all terribly upset!'

'So I understand. Have you—'

'Really, they're in an awful state. Two of them say they're seriously thinking of quitting altogether. I mean, it's not what anyone would expect, is it? To walk into a place and find a body on the floor covered in blood?' Her wide pale-blue eyes fixed his.

I have to expect it. It happens to me quite a lot, thought Stubbs resentfully.

'Mr Crosbie has had to give them the rest of the day off,' continued Misty in an even lower voice so that Stubbs had to lean forward to hear her. 'It's upset our schedules something awful. I'd go home myself, if Mr Crosbie would let me. But he won't.' She leaned towards Stubbs, so that their heads almost touched. 'I'm not sure I want to work here now. It's not nice, is it? Being interviewed by the police over a murder.' She gazed at him reproachfully and at disconcertingly close quarters. 'I don't know what my mum is going to say! It's awful.'

'I'm not interviewing you about the murder,' Stubbs assured her, sitting back as far as he could in his chair in order to put more distance between them, and to reassert his grip on the interview. Left unchecked, there was a good chance that Misty would moan on indefinitely. He suspected she was beginning to enjoy herself. 'I only want to know if you have contact details for Mr Harrison.'

She looked bewildered. 'How can I have any, if he's dead? I don't know where the poor man is now! If he's anywhere, I mean.

Here . . .' Misty leaned forward again and Stubbs, unable to back away any further, felt himself trapped. She whispered, 'Do you believe in an afterlife? Heaven and hell and all that?'

'Police training doesn't cover that,' Stubbs told her woodenly. 'Look, about the cottage owner. I understand that not only does your company clean the place in the summer season, through an arrangement your firm has with the letting agency, but all year round by a supplementary arrangement between the owner and . . .'

But his words were clearly not registering. Misty's train of thought was still with the afterlife. 'I've watched those programmes on the telly where people go into haunted houses and *they sense another presence*.' Her voice sank again. 'It's really scary.' She eyed him with renewed interest. 'You're always around murders and so on, have you ever felt a presence?'

'Not the sort you're talking about.' The presence hovering around him was usually Inspector Campbell or, worse, Superintendent Carter. Any ghostly presence thinking of intruding on the scene would suss out the opposition and take itself off immediately.

'Shame,' said Misty consolingly.

Stubbs felt like burying his head in his hands. This was not his day. 'Can I speak to Mr Crosbie, your boss?'

'Course you can!' she told him brightly. In a return to the muted tone, she added, 'But you'll find him in an awful mood.'

I'm rapidly getting into an awful mood, thought Stubbs, as Misty tottered away in high-heeled boots to tell Mr Crosbie the police needed to talk to him.

Crosbie may have been in an 'awful mood' with his unfortunate staff; but he proved a man who wore a coat of many colours. He was gym-buffed, fake-tanned and Stubbs suspected he'd had his teeth whitened. Despite Misty's pessimism, he was far from being

59

in a temper. He radiated professional bonhomie. He gripped Stubbs' hand, and declaimed, 'Murder, eh?' Echoing Misty, he added, 'Don't expect that when you come into work, do you?'

You might not, thought Stubbs, retrieving his crushed fingers. It happens to me a lot. It had happened today.

Woodenly, he said, 'I'm sorry to hear your cleaning staff are so distressed by this morning's events.'

'It's disrupted the schedule no end,' conceded Crosbie. 'I had to send them home. Not the whole crew, you understand, just the couple who walked in and found the corpse.' He displayed his gleaming white teeth in a predatory grin. 'They'll have to pull their socks up and get over it.'

Try it yourself, thought Stubbs. 'We are hoping,' he pressed on aloud, 'you can supply us with any other contact address for the cottage owner, Jeremy Harrison. One he used during the months the cottage was rented out.'

Crosbie sprang to action. He rattled the keys of his computer and announced, 'Correspondence care of his solicitors, likewise all queries. That generally means the owner lives abroad, or spends a lot of his time travelling out of the country. The law firm's not local, I'm afraid. They're in London. Hang on, I'll print out their address.'

'Did you ever meet Mr Harrison personally?' asked Stubbs.

Crosbie showed the first sign of any regret. 'No,' he said. 'Pity about that. I can't tell you a thing about the guy.' Another flash of the whitened teeth. 'The letting agency could probably tell you something.'

'Just one more question!' Halfway out of the door, Stubbs had been struck by a thought. 'Is it normal for the cleaning crew to walk in without ringing the doorbell or announcing their arrival in some way?'

'We hold keys for the property, all the properties, on our books,' explained Crosbie. 'They ring or knock on the door first if they think there's someone there. Or that's what they're supposed to do. Well, you don't want them walking in at inappropriate moments, do you? Never know what you might see. But today they used the key because no one answered when they knocked.'

'And today they saw a corpse.' Stubbs tried not to sound sarcastic and failed.

'What? Oh, sure.' Crosbie frowned. 'Not sure whether the two I sent home will come in to work tomorrow. I may have to start looking for replacements.'

'Well, we all have our problems,' Stubbs consoled him.

'What? Yeah, right . . . Well, you lot do all the time, I suppose.'

'Indeed, we do!' Stubbs assured him, taking the expression 'you lot' to mean the police. 'We now hold the key the cleaners used this morning to gain entry. But if you still hold any more keys to Rose Cottage, I'll need to take them with me.'

'Sure,' said Crosbie. *Misty!*

Misty tottered into the room.

'Bring the keys to Rose Cottage, there's a good girl,' ordered her boss. 'The sergeant needs them.'

'There's only one key here,' replied Misty, sounding unexpectedly sharp. 'It's the spare. The cleaners said the police had kept the one they'd used.' In an obvious change of manner, she turned to Stubbs and bestowed a smile on him. 'I'll be pleased to find it for you, Sergeant Stubbs.'

Attagirl! Stubbs thought.

Chapter 6

Carter had set off to explore the area around the murder scene. He had already spotted a fingerpost, in need of a repaint, pointing down a narrow lane, really more of a track. Its legend read *Location of Roman villa*. It must be the one Eleanor had told him about. Curiosity led him to turn and follow the direction indicated by the wooden finger.

He drove cautiously down the track, hoping he didn't meet another vehicle coming towards him, as there appeared to be nowhere to pull over. Eventually the track widened and he saw a gate and another noticeboard, weather-beaten and slightly askew, announcing *Site of Roman villa.* The gate was open and led into what looked like an area of rough pasture. There was no sign of any villa, but there was a wooden building that looked like a store and, parked by it, a muddy campervan. There were also people, two of them, who appeared to have just exited the van and were standing together, studying a map or plan. Carter turned in through the gateway and stopped just inside. He climbed down from his car, and as he did the two people turned to face him.

The man was probably in his sixties, tall and lean, with a greying beard and a shock of matching hair. For all his well-worn traditional outdoor country wear and weather-tanned complexion, Carter thought he had 'academic' hanging in an invisible sign above his head. The woman appeared some fifteen to twenty years younger, and of stocky build. She wore jeans and a heavy sweater of Scandinavian type. Both wore heavy laced boots.

'I pulled in,' Carter explained apologetically, 'because it seemed more sensible than trying to park up in the lane.'

'No problem,' said the woman with a cheerful grin.

Her companion, after scrutinising Carter, said, 'The site isn't particularly accessible, but that suits us.'

'We don't want a lot of enthusiastic souvenir seekers doing a spot of their own excavating,' explained the woman.

Carter explained he wasn't a casual sightseer but a police officer. He produced his ID as proof, and explained exactly why he was in the area. 'And you are?'

They hurried to introduce themselves as Marianna Holm and Dr Andrew Sullivan. They were, they explained, from a research institute situated in Oxford, 'but not part of the university'. It was a private foundation, they explained, endowed by a wealthy Victorian businessman, who had died childless.

'But rich!' said Marianna briskly. 'He was interested in archae-ology. He had a bee in his bonnet about Roman Britain. Fortunately, he wasn't just a crank. He grew up locally and heard, in his boyhood, that there had once been a large estate hereabouts in Roman times. Chatting to locals, he heard tales of pieces of brick and pottery turned up by ploughing here.' She waved a hand at the field. 'He spent time digging about, when he was a youngster, and came across a few coins. Under the terms of his will, the Institute was set up to seek out and excavate sites like this one, around the country. It's long been felt by the trustees that we have a duty to our founder to investigate this particular field. It was, after all, his inspiration.'

'So, you're planning a dig? I should have thought the ground far too hard at the moment for that.'

'It certainly is!' Sullivan agreed. He folded the map and returned it carefully to a plastic envelope. 'Any actual excavations would be for later in the year. We're just carrying out a general survey, with a view to making a geophysical survey later, to establish if there would be any point in returning to dig. There are records of an earlier exploratory dig, many years ago. It found pottery and fragments of pavement, probably damaged by mediaeval ploughing. No more exploratory trenches were sunk because there are other sites and, well, any dig takes time and labour and money. Allocation of resources is always a thorny issue. But, yes, we'd like to give it another go in the summer, if we can decide whether it would be worth it. The owner of the land is happy for us to try. He only grazes a few sheep here.'

The couple exchanged glances. 'You're a detective?' Sullivan asked, raising his bushy grey eyebrows. 'Your presence is official?'

'Actually, we had heard that someone had been found dead in a cottage,' confessed Marianna, before Carter could answer. 'Or *I* heard about it. I called into that shop, they call it the Minimart, down in the main village earlier, to get some milk. It was full of people talking, not shopping. They were saying there had been a murder. But I didn't know if it was just a rumour some of them had heard. It must be pretty quiet around here and any news like that would really get them going. I thought it might not be true.' She eyed Carter, frowning. 'It's really murder, then, is it? Just as the people in the shop were saying? It does seem hard to believe.'

'A body has been found. The coroner will rule on the cause of death in due course,' said Carter, wishing he didn't sound so much like a policeman. 'But, yes, we are treating it as a suspicious death at the moment.'

And if they cherished the idea that nothing much ever happened in the countryside, they were much mistaken, Carter thought. *Especially with regard to Weston St Ambrose.*

'Good Lord!' said Sullivan. He sounded disapproving. He looked at his companion. 'Perhaps we ought to go back to Oxford, Marianna. If there's a murderer roaming around, we're not exactly secure here.' He turned back to Carter. 'We've been sleeping in the campervan,' he explained. 'Just the last two nights. We thought we'd be quite safe. But, in view of what my wife heard in the shop, and you've just told us, perhaps it isn't a very good idea.'

'There is a small hotel in Weston St Ambrose,' Carter told him. 'It's called the Royal Oak. In the circumstances, if you want to stay longer in the area, you might be safer there. I believe it's quite comfortable. Oh, there is also a pub called the Black Horse. I believe it does do rooms, but I wouldn't recommend it. The pub can get quite rowdy and you wouldn't get a good night's sleep.'

Sullivan nodded. 'Thank you, we'll think about it,' he said. 'But it wouldn't be so convenient as being here, on the spot.' He heaved a sigh of annoyance, 'What a nuisance!' he muttered, and turned away, apparently not interested to discuss the murder any more. That it was a shocking crime appeared to matter less to him than a possible problem for himself.

Obsessive type! thought Carter. *Roman Britain has a greater call on his attention than the present day. He's not worried about someone being murdered in their own home, just the inconvenience to him and his plans.*

Marianna was more curious, still staring at him. She had large, pale-blue eyes, he noticed, that went with her flaxen Scandinavian hair. *A Viking!* he thought with a touch of amusement. She looks pretty strong, as if she could wield a handy axe.

'Domestic, is it, your murder?' she asked. 'Quite a lot of guns in private hands in the country, we've found.'

'What? Oh, we don't know . . .' Carter said vaguely. The victim hadn't died of a gunshot wound, but this wasn't the moment to release any information. Too soon for that. Moreover, the most unlikely people might go running to the local press.

Sullivan, nearby, glanced back and frowned at his co-worker reproachfully.

Marianna put a finger to her lips. 'Sorry! Shouldn't ask questions.'

'I've got one or two of my own,' Carter told her. 'Have you spoken to any of the residents? Have you, on previous visits, met anyone staying at Rose Cottage? It was let out in the summer to holiday-makers.'

They shook their heads.

'Try the local pub,' Sullivan called out. 'We might go there later, to see if they can provide us with any lunch, I mean. Not to snoop!' he added hurriedly.

'They'll tell you all about it, anyway. By the way, our incident room is set up in a barn behind the pub,' Carter told him. 'If you want to chat to any of us, for any reason. Inspector Campbell is in overall charge. If she's not at the barn, then Sergeant Bennison will be there. Oh, just as a matter of routine, should you need to return to your base in Oxford, perhaps you'd let the incident room know.'

'Of course!' Sullivan said.

Carter turned to leave, but then turned back. 'I wouldn't recommend trying lunch at the Waggoner's Halt today. It's pretty packed out with curious local residents.'

Had they sought out Jess Campbell at the barn incident room straight away, they wouldn't have found her. After a quick call to confirm Eleanor was home, she had made her way to Greentrees Kennels.

'Any time during the next three hours,' she was told. 'I'll lock 'em up.'

She didn't explain who 'they' were; she probably realised that Ian would have warned Jess about the pugs. The only indication of their presence on the property now was a commotion behind the house. But Jess's arrival had been noted by their owner, who appeared as the inspector approached the front door.

'They're curious little brutes. They'll have heard your car and want to investigate,' she informed the visitor cheerfully. 'So, I've penned them up. But they don't like that at all. They feel excluded and take offence, hence the noise. Take no notice. Come indoors.'

She led Jess into an untidy sitting room. 'Cup of coffee?'

'Thank you, but I won't, if you don't mind. Superintendent Carter told me he'd met you this morning and you were a close friend of the cottage's one-time owner. Not the murder victim, but the person who lived there before him; we've been told she was his aunt. However, you also knew Jeremy Harrison, her nephew, whose death we are now investigating – or we believe that to be the name of the victim. We're hoping you might be able to give us some information about him.'

'His name was indeed Jeremy Harrison, but I can tell you more about his aunt than I can about him. She was a very close and valued friend. Her name was Lucinda by rights, but we all called her Lulu. We knew each other all our lives. We were at school together.'

Eleanor sighed and looked sad. Then she pulled herself together and added briskly, 'I knew Jerry, who seems to be the victim . . .' She paused and looked inquiringly at Jess. 'That's been confirmed?'

'No,' Jess admitted. 'It seems probable but we are hoping to find someone to identify him.'

'Are you, now?' murmured Eleanor thoughtfully. 'Well, I knew him originally through Lulu. I used to see him about the place when he stayed with her during her lifetime. I saw him more after she died; because he inherited the cottage and retired to come and live here full time. I walk the dogs every day and he used to walk a lot, but always on his own. When we met up, we'd stop and exchange a few words for a couple of minutes. But that was it. He was a strange, solitary sort of fellow. So, tell you *about* him? That's another matter altogether.

'What I do know, I know from Lulu. He never volunteered anything. He just wasn't the sociable sort, as I said. I believe he was invited to join the bridge group here, but he didn't. In the summer he took long holidays and the cottage was rented out. He was an odd fish; I can tell you that. His aunt was fond of him. I suppose she must have been, to leave him the cottage in her will.'

'As a matter of fact . . .' Jess hesitated. 'We may find it difficult to find someone to identify the body. We've no reason to believe it isn't Jeremy Harrison. But we only have the statements of the team of contract cleaners who came to the cottage earlier and found him. That's not really enough.'

'So, do you want me to take a look at him?' Eleanor settled back in her chair and stared hard at Jess.

'It's an imposition, of course, and if you don't want to do it, we'd quite understand.'

'Oh, I don't mind taking a look at the poor blighter,' said Eleanor briskly. 'For Lulu's sake, not for his.'

She paused. 'My name is Eleanor, so I was always called Nell. Later on, only my late husband called me that, he and Lulu Harrison. She always called me Nell.' Eleanor frowned. 'I tell a lie, Jerry Harrison called me Nell, because he heard his aunt call me that.'

She seemed to drift away into memory. 'The really funny thing was that, although my husband called me "Nell" all our married life, the last clear words he spoke were, "Goodnight, Eleanor." Don't know why.' She looked apologetically at her visitor. 'Sorry, Inspector, I'm rambling. It's just that death, any death, has a way of reminding you of all kinds of little things.'

The little things, thought Jess. *It's the little details I want.*

Outdoors, the pugs had fallen silent, as nothing was happening where they could see or hear it. That didn't mean they had lost interest. They knew a stranger was still on the premises. Jess suspected they were waiting for sounds of her departure; and then bedlam would arise again. Eleanor was staring thoughtfully at her visitor.

'To be honest, I did resent Jerry calling me "Nell",' she said. 'Just a bit, you know. It came across as a familiarity. But that was what his aunt had called me, so it was natural enough he did the same. Anyway, I called him "Jerry" and not "Jeremy", so it was tit for tat. He wasn't really taking liberties. It's just that I didn't like him much. But then, I'm a crochety old bat.'

Jess suppressed a smile. 'Any particular reason? For not liking Jerry Harrison? Apart from his being generally unsociable?'

'No, like I said, I'm cantankerous sometimes. Some people might say I'm unsociable. Perhaps it was only the casual way he'd turn up, and make use of Lulu for accommodation, until he went off travelling again.' She snorted. 'He called it "work assignments overseas". I called it travelling.' She gave a wry grimace. 'But Lulu seemed fond of him, so I was careful not to sound critical when his name was mentioned.'

There was a brief silence during which Eleanor didn't add to her words. Jess waited. If you pushed witnesses, they could clam up. Eleanor seemed to be thinking something over. Jess felt a tremor run up her spine. The other woman was about to impart some confidence and that was what Jess had been hoping. When it came, however, it was a long way from what she might have expected.

'That's a death the police ought to have investigated!' Eleanor said suddenly in a sharp voice. She fell silent again and stared moodily at Jess, seeing her very much as a police officer. 'Someone should have asked some questions about that. I nearly told that fellow, Carter, so. But it's old history now and I dare say you are only interested in this morning's gruesome find.'

'Lucinda Harrison's death?' Jess guessed.

'Absolutely!'

'Believe me,' Jess assured her, 'if it occurred at Rose Cottage, I'm interested to hear about it. Any kind of background information can prove useful.'

Eleanor beamed suddenly. 'I understand you don't want coffee; and you're not supposed to drink alcohol on duty. But would a small sherry be in order? Fact of the matter is, if I'm going to talk any more about poor Lulu, I'll need a strengthener.'

'A very small sherry would be fine for me,' Jess told her.

'Good. Hold on a jiff!'

A few minutes later, they were settled with a sherry apiece. Eleanor drew a deep breath, preparing to tell her story.

Before she could begin, Jess asked quickly, 'Do you mind if I record this?'

'What? No, go ahead! Well, Lucinda was a pretty girl and grew into a very attractive woman. My mother always reckoned Lulu would marry well. She never said that about me. I think she believed she'd be lucky ever to get me off her hands. In fact, I married a man I loved, and who loved me, and we were happy for many years.'

Death on the Prowl

Eleanor indicated a wedding photograph with her sherry glass. 'He'd inherited the family farm and we ran it together until he was killed in an accident. I hadn't the heart to carry on without him; and there was someone who wanted to take the place on, a brother-in-law. So I came here, partly to be near Lulu.

'Poor Lulu, she had no luck at all. My mother certainly got her predictions all wrong. Lulu married a real wrong 'un. Bit of a charmer, from a decent family, and, I understand, very highly thought of in professional terms. To sum him up, he was successful, but entirely selfish. That sort very often is, you know. They get used to having everything their own way, issuing the orders, making the big decisions. Being the person everyone refers to. The one-in-charge without whose say-so nothing can happen. Enough to turn anyone's head, I suppose.'

Eleanor sipped her sherry. 'The real problem was that he was a dedicated philanderer. Only to be expected, perhaps. Power is said to be an aphrodisiac, isn't it? At any rate, women liked him and he liked women. Plus, he was used to getting what he wanted.

'Eventually, Lulu got fed up with all his playing around; and they divorced. No kids, fortunately. Divorce is hard on children. Lulu would have made a great mother. She didn't remarry. I understand her ex did, eventually. She mentioned it to me once. "My former husband has got himself a new wife," she said to me. "What they call a trophy wife. That sounds better than a bit of arm candy. I understand he met her abroad. Perhaps she'll have more luck with him than I did!"

'No more, just that. I told her, he was lucky to have found a foreign woman to take him on. Nobody in this country, who knew anything about him, would have done so.

71

'So, Lulu and I settled down as neighbours. She'd resumed her maiden name of Harrison. We had a kind of understanding to regard her brief marriage as a kind of "blip". A lot of our mutual acquaintances thought she would marry again. But she never did. Perhaps she just never met the right man, after all. Or maybe it was an example of "once bitten, twice shy".

'We didn't live in each other's pockets, you understand, but it was nice having her nearby. I think she liked having me not too far away.'

Eleanor drew a deep breath. 'Everything might have continued well, but for the arrival of a cuckoo in the nest, Jeremy Harrison, probably your corpse. I never took to him. He was the son of Lulu's brother. The brother, I can't recall his name, was at least ten years older than Lulu. The brother and his wife died in a car crash, I believe. I never knew them. But Jeremy was Lulu's nephew, and I got to know about him. *About* him, but not know him as a person, I mean. I wonder if anyone did. Perhaps Lulu thought she did. But she was mistaken, if so.'

The speaker smiled grimly. 'You know, Jeremy Harrison always reminded me of Kipling's cat, in the *Just So* stories. You know the story, Inspector? The cat "who walked by himself, and all places were alike to him". Except that Jerry Harrison had his eye on one place – his aunt's cottage! It's my belief that he set his sights on owning that from the moment he laid eyes on it. It's a nice place.'

'You know what he did for a living?'

'He was some kind of engineer, working in the oil industry, largely in the Middle East, so Lulu told me, but actually anywhere where there was a job for him. He used to come and visit her when he was in England. His wandering existence meant he hadn't put down any roots, never married, no kids . . . I suppose

72

she was the only family he had; and he wasn't slow to work out what that meant.'

'He would be the most likely beneficiary of her will?'

'You've got it! At first his visits lasted a few days, but quickly he started hanging around for longer periods. Lulu always said he was waiting to begin a new job abroad, and would be off as soon as he had the details.'

'He didn't have any other English base?' Jess asked.

'Not that I ever heard of. He'd turn up, between overseas jobs, and do pretty well nothing apart from a spot of gardening for his aunt. Then he'd take off again. She wouldn't see him for ages. I used to think that she appeared drawn to unreliable men: first the adulterous husband, then the nephew with wanderlust. They weren't either of them among life's failures, that was the really irritating thing. They had ability, were successful in their line, but deep down they were simply rotters. Who knew what other black sheep might have turned up, but Lulu died.'

Eleanor broke off. She'd finished her sherry and held up the bottle, raising her eyebrows in inquiry.

'Not for me, thanks, one's enough,' Jess told her.

'I'll have another.' Eleanor poured it. 'This suspicious death of Jerry Harrison, that you are investigating now, that's something of a repeat performance. Lulu was also found dead by a chance caller at Rose Cottage.' Eleanor paused and looked sadly down at her hands. 'Lulu's death was very hard to accept. It really shook me. For a long time, I had feelings of guilt, you know, that I should have been there, prevented it somehow.'

'Feelings of guilt after someone has died are quite common,' Jess assured her. 'But death, well, it comes to us all. Not always violently, of course, and not always in suspicious circumstances.'

'You'd know more about that than I do. In Lulu's case, the

postman found her dead. He'd arrived with a parcel of some sort. She used to order clothes from catalogues. He knocked at the door, didn't get an answer. The door wasn't locked. He pushed it open and called out to her. No reply. He got a bit concerned because he knew her as someone he'd delivered to before. All those catalogue clothes, you see. He knew she lived alone. He went a bit further in, called again, and saw her on the hall floor, quite cold.'

'There must have been an inquest,' Jess said.

'Oh, yes, there was. She was still wearing her dressing gown; and the theory put forward was that she'd stepped on the hem while coming downstairs during the night for some reason. She lost her footing and plummeted down. Knocked unconscious by the fall. Cold night. The weather was rather like it is now, only even colder. So she lay there and froze.'

'I've been in the cottage and seen that staircase,' Jess said. 'It looks tricky to me. The treads are really narrow.'

'Yes,' agreed Eleanor. 'It's often the case with old properties. Anyway, I never really bought the explanation of Lulu's fall. I mean, I agree it wasn't impossible, but I just had a feeling that it was all wrong.'

'Where was Jeremy, or Jerry, the nephew?' asked Jess. 'At the time this happened.'

'Oh, the proverbial bad penny? Out of the country again, as he so often was. He hadn't been around for a couple of months or more. But here's the thing! He turned up almost immediately after she died.' Eleanor uttered a growl not unlike that of one of her pugs. 'He was supposed to have been working overseas at one of his oil jobs, in the Middle East. His story was, he'd come home a few days earlier than expected, and had been staying at a hotel near the airport. But Lulu hadn't mentioned to me that he was back in England, let alone said anything about expecting a visit from him. I taxed him with it when I saw him. He was pretty glib in his explanation. A flight back became available earlier than he'd expected. He'd jumped on it and hadn't had time to let his Aunt Lucinda know of his arrival. He had tried to phone her from his airport hotel, to let her know he was back, and would be coming to see her soon. When he got no reply, he became concerned and hurried down here in a hired car. He arrived to find she'd had her "accident" the previous day. He was the heir. When all was settled, he moved in. I thought the whole thing fishy, but I had no evidence I could give at the inquest. Lulu was gone. Jerry Harrison was here, literally, living in her home.'

Eleanor scowled into her empty sherry glass. 'It all happened so fast, or seemed so to me. When things happen unexpectedly, events often pick up speed afterwards. Have you found that in your work?'

'But he carried on with the pattern of lifestyle,' Jess said thoughtfully, ignoring her question. 'Only staying here from time to time, mostly in the winter months now he was the cottage owner, and travelling abroad for the rest of the year. Or was he still working in the oil industry?'

'No, my understanding was that he retired quite soon after Lulu died. I suppose that meant he'd made enough money and, I dare say, Lulu left quite a bit. Jerry was approaching the age when he could take early retirement. I imagine one needs to be very fit and active in the oil industry. Maybe he was finding it harder to keep up with the younger ones,' retorted Eleanor. 'There's no reason to suspect that wasn't the truth. But he still had restless feet. It was a quiet life here, too quiet for his taste. Letting out the cottage in the summer gave him a supplementary income. It also meant he could go where he pleased, knowing that the place was occupied and the letting company was keeping an eye on it.'

'Did he inherit everything?'

'Oh, yes, the lot, every last penny, apart from a Dresden coffee service she left to me.' Eleanor leaned forward. 'She just made rotten choices when it came to men. Poor Lulu, she was a very trusting sort of person. She never learned.'

'Well, thank you for telling me about it,' Jess said. 'Have you any idea who might have wanted to kill Jeremy?'

Eleanor uttered another of those throaty growls, not unlike that of a small dog. Jess had to suppress a smile.

'No idea!' Eleanor said briskly. 'Perhaps it has something to do with the time he spent abroad? Made an enemy or two? That wouldn't surprise me. As I said, he was a strange sort of chap, a loner, I suppose you'd call him. Even when he was living at the cottage, I didn't see much of him. As I told you, I take the dogs out every day. Occasionally, I'd run into him. I see nearly everyone around here at least a couple of times a week. There are more people living locally than you'd think.'

'I realise that,' Jess told her, with a rueful grin. 'I think most of them have visited the Waggoner's Halt this morning.'

'Only natural,' said Eleanor tolerantly, draining the last of her sherry. 'This is a quiet sort of spot. Not a lot happens. Perhaps that's why Jerry wanted to make his base here. He liked privacy.'

'Very likely,' Jess agreed. Privately she was thinking, *And perhaps he was hiding from someone, or something.*

But the past has a way of catching up with life's chancers; and she was beginning to think Jeremy Harrison had been one of them. All the same, it was a curious coincidence. Two unexpected deaths in the same cottage, within a very few years. Eleanor thought her friend's apparent fall downstairs suspicious.

As an isolated incident, it might not have been. But with a second body . . .

'I don't like coincidences,' said Jess aloud to herself. 'I'm a detective and I like explanations, good, watertight ones, if possible.'

But she was well aware that wanting neat, provable, explanations was one thing. Getting them was another.

Chapter 7

At the barn, the incident room was still receiving a steady stream of visitors, and Tracy Bennison had found herself obliged to help out the struggling single constable trying to take all their information. Or, rather, listen to their opinions, which was by no means the same thing. Apart from the retirees living in Long Lane, others were making their way there, including from Weston St Ambrose village itself, or even further afield. Thus, it turned out that Bennison found herself talking to Mrs Beryl Garley – and Sammy.

Sammy was a small dog of the terrier type and was perched on Mrs Garley's knees. He stared intently at Tracy, who felt that their roles had been reversed. Sammy was interrogating her.

'I'd leave him outside normally,' his owner had announced as she took her seat and Sammy jumped up on her lap. 'That's what I do when I go into the Minimart in Weston. You're not supposed to take dogs into food shops. Well, you'd know that, wouldn't you, being police and that? Mind you, the Minimart is run by my niece, Debbie, and I dare say she wouldn't mind because she knows Sammy and how well-behaved he always is.'

Sammy made a low grumbling sound that might have been a growl or just signified impatience. Tracy felt the same way. 'Mrs Garley . . .' she prompted.

The witness took no heed but rolled on placidly at her own speed. 'But, being as this is a strange place for Sammy, and he doesn't know most of the people here, it's different. So I brought him inside with me, or he'd just sit outside and howl. He's sensitive. Well, no more do I know most of these people,' added Beryl. She gave a dismissive glance around her. 'They're incomers, a lot of them, the ones who live in those big new houses along Long Lane. The real local people all know one another. But these other people come from all over the place. It makes you wonder what's brought them to live out here. It's not like they've got any connections, is it?'

Bennison tried again. 'Quite so, Mrs Garley, I understand. Now then, what did you want to report?'

The witness – if, indeed, that was what she was – leaned forward.

'We're a local family, like I was saying,' she confided to Tracy, and smiled kindly. 'I thought I'd just pop in and tell you.'

'Tell me that yours is a local family?' Tracy felt she'd got that message.

But Beryl was looking at her pityingly as if the sergeant had a problem grasping the narrative.

'No, dear, tell you that I used to clean for Mrs Harrison.'

Tracy glanced at her notes. 'We understand that the victim, Jeremy Harrison, was not married.'

'No,' agreed Beryl. 'And he might have been a nicer and happier person if he had been. But I was more than willing to clean for him, just like I did for his auntie, when she lived at the cottage. That's the Mrs Harrison I'm talking about. But no, he didn't want me. He was downright insulting. He said he'd arranged to use one of them cleaning services, so I wouldn't be required. That's his words. "Not required!" "It's letting complete strangers into your house," I told him. "Your auntie would never have done that." But it made no difference. He wanted the cleaning company. It wasn't as if he didn't know me. I'd cleaned at the house when he'd been visiting Mrs Harrison. He used to come and stay with her every so often, you know. Now then,' added Beryl Garley, lowering her voice to a confidential undertone. 'If you ask me, he'd be alive today if he'd let me clean for him, like I did for his auntie.'

'Because?' prompted Bennison,

Mrs Garley stared at her. 'Because it's never a good idea to let strangers into your house, is it? That's what he did. He let strangers into his house. Now he's dead, murdered. That's what comes of being careless.'

'Let me get this right,' Bennison said slowly. 'Are you accusing someone employed by the cleaning company of murdering him?'

Mrs Garley eyed her with exasperation. 'No! Of course I'm not. But if you go letting strangers into your house, you don't know what they might do, do you? I reckon he let a stranger in that evening, and it got him killed.'

'I see, well, thank you, Mrs Garley . . .'

'He was a miserable git,' Beryl added without rancour, as she rose to leave. The movement dislodged Sammy, who leaped to the floor. 'He had no friends, no visitors, and he went off on holiday every summer and left the house full of strangers. A "holiday let" they call it. Now then, is that normal? Poor Mrs Harrison must have been spinning in her grave. It's got to be asking for trouble. He was always allowing strangers into his home. No wonder he ended up like he did. *As you sow, so shall you reap*. It says that in the Bible. God rest his soul!' she concluded piously.

'Well, thank you, Mrs Garley. I've made a note of all you've said.'

'Just thought I'd come in and tell what I thought,' said the would-be witness. Sammy shook himself vigorously. 'It would never have happened if he'd let me clean for him; like I did for his auntie. Cleaned for her for fifteen years, I did. She was the nicest person you could hope to meet.'

'What was all that about?' asked the constable who was on duty with her, when the witness had marched out, Sammy trotting alongside her.

'Goodness only knows,' said Bennison. 'She didn't have anything to tell me. Waste of time!'

But there, had she but known it, Bennison was wrong.

Millie had not been the only one to reach the Waggoner's Halt by bike. Beryl Garley, too, travelled the local area by means of a large, old-fashioned delivery-boy's bicycle, with a large metal frame containing a wicker basket attached at the front. The basket was lined by a blanket and this was where Sammy travelled. He was well used to it, having done so since he was a puppy. After her visit to the incident room, Mrs Garley rattled down the lane to Weston St Ambrose; and left the bicycle parked at the rear of the Black Horse public house. Sammy jumped out of the basket and accompanied his owner into the pub. In fact, he led the way into the low-ceilinged public bar, because he'd been there so many times before.

The bar's beams were hand-hewn and irregular. Some had brass tankards hanging from them. The presence of a large-screen television on one wall jarred with these old-world touches. The little dog also knew the person Beryl was seeking and had spotted him seated in a corner. Sammy scurried towards a lean, weather-beaten and tanned sinewy figure. This was Wayne Garley, handyman and Weston's general Mr Fixit. From his seat Wayne had a clear view of whoever entered the room. Now he raised his beer glass in salute to Beryl, before leaning down to scratch

Sammy's ears. Beryl, having paused to order a small gin and tonic, not too much ice, followed.

Beryl was a widow. She had once been married to Wayne's brother; until the said brother fell off a roof he was helping to tile. She still considered Wayne to be her brother-in-law. He was also a distant cousin because, as locals who knew the clan would tell you: 'The Garleys are like that. They marry in the family.' Wayne's daughter, Debbie, ran the only shop in the village. Thus, new arrivals soon found that, wherever they went in Weston St Ambrose, they wouldn't be able to get away from the Garleys. They also found that whatever they did, the rest of Weston St Ambrose knew about it pretty fast, courtesy of Debbie, who operated an information service the police might have envied.

Wayne put aside the *Daily Express* he'd been reading and said placidly, 'Hullo, Beryl, all right?'

Mrs Garley didn't waste time on trivia. 'I've been up to the incident room they opened in Barry Wilson's barn.'

'Oh, yes?' said Wayne. 'Doing good business, are they?'

It went without explanation that 'they' referred to the police.

'Wasting their time,' Beryl told him.

'You don't reckon they'll find out who did for the bloke who lived in Rose Cottage, then?'

'Not unless somebody tells them,' Beryl sniffed.

Wayne raised his glass to his lips. 'Well, they shouldn't get their hopes up that anyone is going to do that,' he said, before taking a generous swig. 'Wasting their time, that's what those cops are doing. Incident room!' he snorted. 'Are they paying Barry for the use of his barn?'

'I don't know about that,' said Beryl regretfully. 'I didn't ask him. He probably wouldn't say, if they are. You know how close he is about money. Perhaps he hopes everyone is going to buy a drink at the Waggoner's. There's a fair crowd of folk there, all curious to see a real investigation at work, so the trade is there. But, as for the incident room as they call it, there's nothing to see except a couple of coppers sitting at desks chatting to anyone who wants to talk to them.'

Beryl gazed thoughtfully into her emptied glass. 'The only thing is that, as well as the couple in the barn, two more senior coppers have been back again. You remember, the superintendent and the red-haired inspector? They came before, the last time there was a bit of trouble hereabouts. They're not sitting in the barn. They're wandering around outside.'

'Ah,' said Wayne. 'That's not so good. Nosy pair. But they're not doing the questioning in Barry's barn, you say?'

'No, less important ones are doing that, like I told you. But I saw the superintendent talking to Eleanor Holder. They were standing outside Rose Cottage. Mrs Holder had those little dogs of hers with her. I cycled off before they spotted me.'

There was an interlude during which both drank and said nothing.

'Asking does no harm,' opined Wayne at last, setting down his empty glass. 'It's the answers can do that.'

Mrs Garley frowned. 'I don't like them bothering Mrs Holder. She was Mrs Harrison's friend.'

Wayne chuckled. 'You don't need to worry about Mrs Holder! She's got her head screwed on the right way. You want another gin, Beryl?'

'Better not,' said Mrs Garley regretfully.

'Is Millie back?' Carter asked Monica later that day, when he arrived at her cottage. He knew he was trying and failing to sound nonchalant.

'Upstairs, having a really good sulk,' returned Monica cheer-fully. 'Don't worry about it. She'll get bored up there on her own, and hungry, and come down.'

'Did she tell you all about it?'

'Not really, only that you ordered her away from the scene of the investigation. I didn't ask why. It's not my business.'

'She was hanging about there,' Carter defended himself. 'I can't have that!'

'Why not?' asked Monica mildly. 'No, don't tell me. I only suggest that when you get back to your flat tonight, you have a talk with her.'

'I'm certainly going to do that,' Carter said grimly.

'I mean a two-sided talk. Listen to what she has to say! You might be interested.'

That sounded worrying. He would have liked to press Monica for more details, but knew it would be futile. If she had wanted to tell him more, she would have done so.

Monica stooped to peer into the oven. 'We're having cottage pie, all right?'

'My favourite,' said Carter glumly.

'Jess isn't joining us?'

'There's a lot going on down there, and I forgot to ask her,' he lied. 'You think I've handled this all wrong, don't you? With Millie, I mean.'

'What I think is of no importance. There's a beer in the fridge. Bring it into the sitting room. There is something I need to talk to you about, something else. Millie being upstairs, it gives us a chance.'

Carter followed her into the comfortable, cluttered sitting room, wishing he didn't feel so apprehensive. He managed to find a comfortable chair that didn't already have a cat in posses-sion of it, and accepted the glass of beer his hostess held out.

Monica glanced at the door to check it was closed. 'I've had a long chat with Sophie, on the phone.'

'All well there, I hope?' Carter asked tersely. This, he felt, was going to be bad news in some form or another.

'I understand,' continued Monica, 'that she and Rodney haven't been getting along too well lately.'

'They aren't splitting up, are they?' Carter sipped his beer to disguise his alarm. That would be the last thing he needed. Sophie might have chosen to cut him out of her life. But that was while Rodney was around. Rodney out of the picture and . . . The scenario didn't bear thinking about. Sophie was not the sort to suffer in silence, or alone.

'I'm not sure. It's something you ought to know about, because of Millie. They have a beautiful home in France, as you know. I've visited. Rodney has apparently been able to work from that base quite comfortably. Sophie, I suspect, has begun to be bored.'

'What about their son? Doesn't he keep her occupied?'

'Well, he did, when he was a baby. But now he goes to a play-school of some sort. He's talking well, chattering away, I gather. In French, of course, although they speak English with him.'

'Only to be expected. Didn't Sophie and Rodney consider the possibility? The kid was bound to be going to local schools in time. Of course, he'll be bilingual. Rather an advantage in life, I'd have thought.'

'They didn't think it through deeply enough,' retorted Monica. 'He's even started talking to *them* in French. They don't mind, in fact, they're rather proud of it. But it's reminded them that when they moved to France it was a permanent thing. This wasn't a holiday home. It was their future base. I guess it's concentrated their minds. Or, at least, it's given Sophie food for thought. Rodney doesn't have any problem.'

Monica paused and added, 'I don't think Rodney sees problems. Not domestic ones, anyway. Business ones are another matter and he concentrates on them.'

Ian managed not to make any comment on that, at least not aloud. He concentrated on his beer glass. *We're above all that domestic trivia, are we, Rodney, old boy? Sophie didn't let me get away with that; and she won't let you off the hook, either!*

'He is able to run his business online, as people do nowadays. It doesn't matter any more where they live.' Monica sighed. 'All that technology. It really is a different world.'

I don't doubt Rodney could run his business from the moon, snarled the inner Ian, and then reproached himself for feeling so resentful.

'They have a very decent income; and there has been no difficulty about their living in France, even though now we're out of the EU. They've been granted residence and they have been talking of applying for French passports. No mention of coming back here.'

With a sinking heart, Carter asked, 'But you suspect that something has changed, and now they are thinking of coming back here?'

Monica hesitated. 'Things haven't reached that point yet.'

Carter felt himself the proverbial drowning man grasping at a straw. The moment was fleeting. Monica had taken a deep breath and was about to make some momentous announcement. Or perhaps she wasn't, but Carter just feared she was.

'As I understand it, Rodney wants to stay in France. Sophie is thinking that perhaps they ought to return to England, set up a new base. Keeping the French house as a holiday home, or letting it to friends for short breaks. Not to strangers, of course.'

Jeremy Harrison, thought Carter, *whose death we're investigating. He let out his house, to people who were strangers, for nearly half the year. Rodney and Sophie should think it over carefully before they did anything similar.*

But who am I to advise them? Ian forced consideration of their problems from his mind. *I'm just a copper who sees life at the grubby end of things. There is no reason why Rodney and Sophie should have any trouble at all. So far, they've organised their lives pretty well. Unlike me. My daughter apparently thinks I'm a lonely old guy living in a hovel.*

Monica was still doing her best to represent Sophie's point of view. *Frankly,* thought Carter, *I can do without all this.*

'She misses her old friends, all kinds of little things she probably didn't even think about when they left. If Sophie isn't happy, she—' Monica broke off, probably not wanting to sound disloyal to her niece.

'She complains!' said Ian promptly. 'I've had the experience of being on the receiving end of Sophie not being happy.'

'I gather things between them haven't been harmonious.' Monica was ever tactful.

'Monica,' Carter said quietly. 'You know, this really hasn't anything to do with me.' Did he sound defensive? To his own ears, he did. 'I'm not married to Sophie now. She's married to Rodney. It's Rodney's problem, not mine.'

'You have nothing to do with Rodney, or Rodney's son,' Monica agreed. 'But you and Sophie share Millie. Her life has been upset enough. She doesn't need more rows, arguments, uncertainty. It would make any child feel insecure. And Millie feels insecure enough as it is.'

'Does she?' Carter asked. 'I should have realised. Sophie always complained life is all work for me. Perhaps she was right.'

'Just thought I'd mention it,' said Monica. 'To keep you in the loop, so to speak.'

She bustled out of the room, probably leaving him to digest the news. Carter stood up and went to the window, looking out into the small but immaculate front garden. One of the cats, a stripey one, was doing its best to upset the carefully weeded and maintained beds by making a neat heap of earth on one of them. It saw the movement at the window, stopped what it was doing and directed a defiant stare at him.

'Fair enough,' murmured Carter. 'There are private moments when no one needs an audience.'

But he had enough on his plate at the moment, and could do without Sophie's problems.

There was sound of someone coming down the narrow staircase, followed by rattling from the kitchen. The sitting-room door opened.

'I've taken the cottage pie out of the oven,' announced Millie from the doorway. 'It's starting to dry out.'

Is that what's happened to me? wondered Carter. *Have I started to dry out?*

Millie sat silently beside him as he drove them home. That, in itself, was a very bad sign. She had always been a chatterer. As soon as they were indoors, and before Millie could shut herself in her room, he opened proceedings.

'I'm sorry if you were upset that I sent you away from the incident room, but I was very surprised to see you there.'

'I wasn't in the incident room,' she corrected him. 'I was outside.'

'Yes, that's true, but had you intended to go into the incident room?'

She looked a little embarrassed. 'I might have done.'

'A murder investigation is a very serious matter. It doesn't need sightseers.'

That really did anger her. She turned scarlet and snapped, 'I wasn't sightseeing. All those people at the pub were sightseers. I was observing, with a view to making notes.'

That stopped him momentarily in his tracks. Millie pursued her advantage.

'You didn't even ask me why I was there!'

'I didn't, that's true,' he admitted. 'So, why were you keen to make notes?'

'Because I want to join the police force one day.'

Afterwards, thinking the conversation over, Carter had to admit to himself that she'd delivered a knockout blow. It left him speechless. When he was able to utter a word, it was simply, 'Why?'

'Well, we had a talk from a careers adviser. She came to the school. She asked us all if we had any ideas for our future. I told her what I was thinking of, and she said the same thing. She asked me why. So I told her my father was a superintendent in the police and the inspector who worked with him was a woman, Jess, I meant. And I want to be like Jess, work in CID.'

'And what did this careers adviser say to that?'

'She advised me to go for a degree first of all, and after I graduated, if I was still interested, I could apply to enter the police on the graduate scheme. She suggested that, as well as talking to you, I might talk to Inspector Campbell. I referred to Jess by her rank when I was talking to the adviser. I thought I'd better not call her Jess.'

'I'm going to make some cocoa,' Carter said, because he needed time to think. He'd have preferred a stiff drink, but in the circumstances it would have to be cocoa. 'Then we can talk about it a bit more.'

'You're not going to be totally negative, I hope?' she challenged.

Totally negative . . . he recognised the phrase as being one of the criticisms Sophie had levelled at him. Not so much negative as reeling, he thought. 'Have you talked to your mother about this?' he ventured cautiously.

'I did just mention it.' Millie frowned. 'She didn't like it.'

'Oh, well, yes, I don't suppose she did.' *Monica! Why didn't you warn me this was what it's all about?*

Millie's manner softened. 'I can see it's come as a bit of a shock to you too, Dad. I'll make the cocoa. You sit down. You've had a very busy day.'

Yes, you could call it that, he thought.

'This is quite ridiculous,' Eleanor told the pugs. They gazed up at her questioningly. 'After Lulu died, I didn't like walking by Rose Cottage, especially when *he* was living there! Now it's as if I can't stay away. So, come along, you lot, we won't be out for more than half an hour.'

In the end, she took only two of them. The chosen pugs were resentful and let her know, rumbling and grumbling as they trotted along. Eleanor herself was beginning to think it was not such a good idea. It was cold and dark; sporadic spots of rain touched her face like cold fingertips. Having been, at one time, a farmer's wife, she was well used to the countryside at night and the range of sounds unremarked during the day but now, without passing traffic to muffle them, they sounded sharp and clear. The fox was out and about. She heard its distant bark and so did the pugs. They set up another barrage of gruff throaty growls, and would-be barks, that didn't quite escape their throats. She spoke to them reassuringly, but they weren't convinced.

'It's all right!' she reassured them. And even then, as she spoke, she heard the scrape of leather on the road surface a little way behind her. She tried, for a mere instant, to convince herself that it was her imagination. Then she heard it again, heavier, more determined. Someone else was out walking on this inhospitable evening. Eleanor tried to push out of her mind her impression that the person following had quickened his step in order to catch up with her.

The Waggoner's Halt was not that far ahead. Eleanor quickened her steps. The pugs were obliged to hurry along, too, but they didn't like it. It made them even more restless. Instead, she chose the alternative and stopped altogether, waiting. If the other walker were legitimate, he, or she, would catch up. If, on the other hand, the other walker had mischief in mind, he would halt too, and wait. She almost called out, 'Who's there?' but stopped herself. She feared her voice might sound shaky. In any case, she reasoned, the fact that she betrayed alarm would make her more vulnerable. She couldn't rely on the pugs to defend her. They would try, certainly, but they couldn't do more than nip an assailant's ankles.

The follower didn't stop. He – she felt instinctively that the other person must be 'he' as the footsteps were too heavy for a woman – came onward and now she could see his darker outline against the moonlit sky. It was strangely shaped. It – he – wore a very baggy coat. It rang a distant bell in Eleanor's memory. She had seen such a garment before, long ago. Back then, the coat had belonged to a poacher. But a poacher wouldn't be walking boldly down the road. He'd be seeking the camouflage of trees or hedges. Then the figure spoke.

'What are you doing out at this time of night, Mrs Holder? You'd be better off at home, sitting by the fire with a glass of whisky.'

She thought the voice familiar but still heard herself ask, 'Who is it?'

'Wayne Garley,' he told her. 'Give you a bit of a fright, did I?'

He'd reached her and stopped. 'You on your way to the pub, then?'

She almost replied that, yes, she was on her way to the Waggoner's. But lies had ways of making things more complicated. If Wayne drank at the pub of an evening, he would know she didn't go there normally. With this in mind, she said, 'Just taking two of the pugs out for a last short walk. It might rain tomorrow.' Then, without knowing quite why, she added, 'I intended to go as far as Rose Cottage and then go home. The police will have it cordoned off, of course; I didn't intend to go on to the property.'

'No harm in taking a look at the place,' Wayne said. 'I'll walk that far and back with you.'

Eleanor, suddenly overwhelmed with relief, said, 'Thank you, Wayne, that's kind of you.'

''S'all right,' said Wayne. 'Someone ought to keep an eye on the place.'

They turned their backs to the Waggoner's and set off down the lane to the right. The pugs seemed happier too, now that Wayne was with them. *They've got more sense than I have*, thought Eleanor. *Setting out at night in such a lonely spot, with a murderer still wandering around, for all we know. I want my head seeing to.*

Rose Cottage stood alone and forlorn. The wind rustled the leylandii and the police tape, secured around the edge of the property, snapped and crackled as though it argued about something. Eleanor had the uneasy feeling that voices, not human but of something else, whispered in the foliage. She was more than ever glad that Wayne was there.

'Them trees,' said Wayne now, in brisk, practical tones. 'They need taking down altogether.'

'Yes,' agreed Eleanor. 'They probably do.'

'I told him so, the bloke who was murdered there, I told him I could take them down, very reasonable price, seeing as it would be a local job, or at least take them down to half the height. But he just said, very sharp, that he liked the privacy.'

'He was like that, very private,' agreed Eleanor, without meaning to answer Wayne directly, more talking to herself.

'Miserable blighter, right enough,' said Wayne, not in a way that condemned the late Jerry Harrison, but more in the manner of a fair comment on his character. 'His auntie, now, Mrs Harrison, she was always very pleasant. I did a few odd jobs for her over the years, roof repairs, bit of plumbing.'

'You can turn your hand to anything, Wayne,' Eleanor told him. She was thinking, *And I wonder if that does include a spot of poaching.*

'Got to, living out here. And Weston St Ambrose people have always looked after themselves, as you might say. My sister-in-law used to clean for Mrs Harrison when she lived here.'

'Yes, I remember Beryl,' said Eleanor. 'I see her about occasionally on her bike, with the little dog in the basket.'

'Good sort, our Beryl,' said Wayne. 'You stepping into the Waggoner's for a glass of something?'

'Nice idea, but much better not,' Eleanor told him. 'The pugs have never been in there and might not settle.'

'Then I'll walk you back home,' said Wayne. 'Safer that way.'

'Thank you,' Eleanor said gratefully.

'Weston St Ambrose people always look out for one another,' Wayne told her. 'I remember when you and your husband had the farm.'

So I count as a local, Eleanor thought. *It's good to know.*

As she let herself into her house, she could hear the crunch of Wayne's footsteps heading off back to the Waggoner's Halt. She wondered why he had chosen to drink there, and not down in the village proper, at the Black Horse. Also, why he had walked there, a fair step, and not driven there in his van.

He's not poaching, she decided. *Nor is he out just for a pint or two. He's checking up, keeping an eye on the place, like a village policeman used to do, years ago when such people existed. Pounding the beat. Weston St Ambrose people look out for one another, as he said.*

She took the two pugs indoors with her, not returning them to the kennels that night. She felt she owed it to them; and she needed company.

Chapter 8

The following morning began with a team meeting to review the investigation so far. It didn't take long because, as Carter remarked quietly to Jess, 'We haven't got very far.'

Bennison reported on the interviews conducted at the old barn. That also did not take up much time. Most interviewees had been of a mind with Beryl Garley. They expressed it more elegantly.

'He wasn't a team player,' said a retired colonel, one of the Long Lane incomers. 'Entirely his decision, of course. But sometimes one needs backup. For example, if he had had any threats, he didn't tell any of us. If he had told me, I'd have advised him strongly to go to you, the police. Depending what kind of threat it was, naturally. He might have been better consulting his solicitor.'

Other residents of the large, discreetly screened properties said much the same.

'If you ask me,' opined Tracy Bennison, concluding her report, 'they feel a bit guilty, not knowing any more about him. In my opinion, it's just a reaction to the shock of his murder. I don't know why they should feel any responsibility. He was a private sort of guy, after all. He wanted to be left alone. You can't blame them for not going round to his home and hammering on the door, demanding he come and party with them! Not that they do a lot of partying as far as I can tell. They're a real bunch of stick-in-the-muds.'

'But he went on those cruises in the summer months,' Jess reminded her. 'You're hardly entirely alone on a cruise ship.'

'There's always one who doesn't join in, in any group of strangers thrown together,' countered Bennison. 'Perhaps he just didn't like his neighbours. I can't say I took to them much. Cliquey, you know?'

'One useful thing,' Jess put in. 'Mrs Holder has offered to identify the body.'

'Has she, indeed?' Carter was startled.

'She knew him for a number of years. He visited his aunt before she died and he came to live in the cottage. Mrs Holder was very close to the aunt. I gather,' added Jess, 'that she didn't altogether approve of Jeremy Harrison and viewing the body won't upset her, or so she says. I don't mean she'll stand over the corpse, rubbing her hands in satisfaction, and gloating. But she was a farmer's wife for years and it makes for a practical outlook.'

'We'll take her at her word, then.'

Stubbs was despatched to escort Eleanor Holder to the morgue, to identify the body. It was the first line of action and it needed to be done straight away.

'I always get the old ladies,' Stubbs muttered resentfully to Bennison. 'She's not going to have a heart attack or something is she, when she sees the corpse?'

'No chance of you getting any cake, this time,' Bennison retorted with a grin.

Overhearing, Jess told them, 'She's not the cake-making sort of old lady. She's pretty tough, in my judgement, and I think she'll handle taking a look at the victim without going into hysterics. She was one of many who didn't like him. That will probably sustain her.' She frowned. 'As far as I can make out, almost no one did like him.'

'Quite makes you feel a bit sorry for him,' put in Dave Nugent, who was present at the meeting.

'The impression I get,' said Carter, 'is that he didn't care whether anyone liked him or not. He does appear to have been an odd sort of guy; but that's the way he was.'

Back in the privacy of Carter's office, Jess said, 'As soon as I hear from Stubbs that Eleanor has made an identification, I'll hop on the train to London and look up the solicitors who handled Harrison's affairs. I've phoned them. They're expecting me this afternoon.'

'I don't like the disappearance of all his personal documents, driving licence and so on.' Carter walked to the window and stared discontentedly down into the car park. 'Why?'

'Could be several reasons, all good ones,' Jess said. 'It could simply be down to theft. All this, including the murder, could be down to a burglar being disturbed.'

'We're not talking of a common or garden burglar turning violent when discovered,' Carter muttered. 'The murdered man had been sitting there drinking whisky with him, or so the bottle and glasses suggest. Yet, according to all who had come into contact with him, Harrison was not the sociable type. So what were they talking about? Business? Harrison was apparently retired. He hadn't been a businessman; he had been an engineer.' He shook his head. 'There is something personal about all this. That's what I don't like. A professional housebreaker would wait for a premises to be empty before going about his work. We're looking for someone with a grudge, someone with a reason for seeking out Jeremy Harrison. That person would have no reason that I can think of to take personal documents and any computer, or anything else of value. That's what a sneak thief or burglar would do. Our killer doesn't fit the profile of either of those. We need to know more about the victim.'

'Then we could be obliged to cast a worldwide net.' Jess gave a wry smile. 'He worked in the oil business, everywhere from the Middle East to oil rigs in the North Sea.' She hesitated. 'Perhaps we should take a look at the earlier unexplained death at that cottage.'

'An earlier one?' Carter looked startled.

'Yes, our victim's aunt, Lucinda Harrison. Eleanor told me about her. She lived at Rose Cottage and Jeremy Harrison inherited the place from her. Lucinda was found dead on the hall floor one morning, still in her dressing gown. The postman found her. Everyone assumed she'd tripped and fallen down the stairs.'

Carter frowned. 'I presume the coroner was satisfied at the time. No suspicious circumstances. If she was an old schoolfriend of Eleanor's, with respect, she couldn't have been a young woman and, sadly, older people do have falls.'

'She was an older woman but she wasn't doddery, according to Eleanor. They were contemporaries at school; and you wouldn't describe Eleanor as uncertain on her feet, or those dogs she walks would've pulled her over more than once. What's more, Eleanor told me that Lucinda Harrison's brother, Jeremy's father, had been ten years older than Lucinda, so there wasn't a huge age difference between aunt and nephew. I know she might still have taken a tumble down the stairs; anyone can do that. The staircase in the cottage is narrow and spirals; and I noticed myself, when I first saw it, how narrow the treads are too. It's easy to believe someone might fall. Whatever caused her to fall, she was dead; and within days, Jerry, as he was known, the wandering nephew, was there to claim his inheritance. That suggests to me that he knew she'd willed Rose Cottage to him.' Jess looked at Ian inquiringly, waiting for counter-argument.

Carter spread his hands. 'Unfortunate, but not necessarily suspicious, no matter what Eleanor thinks. She was close to her old schoolfriend, Lulu, and she didn't like Jerry. Again, that's not special. We've already agreed that no one appears to have liked him. What was more, he didn't care.'

'I'll get someone to check out the coroner's report, anyway,' Jess said. 'No harm in taking a quick look at it. Other than the fact that he had a grouchy disposition, we know so little about Harrison. Perhaps the solicitor will have some interesting information this afternoon.'

Carter returned to where Jess stood and said, a little awkwardly, 'I don't know what time you'll get back from your trip up to London, but if it's not too late I was wondering if you'd like to come for a pizza somewhere, with Millie and me.'

'Sounds like fun,' she told him, with a grin.

'I have to confess that Monica had invited you too, last night. I didn't mention it to you, partly because I knew Millie was so cross with me. But she is keen to talk to you. She wants to follow in your footsteps, join the force.'

He saw the grin fade. 'Oh,' she said. 'That's a tricky one.'

'A careers adviser, who visited her school, has suggested she studies for a degree in something, somewhere, and enter as a fast-track candidate, if she still wants to do it.' Carter sighed. 'I suppose I should be flattered, but I'm not. She has no idea what's involved in investigating crime. I'm not talking about the procedure. I'm talking about dealing with seriously unpleasant, often very dangerous, villains; and blood-spattered scenes like the one at Rose Cottage.'

'My mother didn't want me to be a police officer of any sort either.' Jess smiled at him. 'Millie's very young. Give her time.'

'She's mentioned it to her mother,' said Carter gloomily. 'It didn't go down too well; but Sophie doesn't seem to have said too much to Millie. I suspect she's saving up her wrath for me. I'll get the blame for everything.'

'You'll cope,' Jess told him encouragingly.

Carter looked at her smiling face and mop of red hair. 'I'll book us all a table somewhere, for the pizza.'

Suddenly, he felt much happier. He had also assuaged his conscience because he hadn't passed on Monica's invitation to bring Jess to share the cottage pie. He hadn't liked fibbing to Monica, and knew she had sussed him out. But if he'd brought Jess that night, Millie would have wanted to talk about the investigation. In the pizza restaurant, that would be less likely.

Stubbs returned to report that Eleanor Holder had identified the body as being that of Jeremy, otherwise known as Jerry, Harrison.

'She was OK with it?' Carter asked him. Jess had been confident Eleanor wouldn't react badly to the experience; but Ian himself had not been entirely sure.

'Didn't turn a hair,' said Stubbs with a note of wonder in his voice. 'She's a tough old girl, that one.'

'She identified him straight away?'

Stubbs frowned. 'She didn't rush. She stood there looking at him for a couple of minutes. I was just beginning to wonder if she had any doubts, or was upset at looking at a corpse, when she spoke up, quite calmly, and said, "Yes, that's him. That's Jeremy Harrison, poor Lucinda's nephew."'

Jess thought, *Not poor Jeremy, poor Lucinda* . . .

'Did she say anything else of interest?' she asked aloud.

Stubbs consulted his notebook. 'She said, *"Unlucky blighter, not a decent way for anyone to go. But if anyone asked for it, it was probably Jerry Harrison."* I asked what she meant by that; but she only said that she knew nothing specific against him, just thought him generally unreliable.'

Stubbs again read aloud from the notebook. '"*You get a dog or*

100

a horse like that sometimes. It's just a look in the eye. They take a nip at you if they get the chance." Then she pointed at the body and added, *"It doesn't mean I wanted to see him like that. Not a way to go, as I said."'*

Stubbs closed the notebook. 'She really didn't like him. But I don't think she killed him! She was ready to leave, so I drove her home and she invited me in for a glass of sherry. I thanked her and told her I hadn't the time.' He grinned. 'She's probably downed the best part of the bottle by now.'

Carter muttered, 'I still wish we could have asked someone else.'

Stubbs was philosophical. 'If there wasn't anyone else, we had no choice. We were lucky to find anyone prepared to do the job, if you ask me. The victim, Harrison, seems to have been a pretty strange sort of guy. He had no friends. We've not found any other family members. He lived in that cottage all winter, doing what? Nothing much, as far as I can make out. Then, in summer, he let the place out and took off for overseas holidays or cruises.'

Jess, who had been standing by, listening, ran her fingers through her mop of red hair. 'There are worse ways of living out your later years, I suppose. He'd had a very active working life, as far as we can make out, travelled the world. Perhaps he'd thought he was ready to put his feet up, but then missed the new sights and so on. The cottage is lonely; but it's a nice little place, and comfortable.'

The cat who walked by himself . . . Eleanor's voice echoed in her brain. Jess dragged her attention back to the here and now. 'He was lucky that his aunt left it to him, I suppose.'

'Fair enough,' said Stubbs. 'Anything else, ma'am?' On being told *No, not at the moment,* he took himself off to write up his report.

Jess resolved to talk again to Eleanor. *If anyone deserved it, it was probably Jerry Harrison.* Eleanor hadn't liked the late Jeremy; and had thought him a sponger off his aunt. But there's a leap to be made between simply being not a very nice person, and deserving to be murdered.

But that would have to wait. Jess set off for the train station and her trip to London.

She had told herself that, although there is still an instinct, quite unfounded, to think of a solicitor as a middle-aged man in a tweed jacket, she should be prepared for something quite different. It was as well that she did, because the solicitor was probably younger than Jess herself. She was also Asian, glamorous, and formidably well dressed and poised.

'Do take a seat, Inspector Campbell,' she invited Jess. 'Train journey OK? May I offer you a cup of tea or coffee? Both from a machine, I'm afraid.'

'I had a cup of coffee on the train, thanks, so I'm OK. I appreciate that you've agreed to meet me so quickly.'

'Well, we are always very sorry to hear of the death of a client, but we deal with a lot of wills, so it happens quite bit,' returned the solicitor with equanimity. 'We are prepared for it. Not all of our clients are murdered, of course, and we are, as a firm, very sorry to learn that is apparently the case with Mr Harrison.'

'Did you ever meet him personally?'

'Just the once,' said the. solicitor cheerfully. 'Pleasant to talk to, as I recall.'

Now that, thought Jess, *is the first kind word I've heard said about the victim. But perhaps he wasn't indifferent to a beautiful woman.* 'We understand,' she continued, 'that he worked abroad before he retired and that your firm kept all his legal documents and forwarded his mail.'

102

'We hold his will, paperwork relating to some shares, and the deeds of his house. Yes, we did occasionally forward some correspondence for him, but that's less common nowadays than years ago. Once upon a time, a firm such as ours would handle all kinds of work on behalf of overseas clients. The personal computer has changed life so much. Wherever he was in the world, Mr Harrison was able to handle any business himself.' She smiled brightly.

The computer that was missing: its loss was perhaps more important than Jess had first thought. Not just a simple opportunistic theft, but taken because it made it easier to trace the recent history of the victim, with names and e-mail details for all his contacts.

'Did you draw up his will?' Jess hoped a note of despair had not found its way into her voice.

'Personally? No, that would have been Mr Prendergast; and he's retired now.'

'Then perhaps I could get in touch with Mr Prendergast, if he knew Jeremy Harrison, and have a word with him about Harrison?'

That gained her a sympathetic smile. 'Retired to Malta, I'm afraid. His wife is Maltese and has family there, I understand. And they fancied a warmer climate.'

Jess glanced towards the window and the grey view of a wintery London street. She understood the Prendergasts' decision to relocate.

'Then can you at least tell me who the principal beneficiaries of his will are?'

'He left everything – proceeds from the sale of the property and its contents – to various charities.' The solicitor looked suitably sad. 'I can only suppose that he had no family members left – or that he had fallen out with them.'

Falling out with people – or simply failing to connect with others in the first place – seemed to have been Harrison's way, thought Jess. She felt suddenly saddened by the realisation of what a lonely life the victim must have led. Working abroad, going on cruises . . . that's what had filled his life. To some, the cruises might appear an attempt to be sociable. But had it really been so? Jess would have liked to meet some of his fellow passengers and hear their opinions. But tracking them down now would not only be very difficult, it would probably be pointless. They would have forgotten him, once the holiday was over. *Ships that pass . . .*

All the same, Jess couldn't help wondering why he'd made no effort to make friends once he'd moved into the cottage. Perhaps he had been one of those individuals who are solitary by nature. A wandering working life had meant he'd lost the knack of forming permanent relationships.

The solicitor said, 'We would appreciate it if, when the police have finished with the property, you could let us know? We have to send a team down there to list the contents, before making arrangements for the sale. It will take some time.'

On the way home on the crowded train, Jess again thought over this conversation. It was not just that Jeremy Harrison had no close friends. He would seem to have had the knack of falling out with everyone. Had he ever been different? Or always that way? Had something happened to sour his view of his fellow beings?

He could well have been closest to his Aunt Lucinda. He had stayed with her, on his visits to the UK between overseas jobs, and she had left him all her worldly goods. It had paid him to stay on good terms with her. But that also suggested there were indeed no other surviving family members; or Lucinda might have included them among her bequests. *We called her Lulu . . .*

Eleanor Holder's voice echoed in Jess's head: *Now, that's a death the police ought to have investigated.*

Eleanor herself had been dropped off at the kennels by Stubbs, after identifying Jeremy Harrison's body. It had not been a pleasant experience; but she had felt she owed it to Lulu. Now she braced herself to return to the normal daily routine. The dogs had been left in the care of the part-time kennel helper, Jade Wilson, whose father was the landlord of the Waggoner's Halt.

Eleanor knew that Jade did not particularly enjoy the work at Greentrees Kennels ('clearing up a lot of dog mess!' in her words). But without the excuse of having a part-time job at the kennels, her father would have expected her to help out more at the pub. Jade didn't relish spending all her time under her parent's watchful eye; and found bar work 'dead boring'. There was more going on at her dad's establishment at the moment than usual, due to the police having taken over the barn as an incident centre. That might have made Jade keener to hang around, hopeful of learning something new and interesting. But Eleanor had been to identify the body; and that, as a source of information and novelty, was hard to beat. Thus Jade appeared as soon as Eleanor returned, with the pugs clustered round her feet. They immediately deserted her for their owner, whom they greeted ecstatically.

'Everything all right, Jade?' inquired Eleanor, once she had returned the pugs' greetings.

Jade had been bouncing around in the background, nearly as eagerly as the pugs. She had tied back her multi-coloured hair. Eleanor was glad of her help, because finding another kennel maid in the area would be difficult. And, in her own truculent way, Jade was reliable. The pugs – and the other dogs boarded at the kennels from time to time – liked her. That was the main thing. Perhaps they recognised a being with a similar disposition to their own.

'No probs!' Jade assured Eleanor now. Her eyes shone with excitement. 'Was it him? The old bloke who lived at Rose Cottage?'

Jerry Harrison would not have liked to hear himself described as 'old bloke', thought Eleanor wryly. Middle-aged was one thing. 'Old' suggested a higher level of decrepitude. She wondered whether Jade described her, Eleanor, as *old.* But anyone aged over fifty was old, in Jade's book. She almost certainly thought of Eleanor as being in that class.

Eleanor felt a spurt of annoyance and snapped, 'It was Mr Harrison's body, yes.'

'Was he all beat up?'

Eleanor sighed. There was no point in getting cross with the girl. Criticism didn't touch her. *But, what the heck?* thought Eleanor. *It doesn't touch me.*

She drew a deep breath. 'The body was covered and they only showed me his face. The wound on his neck was hidden beneath a cloth, so I couldn't see any sign of his injuries.' She almost apologised, because Jade was so clearly disappointed.

'Poor old feller,' said Jade, in the nearest she would ever come to any expression of regret or condolences. 'You were friendly with his auntie, weren't you? My dad said you were.'

'Your father is right. I was a close friend of his aunt. I knew her all my life.'

'Gosh,' said Jade. 'That was a pretty long time, then.'

Eleanor left her and walked briskly into the house. She needed a drink. Something stronger than sherry. There was a bottle of whisky somewhere.

Chapter 9

The pizza restaurant was in Gloucester. It offered other Italian dishes also. Ian Carter was secretly pleased about this as he wasn't the greatest fan of pizzas. He ordered the cannelloni. The place was busy and everyone else around him seemed more than happy to tuck into pizza, so he felt a little embarrassed, but Millie and Jess made no comment. He thought Jess looked tired and that wasn't surprising, as she'd made the trip up to London that day. Admittedly her visit to the solicitors on the matter of Harrison's personal details, including possible other family members, hadn't yielded much that was of help to their inquiry, not so far, anyway. It was interesting that Harrison had apparently willed his entire estate to benefit various charities. Had he no one else? If not, then possibly he and his Aunt Lucinda had been the sole survivors of their family line. Eleanor Holder had told them that Jeremy's father, Lucinda's brother, and his mother, had both died quite some time before Jeremy had appeared at Rose Cottage, visiting his aunt. Jerry had had no siblings, it seemed. So, unless a relation or two appeared out of the woodwork, as sometimes happened when someone, previously believed to be without family, died and an estate was up for grabs, Jerry had only to wait.

But waiting can take a long time. Lucinda's fatal fall down the staircase might, after all, be suspicious, as Jess had reported Eleanor Holder thought it. But, without proof, or even a witness who'd seen someone hanging about the cottage and taking an unusual interest . . . Jess was glad now that she'd agreed to accompany Ian and his daughter that evening. At least it stopped her thinking about Rose Cottage, and the sad demise of its last two occupants. She made an effort to listen to Millie's stream of questions and, where possible, answer them.

Ian, for his part, was studying Jess surreptitiously across the table. Millie was chattering away to her. He did feel guilty at asking her to join him and Millie that evening. She had probably wanted only to go home and put her feet up. Moreover, Millie seemed intent on quizzing her about Jess's own career; and some of the questions were more than a little personal. But Jess seemed to be coping well. Ian himself was pretty well cut out of the conversation. He had other things on his mind, so it was a blessing.

The other matter occupying his mind was not work-related. It centred on his ex-wife. He was resigned to the fact that Sophie turned up from time to time from her French base, and they met. They shared a daughter, so it was incumbent on both of them to keep civilised contact. Once Millie had left school, and the fees no longer needed to be paid, he had presumed his contact with Sophie would cease. He certainly hoped he'd always be in contact with his child.

But his recent conversation with Monica Farrell, during which he'd learned that Sophie was unhappy in France, had given him food for thought and, frankly, got him worried.

If Sophie were to return to live in England, that might throw a significant spanner in the works. If Rodney returned also, things would probably be all right. But if her second marriage broke down and Sophie returned on her own, perhaps with her young child, she would find herself coping alone with any problems.

When that happened, Sophie's way of dealing with difficulties was to unload them on to the shoulders of someone else. Ian had a sinking feeling that the recipient of Sophie's woes would be himself.

There was an even worse scenario. If Sophie left the comfort of her French chateau and returned, perhaps with her younger child, she would be homeless, initially at least. She would need someone to help her hunt for a new place to live. While this was going on, she would have to leave the child with someone – what was the kid's name? Tristan, wasn't it? Or something like that. That might mean she'd move in – temporarily, of course – with her aunt at Weston St Ambrose. That was far too close at hand for comfort. Monica herself probably wouldn't be keen. (The cats would hate it.) *Heaven help us!* thought Ian, alarm rising in his chest. *She wouldn't want to come and stay with me, would she? Even worse, she wouldn't want to come back permanently? For them to get together again?* He felt himself gripped by panic at the mere thought.

'Too much pasta?' asked Jess. She had not been so involved in conversation with Millie that she hadn't noticed he'd stopped eating.

'Er, just a little.'

'You're not worrying about the case?'

'No, no, something else altogether.'

Even his daughter's attention had been prised away from her own future plans and she was looking at him suspiciously. She opened her mouth.

He was saved by the bell – or another interruption.

'Hullo, Superintendent!' said a cheerful voice above his head.

They all looked up, startled. Standing by their table was a woman. Jess looked puzzled. Millie looked suspicious. Carter managed to recall who she was. It was that female archaeologist from the Institute, Marianna Holm. She wasn't wearing her outdoor clothing and sturdy boots; but dressed casually yet smartly in a Scandinavian pullover, clean trousers, and slip-on shoes. A little behind her lurked a bearded figure, Sullivan, who, in contrast to his companion, managed to look this evening much as he'd done at the Roman site. *Not exactly scruffy,* thought Ian, *but weather-beaten and somehow out of place in this setting, whereas at the site he'd fitted in perfectly.*

'Family night out?' inquired Marianna cheerily.

Millie beamed at her and looked about to reply.

Ian cut her off. 'Not quite, but this is my daughter, Millie.' He indicated Jess. 'And this is a colleague and, um, friend, Jessica Campbell.'

'Another copper?' inquired Marianna, who did not appear to have the gift of tact.

Jess got in her reply ahead of him. 'Yes, another copper.'

'I'm going to join the police, too!' declared Millie loudly. 'Well, possibly.'

'Keep it in the family, eh?' Marianna grinned at her.

Carter knew himself obliged to explain to Jess who these people were. She looked startled at learning they were both working near the location of the murder scene.

'We won't be under your feet!' It was Sullivan, who spoke at last, addressing Jess, and managing to raise a smile. 'We're just checking out a possible project for a dig, later in the year, as we explained to Mr Carter. We'll be gone in a day or two. Oh, we took your advice, Superintendent, and have moved ourselves into the hotel at Weston St Ambrose for a couple of nights. In the circumstances, we decided it wasn't wise to sleep over in the campervan.'

'Good idea,' said Carter.

'Have you dug anything up yet?' asked Millie, diverted at last from her own prospective career.

'Not yet,' Marianna told her. 'We're not actually doing any digging at the moment. We're drawing up plans for when we do dig later in the year, as Andrew said. But we've finished doing that. We'll be leaving any day now and going back to Oxford. You asked us to let you know when we intended leaving the site, Superintendent, if you remember.'

'To Oxford?' Jess asked, surprised.

'Yes, it's where the Institute is located, although I must stress, we are in no way part of the university. The Institute is fully independent. We both work there nowadays. We also live there.'

'Oh, yes, you did tell me,' Carter heard himself mumble belatedly. 'Right, I'll make a note that you'll be returning there. Have you been comfortable at the Royal Oak?'

'Very comfortable, they looked after us well,' Sullivan told him. 'But if we can't be at the site, there is little point in us staying in the area.'

He seemed as anxious to get out of the restaurant as Carter was keen to see them both go. He made an awkward bow in Jess's direction. 'I apologise. I don't know your rank.'

'Inspector!' Millie told him loudly and clearly.

The people at the next table turned their heads towards them.

'Yes, of course. Come along, Marianna.' Sullivan, with a farewell nod, pushed his wife and fellow expert towards the door.

They left, thank goodness. Jess was looking at him inquiringly.

'I just came across them when I was driving round, getting a feel for the general location,' Ian defended himself. 'They'd been doing a recce on the site and sleeping there in a campervan. As you heard, they've moved to sleep in the hotel at Weston St Ambrose. I'm quite relieved to hear it.'

'Archaeology . . .' murmured Millie thoughtfully. 'That might be interesting, too.'

A spark of hope entered Carter's heart. Diversion, that was it. Get his daughter interested in something else, other than police-work.

'Don't you like pizza?' asked Millie, as they drove home.

'I just prefer pasta,' he told her.

His daughter missed nothing. He was beginning to think he, on the other hand, missed an awful lot. *Are all fathers like me?* he wondered. *Do we all cherish a picture of their little girl, aged, oh, around seven or eight, and close their eyes wilfully to the fact that young children grow up?*

Aloud, he asked, 'I hope you enjoyed your meal?'

'Oh, yes, mine was fine. And it was great talking to Jess.' In the tone of one making a reasoned judgement, Millie added, 'To be fair, those archaeologist people might have been interesting to talk to as well.'

'Yes, well, lots of possible careers ahead of you, sweetheart. Take your time thinking about it.'

'You don't want me to join the police, do you?'

She was staring through the windscreen at the road ahead as she spoke. A sideways glance from Carter showed her profile, features set. *She grows more and more like her mother,* he thought.

'I don't want to stand in your way, whatever you choose to do with your life,' he told her. 'It's just that, well, policework is tough. You see a side of humanity that is not pretty. You're called out to murder scenes, for example. How do you think you'd cope with that?'

'I'd just have to learn to, wouldn't I?' She sounded frighteningly worldly. 'We all have to learn to cope with things. I had to learn to cope with you and Mummy splitting up.'

'Yes, that was hard for you. Sorry . . .' he mumbled.

'It's all right. I've got over it.'

He heard himself ask suddenly, 'You used to have a toy bear call MacTavish. You carried him with you everywhere.'

'Oh, I've got over that, too!' was the indignant reply. 'I don't carry him around with me as I did when I was little. But I've still got him. He's my mascot.'

Carter felt his heart rise. *We're still needed, you and I, MacTavish, don't worry. There will always be a place for us!*

'When we get indoors, I'll make the cocoa,' Millie told him.

Is that the final stage? Ian wondered. *We start out as the carer and become the cared for?*

Daylight faded early at this time of year. It was something to keep in mind if she wanted to walk the pugs again. But Eleanor's previous evening's short excursion to Rose Cottage had dampened her enthusiasm for walking the pugs after dark. She couldn't rely on Wayne Garley appearing to escort her, as on the previous occasion. Anyway, the day's trip to the morgue to identify Harrison had taken more out of Eleanor than she wanted to admit. Keeping up a brisk front in the company of the police detective who had escorted her – (Stubbs, that had been his name, like the painter of horses) – that had not been difficult. But now, in the early evening, alone, Eleanor found herself thinking about it more than she would have wished. It wasn't the sad sight of the dead Harrison that bothered her. It was the memories of Lulu's tragic death, reawakened now because of all the fuss being made about Harrison's demise. It was the contrast between all the hullaballoo around the investigation into his death and the way in which his aunt's demise had been dealt with so briskly by the coroner at that time.

Brisk was not the same thing as comprehensive, thought Eleanor crossly. *I should have made more protest about it all than I did; asked for more time spent on inquiries. I was so shocked at the time that I suppose I didn't have the wit to speak up at the inquest. Of course she didn't fall down those damn stairs! I should have stood up and said so. She was tripped by some device or pushed or – or some-thing. I know it! I feel it in my bones. But that isn't the same thing as having any proof;* and sadly, Eleanor had to admit to herself, she could not have produced any proof to interest the coroner enough to grant the police more time to make inquiries. Nor had the police at the time appeared keen to have anyone hold up the coroner's conclusion. They'd been satisfied; the coroner had been satisfied. Only Eleanor had been filled with rage and grief.

She missed Lulu more with each passing day. They hadn't lived in each other's pockets. But they had each known the other was there, near at hand, and that had been immeasurably comforting.

How much longer, she wondered, *am I going to be able to run the kennels? Without Jade's help, it would be difficult; and Jade wouldn't be around much longer. She was young and she wanted to see more of life.* Eleanor knew she couldn't count on Jade indefi-nitely. Nor could Barry Wilson hope always to have his daughter work in the bar at busy times. Barry must realise this. Eleanor wondered how much he worried about it.

She hadn't time or the inclination to spend much time brooding on Barry's problems. She'd never really liked him. Besides, she had her own future to consider. In the summer the boarders made the kennels profitable, as holiday travellers hastened to leave their pets in the care of someone else. The other side of the business was the breeding of the pugs, which she did in a limited way. Well, as long as pugs remained a popular breed, she could sell any litter of pups. But she didn't depend altogether on Greentrees. Her brother-in-law had paid her a good price for the farm. Her own outgoings were modest. *I could retire*, she thought. *But retire and do what?*

She had probably drunk enough whisky on her return home; and couldn't allow herself to start again that evening, not even another glass. But she had to do something; not just sit here brooding and feeling so helpless. Despite the decision she had just made to give up on late-night walks, she decided to walk the pugs one more time.

It wasn't a good idea. She realised it as soon as she stepped out of the house. It was the whisky that had made the decision, not her. It was cold outside and damp. The poor little beggars would not like being dragged out of their snug kennels. She couldn't rely on finding Wayne out there to escort her. Too bad. The streak of obstinacy in her character which had helped her through so many difficult times in her life now urged her to make what was surely a mistake. Eleanor struggled to her feet and pulled on a thick jacket.

The pugs certainly did show a lack of enthusiasm. In the end, she decided to leave the older ones behind and just walk the two younger ones. This time she allowed for it being so dark and brought a torch.

'Come on, chaps!' she encouraged them.

They muttered and grumbled to themselves, snorting and snuffling their disapproval, but they trotted alongside her without actually going on strike by sitting down or turning back. Inevitably, her steps took her in the direction of Lulu's cottage. She always thought of it as Lulu's home, despite it passing into the ownership of the late Jeremy Harrison. 'And now?' she wondered aloud. 'Who's going to live there now?'

En route, she passed not far from the Waggoner's Halt again. The ground floor of the pub was blazing with lights in the darkness; and she caught the faint sound of voices, followed by the slamming of car doors. The Halt would be doing well out of all this. She wondered whether Jade was behind the bar; and whether Wayne Garley was in there.

As for the police, they would have gone home, she supposed. They would be back in the morning, in their incident room in the barn. And the crowd of curious sightseers would probably be back, too. Not so many, perhaps, nor so excited by the gruesome novelty of it all. After all, nothing else happened around here. So some would return, and perhaps even a journalist or two might put in an appearance. Not from the television, of course, or the bigger circulation press. But just a local journo or two. Just to see if there were any developments. If any did, the likelihood was they would each buy a drink or even a lunch. That would please Barry. As if to support her line of thinking, an aroma of cooked food drifted towards her.

The Waggoner's kitchen was run by an energetic, taciturn man who hovered above his seething and spattering pots and pans with an air of ferocious concentration. He was assisted by his small, energetic and voluble partner. Their name was also Wilson; the husband was said to be a cousin of Barry Wilson's and to owe him money. Quite what the money was owed for, if this was true, nobody knew. Eleanor thought the rumour unlikely to be correct. What was certain was that the food was very good, and, as a business, the restaurant part of the pub did very well.

The lights and the sounds faded into the silent darkness of a winter's evening. It was broken only by the swoop of wings above her head. One of the pugs growled. *An owl*, thought Eleanor, *investigating the possibility of prey.* But it had quickly sussed out that this small beast on the ground below was accompanied by a human. And either of the pugs would probably have proved too heavy to be snatched up and away by an owl. But the night was not a quiet or empty time. It wasn't an interlude when nothing happened. Different things happened, that was all. Her ear caught the sound of a bark, not a dog's bark, a fox's, with an overtone of a yelp in the sound, the call of something wild. The older of the two pugs growled.

'OK, guys,' she reassured them both.

They had reached Rose Cottage and here they stopped. The pugs started snuffling around the base of the leylandii. The trees had grown too tall, of course. Wayne was right about that. She had not known, before he told her the previous evening, that Wayne had offered to trim them and Jeremy Harrison refused. She wasn't surprised at the refusal. The seclusion had probably suited him. Now blue-and-white police tape was wound round the trunks and rippled in the wind; adding its own faint crackle to the other sounds. A notice informed those taking an interest that this was a crime scene. *Anyone having any information . . .* She sighed and was about to turn and start back homewards when she saw the light.

At first it was just a glimpse and she wasn't at all sure. Perhaps it was just something shiny reflected in the pale moonlight. But then she saw it again, more clearly, stronger, a definite pinpoint. It was moving; and it was on the other side of the police tape.

'Hell's teeth!' she muttered. 'Someone's in there, walking around in the garden with a torch!'

What to do? Should she ignore the admonition to stay outside the tape, and go and investigate? No, that would be foolhardy; and not just because that would be contravening police instructions. It could be anyone in there. The intruder could be armed.

The pugs were loyal and tenacious little beasts, but they weren't guard dogs. Wayne Garley, where are you tonight? Eleanor moved behind one of the leylandii and peered through its lower branches. The pugs were quiet and she felt their gaze fixed on her. She was their leader and they were waiting to see what she would do. Whatever it was, they would follow her lead.

The torch beam swivelled and briefly swept across the trees. Eleanor froze and the pugs might not have been there at all, they were so quiet and still. But she sensed their tenseness. Whoever held the torch was moving again; this time across the front of the cottage. A dark human shape was briefly to be distinguished before it and the torch beam turned the corner and disappeared down the side of the building.

The obvious explanation popped into Eleanor's head and she sighed in relief. This was, of course, Wayne again, doing his security patrol. Or, even though she and Wayne had not seen anyone else out here the previous night, the police might well have left someone on guard over it, a watchman of some sort. Eleanor didn't know much about procedures, but she supposed that a crime scene would attract unwanted attention from the ghoulishly minded. Or, come to that, an empty property might tempt those intent on burglary.

'It's all right, you two, let's go home,' she murmured to the pugs.

They were only too pleased to fall in with this suggestion.

As they passed within range of the Waggoner's Halt again, with its lights and voices, she did wonder whether she should call in and ask Barry Wilson if he knew about a watchman being left at the cottage. But he'd be busy, he couldn't leave his bar, and if Jade were there to help out, she'd be busy, too. If Wayne were in there, she could ask him to walk her back again to Greentrees.

But Wayne wouldn't be pleased to see she had ventured out again. *What is the matter with me?* she asked herself. *Why am I drawn back here? It's as if the cottage is some sort of magnet.*

She set off back home again as fast as she could go. By the time she and the pugs reached Greentrees she was almost running; and the poor little pugs were scampering along as fast as they could go, panting. They didn't even have the breath to utter their usual grumbles.

They turned into Greentrees. Salvation! She wouldn't venture out again after dark. Perhaps, in the morning, if she saw either Superintendent Carter or Inspector Campbell again, or pleasant Sergeant Stubbs, she might mention it. It couldn't do any harm.

Chapter 10

For others, the days immediately following the grisly discovery of a corpse at Rose Cottage gave rise to mixed emotions; chiefly how all this would affect the pattern of their well-regulated lives. The Plunketts and the Pickerings were cardplayers and had formed a small bridge group that was gathered now at the Pickerings' house. The late Lucinda Harrison had also been a member. But if they had thought her nephew might have replaced her, when he moved into the cottage, they quickly realised he wouldn't. He'd made it pretty clear. They played alternately in each other's houses. This simple, practical arrangement was suddenly under threat.

In such a normally quiet area, the setting up of an incident centre by the police could hardly be ignored. For the bridge group, as for others who had been living in comfortable seclusion around the immediate scene of the crime, it had come as a real shock. Initially there had been disbelief, followed by a rush to consult others and confirm that this was not a hoax. It was natural that everyone had gathered at the Waggoner's Halt, on the first day when the police arrived, to find out if there was any more news. And then the police officers themselves had arrived and taken over the barn behind the pub to serve as an incident room. That one practical detail had served more than any other to convince everyone that this was no wild rumour. This was in deadly earnest. Only now words like 'deadly' could not be used carelessly.

Understandably, there was a heightened degree of alarm

regarding individual personal safety. They told one another that they had every reason to be disturbed. None of them used words like 'frightened' or 'terrified', as that would have made things worse. A genie like 'terror' had to be kept firmly stoppered inside the bottle. Secretly, each of them knew the genie had escaped. He hadn't been one of their bridge group, that fellow living at Rose Cottage, unlike his late aunt. Admittedly Jerry Harrison had been something of a recluse. But no less a local resident for all that: a neighbour, and he'd been murdered.

'And it isn't as if there are that many people living here, not like in a town', said Caroline Plunkett.

All of their own secluded homes were alarm-protected, naturally. Of course, no one knew yet at what time of day the murderer had carried out his dreadful crime, but it seemed to have been after dark. It was a timely reminder to set the security alarm as soon as dusk closed in, not to wait until bedtime. Harrison, rumour had it, had sat drinking with his killer before the attack. That detail was the worst bit of all. Logically, he knew him, must have done. That could mean that any one of them— No, no, impossible! Their thoughts ran parallel to those declared by Beryl Garley. The killer had come from outside.

There was no denying, however, that the activity in the barn provided a break in the humdrum day-to-day routine. Many of the retirees had lived active, responsible professional lives. While none of them wanted to return to the daily grind – all that behind them, thank goodness! – life in rural retirement could be a bit, well, uneventful by comparison. So, it wasn't altogether too bad to have a new subject of conversation and speculation. A bit of excitement, really. Of course, they didn't want the whole circus around for too long. Perhaps it wouldn't be wise to go out after dark until the dreadful business was over and settled.

Thus, they had just reluctantly agreed to suspend their regular bridge gatherings, after one meeting just to have a drink and discuss events. During the Covid restrictions they'd played online. But it wasn't the same; and no one wanted to go back to that again. All the same, better safe than sorry. After all, who could concentrate on the cards and not talk about the horrid business?

But it all provided a distraction and an undeniable frisson of excitement. Besides, it was very interesting to see a murder investigation at work. That, too, had drawn them all to the Waggoner's Halt on the day the incident room was established. In retrospect, a few of them felt a little ashamed of being members of that enthusiastic mob.

Not that any of them had any information to give to the police, they told one another. None of them had known the victim really well. But they'd done their duty and gone along to speak to the police in the barn. In contrast, most of them remembered his late aunt. Dear Lulu, such a loss.

'I know Eleanor Holder misses her dreadfully,' said Mary Pickering. 'They were friends all their lives, from their schooldays, as I understand it. Not that Eleanor talks about it much, that awful accident, I mean, when poor Lulu took a tumble down the stairs and lay there, I suppose knocked unconscious. And died . . .' She shivered. 'I used to think about it sometimes when I walked past Rose Cottage with Billy. Now, I suppose, I shall think about Jerry.'

'Don't walk past the cottage, then!' recommended her husband briskly. 'It's a shock. Of course it is. But dwelling on it won't help.'

'Billy would do his best to protect us,' continued Mary, gazing down at her pet. 'But he is quite old and his teeth aren't much good.'

Billy, the elderly spaniel, had looked up at hearing his name; but decided that whatever was going on, it wasn't going to involve his being dragged out into the cold. He closed his eyes again.

'I know,' agreed Caroline Plunkett, her neighbour. 'But it's no use pretending we've nothing to worry about. In Lulu's case, just to think of her lying there all night, no one to help. Not able to get to the phone – it's awful.' A little awkwardly, she added: 'I don't feel the same sense of loss for Jerry Harrison as for Lulu. I do feel sad, because . . .' Failing to find any reason for feeling grief at the death of Harrison, she finished her speech with an incoherent mumble.

There was a murmur of agreement. Mary's husband, Philip, spoke up in support. 'Murder is a terrible thing. It affects us all. But it would be simply untrue to say any of us should feel that same sadness we all felt when we heard his aunt had died. Besides, her death was a dreadful accident; and his was, well, not an accident or so we're told. He's – he was – so remote somehow.'

'Strange fellow,' opined Harry Plunkett. 'I've met the type before, mind you. He wouldn't have lasted in the army. He wasn't a team player.'

'Perhaps that's why he spent all that time abroad,' said someone else.

'Had to be a reason for it,' was the general opinion.

It was followed by a short silence during which they all considered why Harrison had spent his working life travelling the world.

'Something to do with oil, wasn't it?' Philip Pickering said at last.

'So I believe,' confirmed Mary. 'In fact, he told me so himself.'

The others looked at her in surprise, not least her husband.

'You didn't tell me that!'

'Of course I did, Phil. You've forgotten.'

'If you had told me he was in the oil business, I most certainly would not have forgotten!'

'Well, clearly, you have, dear.'

Philip was turning rather red in the face and Caroline Plunkett asked hurriedly, 'You chatted with him? I never managed to get a word out of him.'

'Well, not chatted, exactly,' said Mary carefully. 'He wasn't the chatty sort, was he? You've just said so, and I agree. Actually, it was when Lulu was still alive and he used to turn up from time to time, visiting her. He had taken her to lunch at the Waggoner's. They were walking back to the cottage, and I was out with my dog. Not Billy, then. It was the dog I had before that, Casper. When Casper died, Eleanor very kindly offered me one of the litter of pugs she'd bred at the time. It was very good of her, but I explained I'd always had spaniels and understood them. Anyhow, as I was saying, I had stopped really to say hullo to Lulu, as one does. She indicated Jerry, as she always called him, saying he had just come back to England. He'd been out in the Middle East. He had to say something then, so he did. Just the minimum. Yes, he was between jobs. He'd be going back again soon. That was that, really. He didn't volunteer anything about his time there and he wasn't the sort of person one felt one could ask. Lulu seemed fond of him, but he was a family member, so that was normal. I was never sure,' Mary added, looking a little embarrassed, 'how fond he was of her. It was hard to tell. He was a very buttoned-up sort of person; that's a phrase my mother used to use for someone who didn't give anything away.'

Caroline said, quite sharply, 'Lulu gave something away. She gave him Rose Cottage!'

'Oh, yes, but after her death, in her will. Not while she was alive.'

At this last remark, they all seemed afflicted by unease.

It was broken by Philip, who asked with slightly forced heartiness if everyone was ready for another drink.

'You definitely didn't tell me anything about it!' muttered Philip as he set off for the drinks cabinet; and his wife to the kitchen to collect the sausage rolls.

Somehow, that last drink together before 'it was all over and the police left', caused an air of deep melancholy to descend on the group. Even Mary's much-praised sausage rolls didn't help. Nobody said very much more. They just drank up and left. Their departure was Billy's gain. He ate the leftover sausage rolls, while the humans were at the front door. For once, he wasn't scolded.

'I don't know about you,' Caroline said to her husband as they walked home. 'I feel as though we've been to a wake.'

A couple of miles down the road, the residents of Weston St Ambrose village itself viewed events with varying degrees of interest. But their views were from a slightly different perspective. Most only vaguely remembered Lucinda Harrison and had not really known her nephew, the victim, at all. The murder had taken place just outside the village, after all, at the far end of Long Lane, amongst the well-heeled residents of those large, secluded houses. Most of the residents in the village had some family connection with the area. But the Long Lane lot were an unknown quantity.

'I don't know why they've all come to live up by the Waggoner's Halt!' declared Debbie, from her station on the till at the Minimart. 'You'd think, with pots of money like they've all got, they'd buy a place abroad, in Spain, or somewhere. They wouldn't have to put up with a cold winter like we get here. You can sit outside at cafés, and just watch the world go by. I've seen those telly programmes about houses for sale abroad. There are some lovely places.' Debbie sighed wistfully.

The customers agreed. 'But they don't mix with us, do they?' said one of them, meaning, presumably, the Long Lane residents and not the expat community, in Spain.

'My Auntie Beryl used to clean for Mrs Harrison when she was alive,' Debbie told them, abandoning her Spanish dream. 'But she didn't clean for *him*. He used one of those companies that come out and do it. Don't know why. My Auntie Beryl would've done the job better than a bunch of outsiders, half of them foreign.'

Those present agreed with this. No one seemed to think that Debbie's dream of a home in Spain did not quite fit with her resentment of outsiders buying houses in Weston St Ambrose.

Debbie herself then claimed to recall Harrison coming into the Minimart and buying odds and ends. 'But he never did a proper shop,' she added. 'He probably did that online. He wasn't the chatty sort, either. Of course it was horrible, what happened to him. But, well . . . he was a weird sort of bloke.' At this point Debbie would lower her voice dramatically. 'If you ask me, he had a past.'

But Debbie had no idea what that past might have been. Customers at the till speculated wildly: but in the end no one could agree, and so no satisfactory explanation could be arrived at.

One resident, however, was made very uncomfortable, both by the establishment of the incident room at the Waggoner's Halt and the police vehicles continually passing back and forth through the village. He didn't want the cops around for any reason because, whatever it was caused all the hoo-hah, attention eventually had a way of turning to him, whether or not he had anything to do with it. You could safely put a bet on it. At some point one of the pigs would knock at his (actually, his mother's) front door, in the course of 'making inquiries'. That person was Alfie Darrow.

Alfie had been in trouble since childhood. Now, still not quite twenty-one, he had built up an impressive record of petty crime. He did not consider this to be his fault. Unjustly persecuted, that's what he was. He'd heard the phrase during a documentary about Eastern Europe on the telly, and it had stuck in his mind because he felt it applied to him, as much as to some dissident or other. Whatever a 'dissident' was. For example, it wasn't just from the Waggoner's Halt that he was banned. He couldn't now go into the Minimart because of a misunderstanding with Debbie Garley. His intentions in going into the shop had been quite legitimate and even romantic. He wanted to give some chocolate to his girlfriend. Boxed chocolates were expensive and you couldn't slip a box into a pocket. But a bar was easier. And what had happened? Debbie, who had appeared to be fully occupied behind the till, had suddenly left her station there, shot across the shop like a human rocket, seized Alfie by the back of his sweatshirt, nearly throttling him, and frogmarched him in an undignified way at top speed across the shop and out into the street.

'What did you do that for?' he'd managed to gurgle when she released him.

'I can do without shoplifters!' snapped Debbie.

'I wasn't shoplifting!' he retaliated. 'I want to buy some choc—'

'I know what you wanted to do,' Debbie told him. 'And you're not going to get away with it in my Minimart!'

Alfie had rallied. 'You can't accuse me of shoplifting until I leave the shop without paying for whatever it is. Until I get through the door there –' He pointed to the shop entry – 'you've got to presume I'm going to pay for it!'

'What, *you?*' retorted Debbie disagreeably. 'I've known you too long. The cops know you, too. Who are they going to believe, you or me? So, stay out of my shop!'

She marched back to her empire, leaving Alfie fuming but helpless.

He uttered the phrase aloud now. 'Unjustly persecuted.' It had a ring to it. Alfie had a limited vocabulary; this new addition to it gave him a glow of pride.

Apart from this incident, he felt particularly persecuted at the moment, and for once, it was not just by the cops or the Garley family. The impetus behind his wish to acquire the chocolate was that Alfie was in love, or what passed for that in his emotions. Like other lovers before him, he could think of no one else other than the object of his desires – and how to engineer a meeting without her dad finding out.

In Alfie's case, the object of his obsession was Jade Wilson, the intended recipient of the bar of chocolate. His interest had not gone unnoticed by her father, who had cornered him one morning about a week earlier, coming out of the Minimart, and threatened him with dire consequences if he didn't stay away from Jade. See? Unjustly persecuted. What if the Wilsons were an old local family? So were the Darrows. They'd never got on well, of course. It made no difference to Alfie – or to Jade.

Romeo had faced the same difficulties, had Alfie but known it. Perhaps it was as well that he didn't know it: things had not turned out well for Romeo.

His encounter with Barry had been observed from within the supermarket by Debbie, who passed it around customers who, to their regret, had missed it. General agreement was that Alfie needed to watch out. Barry Wilson would sort him out otherwise. But those who had daughters agreed that Barry was right to warn

Alfie off. 'He's not the sort I'd want hanging around my girl!' said more than one of them.

Alfie, oblivious to the fact that half of Weston St Ambrose was following the progress of his romance with Jade, or lack of it, was not giving up. He'd cut across the fields to avoid the police presence around the pub; and had been lurking around the Waggoner's Halt, in the hope of a chance to speak to her, on the first day of the police inquiry.

This was how he came to witness the cops setting up the incident room in the old barn. He'd watched as Barry Wilson led them out to it. He'd hoped that Barry would stay in the barn for a while, leaving the field clear for him to sneak into the pub and speak to Jade. But no such luck. Barry had left the law to do what it wanted and returned to his bar straight away. Alfie couldn't go into the pub in normal circumstances, because Barry Wilson would have ordered him out immediately. He had hoped that the confusion caused by the discovery of a murder victim might have played to his advantage, but no such luck. Alfie had done the best he could and texted Jade to let her know he was outside. She, however, had texted back that they were very busy, and her father insisted on her helping in the bar. Her message actually was: *No chance. All gone mad here*. Alfie translated that easily.

However, he had lingered a little longer, just in case. Although he'd had no luck in snatching a moment or two with her, he had seen something interesting. A girl on a bike had come pedalling along. Alfie didn't recognise her. She wasn't a local girl, and she was a bit young for him. He wouldn't have paid her much attention but for one thing. She was as interested in the incident room as he was. She had stopped to watch the coming and going around the barn for a while, then moved off briefly to chain up the bicycle among nearby trees. Why she had bothered to do that, he had no idea. Who was going to pinch that old heap of scrap? (Alfie himself might have done that. Scrap metal was worth money. But he wouldn't take the risk with so many coppers about.)

The girl cyclist had returned and approached the police incident room on foot, being a bit cagey about it. He watched to see if she was going to go inside. And then – this was the really surprising bit, and one Alfie had brooded on since – that senior copper, Carter, had arrived on the scene. Alfie knew Carter of old; and it was a mark of how curious he was about what would happen next that he didn't immediately make off before Carter spotted him. The superintendent had stopped the car, leaped out of his vehicle and made straight for the girl. He looked really mad. There had been an argument. The girl stood up to him, Alfie gave her credit for that. There had been no arrest, but Carter had won the argument, as far as Alfie could tell. He wasn't surprised. The cops always did. They never listened to anything Alfie said to them; and the girl wasn't having any better luck. She had taken Carter to where she had left the bike. More argument and finally she had ridden off, back in the direction of Weston St Ambrose village.

'Now what,' wondered Alfie at the time, 'was all that about?' His attention span was at best limited. His thoughts had soon returned to what all this might mean with regard to his efforts in securing a one-to-one meeting with Jade. That was when he had had his idea, one of his best ever. He couldn't wait to tell his beloved about it. She'd be really impressed; and that wasn't something easily done. Of late, he'd caught her looking at him occasionally in a critical way. He didn't know what he'd done to deserve that. But instinct told him it would be best not to ask.

No matter; when she heard his plan, she'd gaze at him, her eyes shining with admiration. Only that old bruiser, her dad, mustn't find out. Alfie would have to work it out really carefully first.

He set off home, cutting across the fields to avoid unnecessary encounters with the forces of law and order. Always best.

For the next few days nothing really new happened. Anyone who had anything to tell the officers at the incident room had spoken up and signed their statements. Ian Carter and Jess Campbell held a discussion in Carter's office and decided that perhaps, if nothing new happened to make keeping the incident room open a necessity, they might close it and concentrate on what they'd learned.

'It's really not much,' said Jess regretfully. 'Not when you think about it. Harrison wasn't popular but that wasn't because he'd done anything to upset his neighbours. It was because he didn't contribute anything to the social life of the community. He was a bachelor living there on his own. He didn't give little dinner parties. He'd originally accepted a few invitations from others, but had not been a lively guest. They'd stopped inviting him. In the summer months, he wasn't there at all and the cottage was occupied by temporary visitors. How he kept himself occupied in the winter, let's face it, we don't really know. If we had his computer, we might be able to find out. But that hasn't turned up, nor have we found his missing personal documents.'

Ian pushed aside his notes and uttered a growl of discontent. 'Time isn't on our side. The locals haven't lost confidence in our investigation to date, but if we don't make an arrest, or issue a progress statement of some sort, their confidence in us will wither and disappear. The natives will begin to get restless. They'll start to get very nervous. They want their normal round of activities to recommence. They'll be demanding why we haven't done our job and arrested someone by now or, at least, announced our interest in speaking to someone.'

He leaned back in his chair and sighed. 'They'll be complaining openly soon; and quite a few of those living in comfortable retirement there are the sort who can make their complaints known at high level. Their reaction to our lack of progress will be to write letters. We're going to have the chief constable and the local Member of Parliament breathing down our necks soon, if we can't offer some visible sign of success.' He drummed his fingers on his desk and stared glumly into the middle distance.

As the pause was lengthening, and Ian appeared to have retreated into his thoughts, Jess asked, 'Millie gone back to school?'

'What?' He looked up, startled. 'Oh, yes, I drove her back on Sunday.'

'Still talking of joining the police?'

'Not so much. I'm hoping those two archaeologists have given her another career idea.' He sighed. 'But, with Millie, that doesn't mean she's given up on the police force. It's more likely she's remarshalling her arguments.'

'Any news from France?' Jess didn't want to appear to be prying but she had a strong suspicion the lack of progress in the case was not the only thing on Ian's mind. Ian had confided in her about his former wife's dissatisfaction. She had felt like advising him to tell Sophie to keep her problems to herself.

But apparently Sophie didn't do that. Jess had realised that Ian Carter, who could be so brisk and resolute in professional matters, could in her view dither annoyingly in personal ones. Not, of course, my business! Jess told herself. But it was of concern to her, because she liked Ian a lot and, frankly, cared about him.

He was speaking again. 'Not as far as I know. Monica may

know something more about that. But she hasn't spoken to me about it, not since that one time. Perhaps she's being tactful.'

'So,' Jess asked him after a pause. 'Do we close down the incident room at the barn?'

'We might as well. I don't think anyone else is going to come forward. Get Bennison on to it in the morning.'

It was never a good idea to express the opinion that an investigation had stalled. It often made things happen; but they weren't the sort of things that helped. If anything, they muddied the water and made things worse. Carter had been told that by an older and wiser colleague when he was young. He remembered the advice later. Because, as it happened, the evening following this discussion with Jess was the evening Alfie Darrow decided to make his move.

Even though Alfie firmly believed that his idea was perfect, even he knew it had to be carried out with care. It centred on Rose Cottage. As he saw it the cottage was now, to all intents and purposes, abandoned. The cops had been crawling all over it at first. But either they'd found all they wanted, or no longer looked for direct evidence there, and had instead taken themselves off to the barn and their incident room. The front and back doors of Rose Cottage were still barricaded with police tape warning that this was a crime scene; and access to the whole area of cottage and garden was still denied to the public by a notice. They'd probably forgotten to take it down.

But Alfie reckoned he could get in, if he planned things carefully. To this end he had already carried out a recce one night with the aid of a torch. He first established that the cops hadn't left a guard overnight. Out here, in the middle of nowhere (Alfie's opinion of the Waggoner's Halt community), they had probably thought it not necessary. In a built-up area, they might have thought differently. But they had completed their own search of the premises and, possibly to save on manpower, were not maintaining a physical watch overnight.

There was old Wayne Garley, of course. He'd appointed himself the local night watchman and taken to wandering round the place in the late evenings, looking out for what he considered trouble. Alfie had learned to watch out for him. But you could hear old Wayne coming, tramping along like he had lead in his boots. He didn't really have to worry about him. Avoiding him was a doddle.

Mind you, Wayne and the cops were not the only ones to watch out for. The old girl who kept the kennels, and employed Jade part-time, was always wandering around with those funny little dogs. She was apt to turn up anywhere at any time, and lately she had been out in the evenings. She'd actually walked past the cottage when he had been doing his preliminary inspection. He didn't think she'd seen him. He'd switched off the torch the moment he'd realised she was down there, by the gate – with a couple of the dogs, of course. But she'd walked off pretty soon, hadn't called out or anything, so he was safe.

Alfie, with his torch, had circled the cottage and marked the easiest point to break in: a lavatory window at the back of the building. It was an old window, wooden-framed, and could be opened and closed by a simple catch on the inside, operated by lifting and pulling down a handle. The catch had probably been there for as long as the window, so it would be pretty loose. Break the glass, just by the catch, put your hand through and operate the hinge. The window would open and in you could climb. Another doddle, really. Once inside, well, it was Alfie's for the use of: and the ideal meeting place for him and Jade. Fully furnished and comfortable, dry, and probably still reasonably warm, even though the heating would've been turned off. It seemed sort of meant. He realised that Jade wouldn't fancy climbing through a lavatory window. But once he himself was inside, he'd find another way of letting her in. All he needed to do was carry out a dummy run. Tonight, having established there was no copper left on guard duty, he decided to do it, once he'd checked that Mrs Holder was at home and old Wayne had made his nightly tour. There was no one who would disturb him after that.

But first he would try and engineer a meet with Jade, so that he could tell her what he planned, and do so unobserved by and unknown to her father. Barry Wilson had put the word out that anyone who saw Jade with him should tell Barry straight away, against the reward of a free pint. The Wilson clan was like that. The Mafia could have taught them nothing. Somehow, he had to think of a way.

Against all the odds, he was successful. He knew she worked at those kennels most days in the mornings, and from lunchtime on at the pub. So he lay in wait about the time he thought she would be walking home to the pub and waylaid her. He first concealed himself behind some bushes, as a precaution against being seen by someone who might run to Wilson with the information, and stepped out from his hiding place when he saw Jade coming towards him. To his disappointment, her initial reaction wasn't delight. She squealed and struck out at him with her tote bag.

'Oy!' he protested, rubbing his arm where the bag had connected. 'That hurt. What you carrying in that? Bricks?'

'You silly sod!' retorted Jade robustly. 'Why were you hiding like that and jumping out at me? It gave me a real turn. There's a murderer about somewhere and I thought you were him!'

'I didn't want anyone to see me and tell your dad,' he explained. Jade eyed him critically. 'You scared of my dad?'

'Yes!' Alfie told her. 'Everyone is.'

'Don't be daft! My dad is all right. His bark is worse than his bite.'

Alfie didn't believe that for one minute. 'Listen,' he entreated Jade. 'I've had a brilliant idea.'

She was looking unconvinced. 'When have you ever had a really good idea?' she asked unkindly.

'I've had one now and if you'll shut up for a minute, I'll tell you what it is.' Alfie realised he had to stand up for himself. Her dad was her role model. He had to show himself as tough. It worked.

'Go on, then!' she invited.

Alfie explained. 'I've worked out what would be a brilliant place for us to meet: that cottage.'

'What cottage?'

'Where the murder was.'

For once, Jade hadn't an immediate response. She stared at him in disbelief. Then she said in a flat voice, 'You're bonkers.'

'Why?' he asked, hurt. 'I thought it was a terrific idea.'

'You would!' she retorted. 'Listen, in the first place, how would we get in? Secondly, I don't want to go in there. Nobody in their right mind would! It'll be creepy. There will be dried blood all over the place and it'll stink.'

'We don't have to stay downstairs, where the murder was,' Alfie argued. 'We can go upstairs.'

'Where it'd be even more creepy. Mrs Holder's friend used to live there. She fell down those stairs and was killed. The postman found her. *And* she was the auntie of the guy who was found knifed there the other day. The place is jinxed, if you ask me. It's like anybody who lives in that cottage dies horribly.'

'No, they don't,' retaliated Alfie. 'There are different people there every summer. They stay there for their holidays.' He shook his head in wonderment. 'It can't be much of a holiday. They could go to Spain, where there's lots going on, bars, and beaches and all sorts of stuff.'

Alfie shared Debbie Garley's opinion of life in sunnier climes, even though he didn't know it. He was at present barred from the Minimart over those totally false accusations, from Debbie, about shoplifting. He'd always intended to pay, of course he had. It had just slipped his mind. He returned to the subject of the summer visitors to Rose Cottage. 'They must be pretty weird to want to spend their summer holidays in the Harrison place, with nowhere to go but your dad's pub.'

'Well, I'm not weird and I don't want to spend any time there,' said his girlfriend firmly. 'It'll be haunted!'

'You don't believe in ghosts and all that crap?'

'I don't know and neither do you. There will be bound to be an – an aura.'

'A what?'

'You know, a feeling, a presence, evil . . .'

'Hadn't got you down as a scaredy-cat!' Alfie drew himself up to his full height, which wasn't that tall. But if she was going to start babbling about ghosts, it was time to jolt her out of it.

'Come on, Jade,' he wheedled. 'Think about it. As for getting in, that'll be a piece of cake. There's a toilet window round the back that I could get open in a jiffy.'

Jade also adopted a more militant stance. Anyone watching them might have been put in mind of a couple of bantams, squaring up for a scrap. 'You can forget *that*! I am *not* climbing through any toilet window. I might end up falling straight into the loo! It would be really grotty with germs all over the place, as well as dangerous,' she concluded.

Alfie saw that he would have to find another argument. Scorn hadn't worked. Time to try another way. 'All right,' he said. 'Tell you what. I'll go there tonight on my own. I'll get that window open and get into the place. I'll take a good look round to see if it's all right. And I'll find a downstairs window we can climb through, and make sure the catch is off. No one will notice. Then, tomorrow, I'll give you a call and tell you if it's OK. It will be fun,' he concluded confidently. 'Come on, Jade. I thought you'd like an adventure!'

He was starting to win the argument. He could see by the look on her face that she was tempted by the idea of an adventure. Who wouldn't be, living in this dead-end sort of a place? Working at those kennels, cleaning up after those dogs, and then going home to work for her dad at the pub? She was weakening. His hopes soared.

'All right, then,' agreed Jade graciously. 'You go there tonight and see how easy it is to get in, and make sure there's nothing horrible in there. Tell me about it tomorrow.' She paused. 'The cops might be moving out of the barn tomorrow. That black sergeant who's been in charge of it told my dad so. There won't be anyone around after that.'

'There you are, then!' declared Alfie in triumph. He had not expected to talk her round so easily.

'She's got these really great braids,' Jade said thoughtfully.

'Who? What are braids?' asked Alfie, thrown off-course.

'The sergeant. Her name is Bennison. I wonder where she got them done. My hair's pretty long now. It might look good braided in those long sort of plaits. What do you think?'

'How should I know?' complained Alfie. 'I don't know anything about women's hairdressing.'

Jade contemplated him. 'What do you know about?'

'I know how to get into that cottage. I'll show you how easy it is!'

Alfie waited impatiently for nightfall. This time of the year, darkness came early, and that encouraged him to believe his idea was foolproof. There would be nobody about. There would be customers up at the pub, but they wouldn't be aware of anything happening at the cottage. In fact, the activity at the Waggoner's Halt would provide a welcome cover and distraction. As for anyone else living nearby, since the murder they were all too scared of leaving the house at night. They wouldn't be going out visiting one another. They would all shut themselves indoors early and watch the telly. He was confident that the only risks he ran were either of encountering Mrs Holder or Wayne Garley, both of whom had taken to walking around later in the evening.

But by this time of night, Alfie reassured himself, it was more likely Wayne would have given up patrolling the lanes. He'd be in the Waggoner's, having a pint. Alfie was confident he could avoid Wayne. As for Mrs Holder – well, it was far too late for her. Funny old girl, Mrs Holder. As well as walking the pugs at night, she had also taken to standing outside Rose Cottage, just staring at the place. The cottage seemed to fascinate her. But he had to be careful what he said about Mrs Holder when talking to Jade. Not only was she Jade's employer; but Jade was fierce in her defence if she thought anyone was disrespecting the old woman.

It wasn't raining, for which he was grateful. It was bad enough he was already chilled to the bone, without getting drenched as well. But, although he did not encounter any human life, he did encounter the fox. It appeared suddenly through a gap in the hedge. Alfie stopped in his tracks; but the fox didn't. It cast Alfie a warning glare and trotted off into the darkness.

He saw as he approached the cottage that one of the warning strips glued across the front door had come loose. The rain and wind would've done that. He made his way carefully to the back of the cottage and the little window he had marked as being the easiest point of entry. Breaking the glass and reaching through to find the catch halfway up the little frame had been his first idea; and he might yet have to do that. But he was hoping to avoid breaking the glass. It would sound loud on the quiet night air, and leave a visible clue to his activity. He set to with a strong piece of flat plastic, in an attempt to work it between the frame and the surround. However, the task proved trickier than he had anticipated. He was growing more nervous the longer it took. Behind him, the wind rustled the branches of the trees and he kept thinking someone was moving about. He told himself not to imagine things. But it had made him jumpy and lent urgency to his task. He abandoned the plastic and instead gave the glass a smart blow, as he had first intended, with the large stone he had brought along for the purpose, should it become necessary. The small pane broke and the pieces fell down inside with a noisy clatter. He'd need to watch out for the shards when he climbed through. Reaching in carefully he could manoeuvre the latch and achieve his purpose. The window opened.

Climbing through proved hard work, because though Alfie was small and wiry in build, the opening wasn't as generous as he'd judged. At one point, halfway in, he panicked, fearing himself wedged. He couldn't let himself be stuck like this, to be discovered the next day by someone. He'd never live it down. And as for what Jade would think if she heard about it! And she would hear of it.

Desperation lent added urgency to the task. Eventually he managed to manoeuvre himself further in and, at last, he was through. He fell to the floor in an ungainly tangle of limbs, dislodging some sort of air freshener that clattered to the tiled floor and filled his nostrils with the odour of pine. No injury to himself, luckily. There could so easily have been with shards of broken window glass on the floor. One thing was obvious, however. Even if he talked her into trying, Jade wouldn't be able to get through. She was, like all the Wilsons, solidly built. The worst-case scenario would be that she'd become stuck as he had temporarily been, half in and half out, and he would have to go and get help to release her. She'd never speak to him again afterwards. Even worse, Barry would do his best to tear Alfie's head off.

He got to his feet and listened. He knew the cottage was empty, but he had made rather a lot of noise. There was no movement or sound. Alfie felt a glow of triumph. He'd done it!

He opened the door and let himself out into what seemed to be a narrow passage. He had never been inside the cottage and was unclear about the layout. He tried to orient himself but, in the darkness, even working out the ground plan was tricky, as this part of the building was an extension to the original. He decided not to put on the lights, because it was just possible they might be seen by someone leaving the pub. Likewise, he'd brought a torch but decided not to use it unless it became absolutely necessary. To show no light at all was the safest course of action. Now that his eyes had adjusted to the gloom, it wasn't too bad.

The first door he came to and opened led him into a shower room. That was no good. At the next attempt, he found himself in the kitchen. But this was fortunate, because another door opened out into a central hallway. The front door was straight ahead. The living room was to the right. The staircase was behind him. Alfie was confident now, so much so that he decided to go into the living room because that had been the scene of the crime, and he was curious. He'd never get Jade to venture into the room where the deadly attack had taken place. Girls, he supposed, worried about things like that. But he wanted the kick of being in a room where a man had been stabbed to death. Jade's warning about supernatural presences came to his mind, but he dismissed all that. Interesting places like dungeons and castles might have a restless spirit or two hanging about the place, clanking their chains. But not an old cottage just outside Weston St Ambrose.

Even so, a natural nervousness made him hesitate on the threshold. The room was in darkness. There was a strange odour, not just blood, but chemicals. He hadn't expected that. He stepped a little further in. His eyes were becoming accustomed to the gloom now. The furniture was bulky, traditional in style, and there was a big telly. Alfie was tempted to take that with him when he left. He'd open a window in this room; and heave it through. But he decided against it. Despite his bravado when speaking to Jade of the adventure, now he was actually in the cottage he couldn't help but feel uneasy. The next time he came, with Jade's company, he'd be all right. She could help him get the telly through a window.

The moonlight bathed the room in a misty glow. It was difficult to make things out and he dared not switch on a light. There was a tall, straight shape over there in the corner. Alfie reckoned he knew what that was. It was one of those big old standing clocks. People who lived in this sort of home liked old things like that, antiques. 'Grandfather clocks', that's what they were called. Probably because old people owned them. They had another name, too. Long-case clocks, that was it. Those programmes on the telly showing antique auctions called them that and they were worth a small fortune.

Alfie decided to take a closer look. He would need someone's help to move it. Jade wouldn't do that. But he knew a bloke who might help.

He began to make his way towards it. Then the long clock shape seemed to tremble and move, too. To his horror, its shape began to change. It grew arms and legs and this strange new creature, whatever it was, human or monster, began to come towards him.

Clocks don't walk. Men do. He could hear hoarse breathing. There was someone else here: no monster but a human and a dangerous one. He had not been alone in the cottage as he had imagined. Someone, or some creature, had already arrived ahead of him; and he knew instinctively it wasn't Wayne Garley. Wayne would have challenged Alfie immediately, not waited so quietly. How the unknown person had got in, or why he was there, Alfie didn't know. Not by breaking in, as Alfie had. Somehow that added to the threat. Had the other one somehow floated, ghost-like, through the walls? Had Jade been right? Whoever or whatever it was, it had heard him break in and waited for him quietly in that shadowy corner. It had listened as he stumbled about, motionless, controlling its breathing, not betraying itself: a hunter, waiting for him to reach this room, the murder room, waiting to pounce.

In his dismay he was momentarily frozen. Then he regained control over his muscles and turned to run.

He was too late. Strong hands gripped his shoulders and he found himself spun round to face the assailant. He was more terrified than he had ever been in his life. Even a clandestine meeting with Jade wasn't worth this. It, he thought of the other as 'it' because in his panicking mind he still confused the attacker with the grandfather clock he'd first thought the shape to be, was breathing heavily. Its breath was on his face. It growled, or made a sound that, to Alfie in his terror, was so like a growl as to be indistinguishable from one. He found himself longing for 'it' to speak, to prove it was human. But it continued to make those animal snarls. Then the creature hit him. There was no mistaking the impact of a human fist. Alfie reached up and tried to push the assailant away. To add to his panic, his hand encountered hair, strong bushy hair. Alfie was a fan of horror films. Or rather, he had been until this moment. Was this a werewolf? Did such things really exist? He knew now that the idea of breaking into the cottage, which had seemed so brilliant when he had explained it to Jade, was the worst idea he'd ever had. Or ever would have if he couldn't get free of 'it'.

Desperation moved him to change his tactics. He couldn't fight it off. He had to try something else. He stopped trying to push the creature away and, instead, went limp. The attacker, perhaps surprised, slackened his grip. Alfie slid to the floor, like an escaping cat. The creature stooped to grasp his clothing and haul him upright. Alfie rolled away and scrambled to his feet. But there was nowhere to flee to. He could only hope to return to the lavatory and squeeze back through the tiny window. But before he reached the door of the room, the attacker was on him again.

He put his hands over his face to protect that. It was all he could do. Then the blows began to rain down on him again. Alfie started to sob, not in pain or fear, but because he believed he was going to die.

Chapter 11

Beryl Garley propped her trusty steed against the side of the Pickerings' house and plodded round to the kitchen. Sammy had been left at home because Beryl was going to work. She had told him so, before she left. 'Work!' she had said loudly to him. He knew what that meant. He watched her leave despondently but without protest. *He'd be all right,* she thought, *because he knows I always come back.*

For some reason, and for the first time ever, the last thought struck her forcibly. *What if she had an accident on the bike and didn't come back? Someone would look after Sammy,* she comforted herself. *Wayne, her brother-in-law, would make sure the little dog was all right. He had a key to her cottage for emergencies.*

But you cannot predict what's going to happen, can you? You get out of bed in the morning, never knowing whether you'll return to it at night.

'All right, Beryl?' asked Mary Pickering, opening the kitchen door. 'I thought I heard you coming. Something wrong? You look worried.'

'I'm all right!' returned Beryl robustly. 'I'm just fed up, like everyone is, with all these strangers hanging about the place.' Perhaps, fearing she might have insulted relatively new members of the community, like the Pickerings and their neighbours in Long Lane, she added, 'I mean the coppers mostly. Though they've got a job to do, I suppose.'

'I've just put the kettle on, Beryl,' invited Mary. 'Come and have a cup of tea before you begin clearing up. My husband's driven over to Gloucester.'

The spaniel, Billy, had recognised the visitor's voice and came plodding out to greet her. ''Ello,' Beryl greeted him, and rubbed his head.

'I'll take him out for his walk before you start,' Mary assured the cleaner. 'I've had to change the usual way I go with him, because of all the new traffic from the police investigation. I'll probably go down the lane past the Roman site.'

'There's them history people been hanging about there, too,' said Beryl. 'It's like the whole world's come to Weston. Just a lot of strangers poking about. I wish they'd all go away.'

Due to the activity around the pub and the cottage, not to say her disturbing after-dark expeditions, Eleanor had also been obliged to change the route of her exercise walks with the pugs. Thus, when the morning came, she avoided walking near the pub or past the cottage with the dogs, and instead she, too, took the lane that ran past the site of the mythical Roman villa. For the first time, it struck her how straight it was, not the winding English lane such as those of which Chesterton wrote.

"The rolling English drunkard made the rolling English road . . ."' she told the pugs. They snorted, not so much in agreement as because they were wondering why on earth she was dragging them down this way. Left to their own devices, they would have trotted straight home.

But the narrow lane, as direct as the proverbial beeline, made Eleanor reflect. She had always thought of the villa as being little more than a folktale. She couldn't really bring herself to believe in it, though there was of course no reason why it shouldn't have existed. Remains of such places were dotted around all over the country. She knew the story of pieces of mosaic being turned up, but it would take more than that to convince her. People liked a bit of history. (Beryl Garley wouldn't have agreed with her.) They believed what they wanted to. The lane was straight; so what?

As she approached the site, she saw the gate giving access to it was open. A vehicle appeared, a campervan, and began carefully inching out into the lane. There was little space to either side, but the driver, a woman, seemed confident. Once clear of the gateway, she stopped and the passenger got out to close the gate and secure it with chain and padlock. *Aha!* Eleanor thought. *They've finished their survey, or whatever it was.* The woman had remained at the wheel, waiting. Eleanor didn't recognise her, although she was the nearer. Then the man, task complete, returned to climb in beside the driver. The car turned into the lane to face Eleanor, who dragged the pugs up on to the narrow grass verge. She hoped the vehicle would get past them without a problem, as the only other option she had was to jump down, with the pugs, into the ditch that ran along the hedge; and she strongly suspected that was filled with muddy water, rat urine and debris. The pugs didn't care for being hauled into the wet grass and weeds. They grumbled and muttered, turning their round eyes up at her, full of reproach. The vehicle faced away from the direction of the Waggoner's Halt. This meant it was on the far side of the lane and she had a clear view of the driver's window, straight now, allowing her a good view of the woman's strong profile. The pugs were getting alarmed at finding themselves between the campervan and the ditch. But the vehicle squeezed safely past, the driver raising her hand in acknowledgement of Eleanor's cooperation.

Eleanor still didn't know her, and did not think she'd ever seen her before. A sun- and wind-tanned sort of woman, what is generally called 'an outdoor type', *much like me,* she thought. *Bit younger than me, but give her a few more years and she'll be a real old boot. Again, much like me!* The driver had her hair tied back in a ponytail. *Too young a hairstyle,* Eleanor thought unkindly. *She's probably worn it like that for years and never thought to change it. The woman must be one of the archaeologists,* she supposed. In raising her arm, the driver had briefly afforded Eleanor a glimpse of her passenger-seat companion in profile: a grey-bearded fellow, also weather-beaten and wrinkled, with a woollen hat pulled down around his ears. Then the campervan had gone, bumping down the ill-maintained lane, splashing through the puddles, and turning off on to the road that would run past the Waggoner's Halt.

Eleanor watched it until it was out of sight. Then she turned her attention back to the increasingly impatient pugs. 'OK, off we go!'

She did not get much further before she saw another dog walker coming towards her. She recognised Mary Pickering and Billy. The spaniel did not like long walks. He was getting on in age and increasingly stiff. He plodded alongside Mary who was looking down at him and encouraging him with false heartiness. The pugs knew Billy and brightened up as they drew nearer.

'Oh, hullo, Eleanor!' exclaimed Mary as they met, and their respective animals exchanged sniffs. 'I think I'm going to have to give up walking Billy. Poor old chap simply can't manage it. His appetite is good and he's bright enough in himself, it's just general wear and tear of age, I'm afraid.'

'Comes to us all,' said Eleanor with a sigh. She gave herself a mental shake. 'My offer of a puppy from the next litter still stands, Mary, should the need arise. Billy might like company,' she added tactfully.

'Thank you, Eleanor. But I don't know whether I'll get another dog when, you know . . .'

'Quite, I understand. But, well, keep it in mind.'

'I will. How are you getting on?' Mary cast her friend and neighbour a shrewd glance. 'You'll be glad to see all those coppers gone from that interview room they've set up behind the pub. We all shall,' she added hastily.

'The sooner, the better!' replied Eleanor in a burst of energy. 'Nothing against them personally. The ones I've had dealings with have been very civil. I identified Jerry's body for them, you know.'

Mary's hand flew to her mouth. 'Oh, how awful for you!'

'It wasn't so bad. It wasn't as though I'd liked him. He was mostly covered up. I only saw his face.'

'You are very brave, Eleanor dear,' said Mary fervently. 'I couldn't – wouldn't . . . Not ever.'

'Well, I was a farmer's wife. You get used to seeing dead stock. That's how I approached identifying Harrison. I made myself think of him as dead stock.'

'Oh,' said Mary, clearly at a loss how to reply to this.

Eleanor continued, 'As for the cops. I'll be glad to see them go because their presence is a constant reminder of when Lulu was found dead. There was a flurry of police activity then, but nothing so formal as an incident room. When Lulu died, they, the cops and the coroner, all seemed to want to reach a decision and draw a line under the whole thing as quickly as possible. I shall never forget that coroner, a pompous old fellow, intoning totally false regret at the sad event. That's what he called it, "sad event". Sad for whom? Not for him! All in a day's work, as far as he was concerned.' Eleanor uttered a growl not unlike one of the pugs.

'We all understand how you feel, my dear,' Mary assured her soothingly. 'Lulu's – fatal accident – meant a loss to us all. But the present set of police officers have begun to pack up and will be gone soon. And, eventually, new people will move into Rose Cottage. There won't be – well, frankly, Lulu's nephew won't be there to remind you.' She put her hand to her mouth again, this time in a guilty gesture. 'I shouldn't have said that, should I? It was, um, tactless; not to say disrespectful of someone who has only just died, and in such an awful way. Please excuse me!'

'Oh, please say whatever you like about Jerry,' Eleanor replied firmly. 'As I said, I didn't like him either, and it's no use pretending otherwise. It may sound a bit, well, unkind; but if something is true, then it can't be helped. Feelings can't be dictated. I feel – again, no doubt quite unjustly, that he somehow took Lulu from me. There's always going to be something to remind me. Just walking past Rose Cottage . . .'

She glanced beyond Mary, down the lane. The campervan was a dot in the distance and would soon be out of sight.

'Perhaps,' Mary suggested with hesitation, 'it would be better if you didn't walk the pugs that way, past the cottage, I mean.'

'You are probably right. But if I avoid the place, then Jerry really did win. We can't dictate what's going to happen. My memories of Lulu are happy ones, overall. It was only the manner of her death that upsets me. Things happen. That's life.'

There was a silence. It was broken by Mary.

'They're probably very interesting to talk to,' she said unexpectedly. 'Those archaeologists, I mean.' She had followed Eleanor's line of sight down the lane to the campervan.

Eleanor turned back to her in surprise. 'Yes, I suppose so. Although I've always doubted the existence of a Roman villa.'

'They must be confident it's worth their while to investigate it. I had been wondering,' Mary added hesitantly, 'whether it would be worthwhile asking them to come and talk to us, as a group. But now – now all this has happened – it probably wouldn't be a good idea, not the right moment.'

'No,' Eleanor agreed, 'not the right moment.'

Mary surprised her again. 'Beryl Garley doesn't like them. You know, she cleans for me.'

'Oh, yes, she used to clean for Lulu,' Eleanor said.

'That's right. She offered to clean for – him – Lulu's nephew, the – the victim. But he turned her down. He preferred the professional cleaning service to come out. Now she, Beryl, cleans for me.'

'You said "them".' Eleanor spoke quite sharply and Mary looked startled. 'You said Beryl Garley didn't like "them". Not she didn't like "him".'

'Oh, I see!' Mary exclaimed. 'Sorry to be confusing. Of course, she didn't like Jerry Harrison at all, because he wouldn't let her keep her job cleaning Rose Cottage. But she didn't like the archaeologists being here either.'

'Why not?' asked Eleanor. 'I didn't realise she'd had anything to do with them.'

'I don't say she did, not directly. It was just their presence. *"Strangers poking about!"* Those were her words. They don't like strangers around here, the old local families, do they? I don't think they really accept that anyone new has any right to live here. Beryl accepts Philip and me, I think, because we employ her. But I'm still not absolutely sure about it. She is a very good cleaner.' Mary added the last words hastily, as if she felt she'd been overcritical of Beryl. 'In the same way, she accepted Lulu, and I expect she accepts someone like you. You're a countrywoman and you and your husband farmed in the area. Plus, you were poor Lulu's friend. But Jerry was another kettle of fish: he took away her job.'

The thought leaped into Eleanor's head: *and he took away Lulu. Or he might have done. I don't know. I'll never know.*

They had fallen into step during the latter part of their conversation and had now reached the top of the lane, where they parted company. But not before Mary's last words had unsettled Eleanor even further.

'We're all agreed, I think, that we would have been very pleased if the police could have established who the killer is by now. But they don't seem to have made very much progress. Until they do, he could be lurking among us and we can none of us feel safe. Our bridge foursome has even suspended its meetings. That's why it is so very important that he is an outsider, isn't it? Otherwise, he's been among us all along and we have just never suspected his identity. You do lock yourself in as soon as it gets dark, don't you, Eleanor? Night falls so early at this time of year. I know your back door is usually unlocked because the kennels mean you are in and out of the house all the time. But just while all this is going on, and especially as the police are about to leave, perhaps you ought to think about locking the back door each time you walk the dogs. Just until, well, until we *know* . . .'

'Jade is generally there in the mornings,' Eleanor said. 'She doesn't miss much. She'd see anything suspicious.'

It would definitely not be wise to tell Mary about her two late-night dog walks, her encounter with Wayne on the first, or the second, even scarier expedition.

'Oh, yes, Jade Wilson, she's there quite a lot, isn't she? Young people can be very careless about securing a house before they leave the premises.'

'Local people don't lock up during the day,' Eleanor told her. 'They all know one another. They expect neighbours to call round.'

'Just so long as the murderer doesn't decide to call round!' retorted Mary crisply.

Goodness, thought Eleanor as she walked homeward. *This has really spooked Mary. I suppose Billy wouldn't be much use as a guard dog. He'd do his best, mind. But even his teeth are no good. If he tried to bite someone, they would likely all fall out.*

Beryl Garley was just getting ready to leave when Mary and Billy got back home.

'Oh, Beryl, thank you. And I've got a bit of news for you.'

'Oh, yes?' asked Beryl, cocking her head to one side much as Sammy did.

'I think the archaeologists may have left. I don't think they liked all the activity. They drove past Mrs Holder in their camper-van about twenty minutes ago.'

'Good!' said Beryl shortly. 'Let's hope they don't come back.'

Jess Campbell had returned with Tracy Bennison to check the incident room and make sure there were no more visitors come to offer any information, before they began to pack up and vacate the barn. (There had been plenty of visitors; but precious little help, she had to admit.)

Barry Wilson had come to watch them dismantle everything they had installed. *It was his barn, after all,* thought Jess, *and he had an interest in ensuring they left it 'as they had found it'.* He stood just inside the door, with his hands in his pockets, and an expression on his red face that was difficult to read. It certainly wasn't welcoming. She hoped it wasn't scorn. She approached him, and he took his hands from his pockets, but still said nothing, arms hanging loosely by his sides, breathing heavily. Away from his bar, there was something unsettling about him. She had not thought he looked a particularly jovial mine host when she had first seen him leaning on the bar when she and Bennison had walked in on the first day of the inquiry. Now he looked more like a bouncer, employed to keep order and, if necessary, throw troublemakers out. Presumably locals knew him and didn't mind his unsmiling countenance.

'Thank you for your cooperation, Mr Wilson,' she said.

Barry mellowed slightly. ''S'all right. It's been good for trade.' Perhaps it occurred to him that the police might not see things that way. He added, 'Been of any help to your lot?'

'We'll go through all the statements, and see what comes out of it.' She smiled at him.

Barry seemed slightly startled at being smiled upon. Perhaps it didn't happen often. He said, 'Glad to have been of help, I'm sure.'

There was a distracting flash of scarlet and peacock blue. His daughter had arrived. Her thin legs were clad in jeans and terminated in muddy ankle boots. The rest of her outfit was concealed under a vaguely official-looking button-through overall.

'You coming back in, Dad?' she asked. 'I gotta get down to the kennels. Mrs Holder is expecting me.'

'Do you like working at the kennels?' asked Jess with a smile.

It was returned with a scowl. 'Not much. She's nice and I like the little dogs. But in the summer, when people go on their holidays, they bring all sorts of other dogs in to board at Greentrees until they get back. Some of them are huge and they don't half make a mess. I've got to clear it up.'

Barry nodded. 'Go on, then. I'm coming in now.'

Jade scampered away, multicoloured locks bobbing, and her father, with a final nod of farewell to Jess, followed her, setting off back to his pub. He had a slightly rolling gait, Jess noticed, like an old-time mariner. *Most likely it's due to his weight,* she thought. *He ought to lose a bit.*

Bennison arrived at her side. 'He's a bit scary, isn't he?' she said unexpectedly. 'I mean, he's been all right while we've been here. Helpful enough. But I reckon he's the sort it wouldn't be wise to cross.'

'Maybe . . .' Jess said thoughtfully.

'Do you know what I think?' asked Bennison after a pause. She was still looking in the direction of the departing Wilson, who disappeared into the pub as she spoke. 'I reckon he's the shape he is now because he used to be a wrestler, or something like that.'

Jess turned to look at her, startled. 'Did someone tell you that, Tracy?'

'No, it's just a guess.' Bennison began to explain. 'I told you I grew up in a tower block. You get all sorts of people living in those blocks. We had a guy living in the flat above ours who used to wrestle a bit on the amateur side. Monty, his name was. The little kids all thought he was a giant! I suppose he built up a lot of muscle and, later on, when he gave up the wrestling, the muscle turned to flab. Not the soft sort of flab; the solid sort, like Wilson there.

'Anyhow, there were a few skinheads around the neighbourhood in those days; and sometimes they gave my mum or my sisters some hassle when they went out shopping. Then, one evening, Monty turned up at our door. My mum opened it and there he was. He said, "If you're going down to the market tomorrow, I'll walk down with you." And he did. He only did it the once. But word got round and my family never had any more trouble. He was a nice old feller, really, was Monty. He just looked scary.'

Jess wondered whether Barry Wilson was, at heart, a nice old fellow. Somehow, she didn't think so.

'While they're busy here, Tracy,' she said. 'We can walk down to Rose Cottage and take a last look round. I brought the key.'

'We won't find anything that's been missed,' Bennison said, as they approached the cottage. 'Sean Stubbs is pretty good at making sure.'

They stopped at the gate and Jess observed, 'It's a really attractive property and must be worth a bit. It's a shame there's no heir. He left everything to be sold and the money donated to charity, so his solicitor told me.'

'They might have a bit of trouble selling it. It would be a bit of a downer, moving into a place where there's been a murder. You can understand how buildings get a reputation.' Bennison drew a deep breath. 'Do we check the exterior, too?'

'Might as well.' Bennison's words had jogged her memory. Eleanor Holder believed her friend's death had been suspicious. Was the murder of Jeremy Harrison the second such crime to take place in this cottage? Or was Eleanor, overcome with guilt and grief at the sudden death of her friend, simply unable to accept that Lucinda had tripped and fallen to her death in a tragic accident?

They walked down the path towards the front door and then turned off to the right. When they reached the back of the property, they both saw the damage to the lavatory window at the same moment.

'Damn,' said Jess in a low voice.

'Break-in!' said Bennison more briskly. 'Not surprising, I suppose. Wonder if anything is missing.'

'There will be hell to pay if the whole place has been emptied out!'

They completed the exterior tour and arrived back at the front door. Bennison pointed at the loose strip of tape. 'Perhaps whoever broke in tried the door first, but couldn't manage to get it open.'

'We might as well just pull the rest of the tape down,' Jess said.

When the door was bare of tape Jess opened it with the key, and they went in. An odour of dried blood lingered in the air together with that of chemicals and fustiness due to lack of fresh air circulating around the place.

Bennison sniffed the air. 'Pretty musty. Where do we try first? Living room?' She followed Jess into the room and both stopped. A chair had been overturned near the door, also a small table. The air had been disturbed. Jess could sense it. Something had happened here, happened since the murder of Jerry Harrison, something violent. Tracy, beside her, felt it too and muttered, 'Uh-oh!'

To prove their fears were not fancy, a human form was sprawled, unmoving, on the floor.

'Oh, hell,' exclaimed Bennison. 'I don't believe it! It's like we never took Harrison's body away.'

The new body was lying on the carpet in much the same place as Harrison's body had been when found. But whereas Harrison's still form had been curled, this victim lay flat on his – he was clearly male – back. His face was smeared in blood. It caked his features, as if he wore a red mask. His hands, raised to rest on his chest, were also red with blood from the split knuckles, or possibly from his assailant as he had tried to fight him off. He appeared to be young, slight in build, though wiry. Jess knelt beside him, checking for signs of life.

'He's breathing!' she confirmed. She peered at his face, slightly turned to one side, and added, 'I know him, it's Alfie Darrow. He's a local boy, lives down the road at Weston St Ambrose, and he's always in trouble. Never anything heavy. Petty theft, that sort of thing.'

'Then he was probably here to steal. But he wasn't alone. Did the thieves fall out?' Bennison joined her. She had taken out her phone. 'He looks a mess.'

'He's received a really severe beating: numerous blows to the head, and I guess others to the body. Someone really went to town on him. Call an ambulance and then call the incident room and tell them to stop dismantling everything. We may be staying another couple of days. And if Stubbs is down there, tell him to get back up here.'

She went out into the hallway and rang Carter to tell him the news.

'*Alfie Darrow?*' Carter's voice sounded in her ear, incredulous. 'What's he got to do with all this?'

'Aiming to do a bit of petty theft, is my guess,' Jess replied. 'But someone else either went with him, and they fell out, or the other person arrived earlier or a fraction later. Whether the other person was also intent on burglary is another thing. What I can tell you is that Alfie appears to have entered the property through a lavatory window at the back. He smashed the glass and reached through to open the latch. It's a very small opening. That suggests the other person must also be pretty thin.'

'Alfie broke in first through the small window and then let in an accomplice through a door,' Carter suggested. 'But in that case, Alfie would have arranged to meet him there. Why the violent confrontation?'

'Unless,' Jess suggested, 'the assailant had a key and walked through the front door. The keep-out tapes had been disturbed.'

'Who on earth would have a key? Harrison was a loner. I can't imagine him giving his door key to anyone. His aim, as far as we can make out, was to keep the outside community at bay.'

'The cleaning company held a key,' she reminded him. 'One of their employees deciding to pay an extra unofficial visit?'

'Stubbs should have collected any keys they held when he called at the offices. Check with him.'

'It's not like him to forget something so basic,' Jess defended the sergeant. She was struck by an idea. 'The person locally who might have a key is Eleanor Holder. She and Jeremy's Aunt Lucinda were best buddies. Eleanor might have been given one by her friend for emergencies, but never used it. Perhaps it's been just hanging up somewhere. I should've asked her when I was there. She could have forgotten about it after Lucinda's fatal accident; because that was so sudden and dramatic. Someone could have stolen it at any time. After I've spoken to Barry Wilson about extending our stay for another couple of days, I'll walk down to the kennels and speak to Eleanor.' She heaved a sigh of exasperation. 'I wish we'd put a round-the-clock guard on the cottage now.'

'We haven't the manpower!' snapped Carter's voice in her ear.

The ambulance was noisily announcing its imminent arrival. 'Got to go,' said Jess and cut the call.

A small crowd had gathered outside by the time Alfie was carried out on a stretcher and loaded into the ambulance.

A murmur ran round the group. 'That's young Darrow!' said one voice.

Talk about jungle drums, thought Jess crossly. *You couldn't keep a secret round here for long!*

She had a word with the paramedics and, as the ambulance drove away, Jess followed in its wake up the road towards the Waggoner's Halt.

There she was greeted by the formidable form of Barry Wilson, standing outside the main entrance, simmering like a volcano about to erupt.

'Is that right?' he demanded. 'Was it that little tyke Alfie Darrow you found in the cottage?'

There was little point in denying what was clearly common knowledge already.

'Yes, Mr Wilson, but we don't yet know the circumstances around his being there or his being attacked.'

Barry lowered his head like a bull about to charge. 'Here, my girl's got nothing to do with it, right?'

'Jade?' Jess was taken aback. 'Why should she?'

'Because Darrow has been hanging around her. I warned him off the other day. I saw him as I was coming out of the Minimart in Weston. He and all the Darrows are bad news.'

One thing was certain, thought Jess. *Barry couldn't get through that tiny window. He didn't attack Alfie, though in other circumstances I'd not put it past him.*

'I've made a note of your concern, Mr Wilson. I hope it won't inconvenience you to have us around for another couple of days?' she asked politely. 'We had intended to pack up the incident room in the barn today. But in view of this . . .'

'Help yourselves!' growled Barry. He stomped back into his bar.

By the time Jess arrived at Greentrees Kennels, word of the attack on Darrow, and where it had taken place, had obviously reached there ahead of her. Eleanor, Jade and all six pugs were standing in the open gateway in varying degrees of agitation.

As Jess got out of her car she was met by a barrage of questions, with two different priorities. The pugs, swept up in the general excitement, contributed their fourpennyworth by way of grunts and growls with a variety of barks. *They really did do their very best to talk,* thought Jess, amused.

Jade yelled, 'Is it right? Has someone tried to murder my boyfriend? How bad is he hurt? Will he get better?'

'Has someone broken into the cottage?' asked Eleanor, clearly dismayed. 'Have they done any damage? Is anything stolen?'

The pugs continued jumping around in a frenzy, still uttering an orchestral range of noises. Eleanor seemed to become aware of the distraction and told them all briskly to 'Pipe down, you lot!' Unexpectedly, they did. But their excitement at what was going on remained. They fixed their eyes on Jess and obviously expected her to come up with something interesting.

Jade was watching her in much the same way, so Jess decided to begin by answering her questions first.

'Alfie Darrow has been taken to hospital, Jade. We found him inside the cottage. He has been badly beaten up but he is alive and should recover before too long.' She turned to the other woman. 'We don't know if anything has been stolen, Eleanor, but we think probably not. A small window at the back of the cottage has been forced open. We'll secure it.'

'Have you seen my dad?' demanded Jade. 'He doesn't know why Alfie was there, does he? He'll go mad.'

Why should Barry care about Alfie's attempt at burglary? wondered Jess. *Or was he there for some other reason? What's Jade's interest?*

To Eleanor, she said: 'We don't know if the intruders arrived together, and then fell out, or separately.' Jess then turned to the younger woman.

'I have seen your father, Jade, and if you know why Alfie was in the cottage, you should tell me now,' she ordered.

'He didn't go there to pinch anything!' retorted Jade defiantly. 'I don't know about the other bloke, the one who beat him up. He might have been there to thieve. Alfie was only trying to find us a place to meet, him and me. My dad don't like him. He won't let him come to the pub. There's nowhere else private round here. Whatever you do, someone sees you. That someone passes any news on, double-quick, usually at the Minimart. Debbie Garley has got it in for Alfie. So, what are we supposed to do? Your lot had finished at the cottage. Alfie thought we could meet in there. He was just checking it out.'

'Oh, Jade!' sighed Eleanor. 'And you agreed to this crazy plan? I would have thought you had more sense. How could you be so silly?'

'You haven't got to deal with my dad!' retaliated the feisty Jade. 'How bad is Alfie hurt?'

'He is unconscious, I'm afraid, but the hospital will take good care of him, I promise you,' Jess assured her.

'Well, it wasn't my idea he went there,' insisted Jade. 'It's nothing to do with *me*! I'm not saying it was any good as an idea. It was pretty daft. I told Alfie so. But he reckoned it would be all right. Even if he'd not been attacked in there, I still wouldn't have agreed to go there with him.'

'Perhaps you'd like to come into the house, Inspector Campbell,' invited Eleanor. 'Jade! Take the dogs round to the back and pen them up.'

Jade hauled the pugs away with difficulty. From the look on her face, she was as reluctant to leave the scene as they were.

When Jess and Eleanor had seated themselves indoors, Eleanor got her question in first. 'Had this anything to do with Jerry's murder?'

'We have no idea, Eleanor, not yet. If what Jade said is true, then Alfie broke in hoping to find a place he and Jade could meet. Unfortunately, someone else also had a reason – we don't know what – to be in the cottage. That intruder could well have been there to steal, of course. We don't know whether he came with Darrow to the cottage, or arrived separately. The toilet window has been forced, the glass broken, the catch moved up to free it. I can well believe that is how Darrow got in. He's slightly built and would have been able to squeeze through. For the other person to climb in that way, he would have to be as thin as Darrow. Once both were inside, whether they arrived together or not, there was a confrontation. Did they argue, fall out over what to do next? Or had the other person arrived before Darrow? If so, how did he get in? He might have tried the front door unsuccessfully. The police tape stuck across it had been disturbed. But what was his purpose in being there?'

'Burglar!' said Eleanor promptly. 'Empty cottage. Open invitation. He wouldn't know there was nothing in the place of particular value, because Harrison sold it all off when he inherited it.' She reddened and looked embarrassed. 'See here, Inspector Campbell, there is something I need to tell you. A couple of nights ago I was giving the pugs a last walk before bedtime. I took them past the cottage and there was someone in the garden.'

'Who? What was he doing?' asked a startled Jess.

'I don't know who it was, but he had a torch and was working his way round the exterior of the place. Casing the joint,' she added in a sudden and unexpected lapse into jargon.

'You didn't think to phone the police? Or report it to the incident room the following morning?'

'I thought the police might have left someone on guard,' Eleanor told her unhappily. 'You know, a sort of watchman, doing his rounds.'

'Unfortunately not,' Jess confessed. 'Shortage of manpower.'

But we should have done, she was thinking. *An empty cottage in a lonely location was bound to attract the wrong sort of interest.*

Unexpectedly, Eleanor said, 'I don't think it was Wayne Garley.'

'Why should it be Mr Garley?' Jess asked, surprised.

Eleanor looked guilty. 'He's appointed himself a sort of watchman. He walks round the lanes at night. Just looking for anything suspicious, you know. The murder at the cottage has left everyone very jumpy.'

'That's risky,' said Jess. 'It would be better if he didn't do that, not alone. And really, Eleanor, it would be wise not to take the dogs out for a walk so late.'

'Point taken,' said Eleanor ruefully. 'But, as I said, I'm sure it wasn't Wayne. He wears a big old coat, baggy. It makes him look as if he's walking round in a tent. Keeps him warm, I dare say. The person I saw in the grounds of the cottage was a much more slightly built figure.'

'It may have been someone intent on breaking in. It could even have been young Darrow planning his little caper. Just looking for a weak spot; and making note of the small window at the rear of the property,' Jess suggested.

It's what Alfie would do, she thought. She continued, 'If Darrow and his attacker arrived separately, there is a possibility that the attacker arrived first and entered the property using a key.'

'Where would he get one?' Eleanor frowned. 'One of the cleaning company staff?'

'Sergeant Stubbs took charge of all keys held by the cleaners as one of his first jobs.'

'How about Jerry's own keys? His murderer could have taken them.'

'Harrison's murderer seems to have taken a number of personal items, documents, computer. But strangely, not the door keys.' Jess hesitated. 'I have been wondering whether Lucinda Harrison ever gave you a key, to use in an emergency? I'm not suggesting you used it to get in and attack Darrow.'

Eleanor looked embarrassed again. 'Now that you mention it, I believe Lulu did give me a key, oh, years ago. I never used it. I don't recall that she ever asked me for it back.'

'Where did you keep it? Do you still have it?'

'If I remember correctly, I hung it on a nail in my larder. It should still be there.'

Eleanor got to her feet. 'We'll go and look.'

This was an old house and the larder was an old-fashioned, walk-in one, with marble-topped shelves. An ancient meat safe, with its perforated door, dating from before refrigerators became common, and now clearly long disused, was still affixed to the wall.

Eleanor pointed to it. 'I've never used that. But when I was a girl, meat safes were a common fixture in kitchens. The smell of the blood attracted flies; and there were usually several clinging to the door. They couldn't get in, of course.'

Also attached to the wall were several hooks. From one of them hung an assortment of modern keys. 'Dog pen, kennels . . .' explained Eleanor.

'And those?' Jess pointed at another bunch of much older-looking keys, dangling from another hook. Some had faded cards attached to them, denoting their purpose.

Eleanor took them all down and carried them to the kitchen table where she spread them out.

'I do believe some of these came from the farm,' she said. 'Don't ask me why they're still hanging there. I really couldn't tell you now.'

'Rose Cottage?' prompted Jess, as patiently as she could.

'Oh, yes.' Eleanor sorted through the collection. 'No, no Rose Cottage.'

'So, you might have returned it to your friend?'

'No!' Eleanor suddenly sounded firm. 'Not while she was alive, why should I? She'd given it to me for emergencies.' Sadly, she added, 'But when there was a real emergency, and she was lying dead at the foot of her stairs, I was not the one who found her. That was left for the postman to do.' She heaved a sigh. 'Isn't life pretty bloody awful, when you think about it? All the nice people drop off the twig in various ways before you want them to go. The monsters hang around for ages.'

'Which leaves us Jeremy Harrison,' suggested Jess. 'Are you sure you didn't return the key to him?'

'That I am sure about,' Eleanor replied promptly. 'I never did more than exchange the time of day with him while I was out with the dogs.' She frowned at the collection of keys on the table. 'I can't explain why it's not there.'

Jess looked across the kitchen to the back door. 'Is that kept locked during the day?'

'Heavens, no. I'm in and out all the time. Jade is here part of the time, of course, but I don't know if she's even aware of the old keys in the larder. If a stranger came round, I'm sure the dogs would let me know.'

'If Jade knew there was a key to Rose Cottage just hanging up here for the taking, she would have given it to her boyfriend,

Alfie, when he told her his plan to check out the cottage to use as a place to meet.' Jess sighed. 'She wouldn't just leave him to break in, surely, if all he had to do, was open the door with a key. I'll ask her.'

Jade was outside, by the dog kennels, sitting on an old wooden bench outside a sturdy-looking hut. She was wrapped in a grubby quilted coat over her kennel maid's overall, with a woollen head-band covering her ears, top of her head and much of her multicoloured tresses. She held a can of soft drink; and looked cold, sulky and resentful.

'I want to go and see Alfie,' she announced as Jess approached. 'I can do that, can't I? You can't stop me. He's my boyfriend, I've got a right to visit him. Anyway, he'll be expecting me. If I don't go, he'll think I've dumped him.'

'Now probably isn't the time for a visit. You'll have to wait until the hospital says he's able to receive visitors.' (*And*, thought Jess, *I want to talk to him first*.) 'Also, I don't think it would be wise to antagonise your father any further just now.'

'He's never liked Alfie!' complained Jade.

Not a lot of people do, Jess thought. 'Your dad's being protective, Jade.'

'I do not need protecting!' declared Jade, offended. 'I'm almost nineteen, you know. I'm not a kid. I can look after myself.'

'Depends what sort of person you're dealing with. There's a killer around somewhere.'

Jade uttered the sort of growl made by the pugs. 'If he's still hanging around, he's nuts. He must have cleared off by now.'

'Murderers often don't think in the way others do.'

Jade's interest was caught. 'You've known lots of murderers?'

'Some,' Jess admitted.

'What are they like?'

'They often appear to be quite normal. It's what's going on in their heads, that you can't see, that makes them dangerous. I've got a question. You know the old spare keys hanging up in Mrs Holder's kitchen?'

'No,' said Jade, staring at Jess. 'What keys? I never saw any in her kitchen.'

'They're on hooks in the larder.'

Jade shrugged. 'Oh, well, then, I wouldn't have seen them, would I? I never go in her larder. What'd I go in there for?'

'Dog food?'

'Kept separate. In the hut here.' Jade indicated the hut behind her.

'Is it open?'

'What, the hut? Sure. You can go in.'

The hut contained a variety of animal-related items, including stacks of tins of dog food; and a large chest freezer that hummed contentedly to itself in a corner.

'OK if I look in that?'

'Help yourself.' Jade had followed her in. Her tone of voice seemed to suggest that the limits of her assistance had been reached.

Jess opened the lid and peered inside. The chest contained numerous little packages wrapped in foil and labelled with the contents. 'Cottage pie,' Jess read aloud. 'Cauliflower cheese. Fish pie. These aren't dog food.'

'I didn't say they were. Mrs Holder has a big cook-up from time to time and puts it all out here. We don't have any corner shop around here, you may have noticed,' Jade concluded sarcastically. 'Or any other shops.'

'There's the Minimart in Weston St Ambrose.'

'Not got much in it.' Jade dismissed the wares offered at the

Minimart. 'One of the Garleys is in charge of that. What do you expect?' She drew a deep breath. 'It's why our restaurant at the pub does so well.'

Jess closed the freezer lid. 'Jeremy Harrison, the murder victim, did he often eat at the Waggoner's restaurant?'

'On a Sunday, when we do a roast,' Jade informed her. 'Don't know what he did the rest of the time. Well, he had a supermarket delivery every so often. I saw the van go past.'

'When he came to the restaurant at the pub, was he always alone?'

'Yes,' said Jade simply. 'Never saw him with anyone.'

'He didn't greet anyone?'

'He'd say hullo to anyone from the big houses around here, if they were there. But he was never chatty.'

'No special friends?'

Jade considered the question. 'I don't think he had friends. Old Lucinda, his auntie, who had the cottage before, she was good mates with a lot of the posh lot. But not him. He was dead weird.'

She did not seem to realise the tactlessness of her last sentence. *But the art of tact,* thought Jess, *was probably a closed book to Jade Wilson. You couldn't blame her. She was Barry Wilson's daughter, after all.*

'Can we make this clear, Jade? It is important. You didn't know there was a key to Rose Cottage hanging up in Mrs Holder's kitchen?'

'I told you I didn't!' Jade shot back. 'If I had, I'd have borrowed it for Alfie, when he told me he was planning to suss out the cottage, to see if it could be used as a place for us to meet. Not,' she concluded, 'that I would've agreed to go there with him, whatever he said. It would've been creepy. It was a stupid idea, anyway. We might both of us have been knocked on the head by whoever attacked him.'

'From the sound of it,' said Ian Carter later that day, 'Alfie is safe while he's in hospital. If we arrest him on the charge of breaking and entering, we can hold him for twenty-four hours and he'll be safe during that period. But we can't really hold him for any longer unless we can charge him with something more serious. Once we release him, he'll have to watch out for Barry Wilson, who is keen to defend his daughter's honour, from the sound of it. We'll have to warn Barry off. How long does the hospital think it needs to keep the patient?'

'Tracy Bennison is in touch with the hospital. They will certainly be keeping him in overnight, perhaps longer. I'll go there myself tomorrow morning and, with luck, I'll see him and might even be able to speak to him. At least they might be able to suggest a date when he's likely to be released; and when we'll be able to question him at a police station. The hospital will need the bed. They will want to discharge Darrow as soon as possible.'

'He might claim not to remember anything,' said Carter with a sigh. 'Especially if he's got Barry Wilson breathing vengeance down his neck. I take it there is a constable outside the door of his ward?'

Jess smiled. 'I agree, he's safe in hospital. Once they've discharged him, we can't protect him from Wilson for ever. But perhaps we should trust Jade.'

Ian raised his eyebrows. 'Wilson's daughter? How is she going to protect Darrow?'

'Put it this way,' Jess replied. 'Alfie is frightened of Wilson. But Jade is definitely not scared of her dad. She's almost nineteen and Barry knows, if he makes her seriously angry, she might just walk out. Barry wouldn't like that. He'd have to find another barmaid. Besides, he probably likes having Jade around. She is his daughter. There's no sign of his wife. He probably doesn't approve of her friendship with Alfie. But he might not tackle her directly about it.'

'He wouldn't leave his bar during the evening,' Carter mused. 'And Alfie would have known at once if it was Barry who attacked him, even in the dark. I can't imagine that Barry would have kept quiet while he was beating Alfie to a pulp.'

'Put your money on Jade,' advised Jess. 'She's the best protection Alfie's got against Barry Wilson.'

This conversation remained with Carter as he drove home at the end of the working day. 'She is his daughter!' he said aloud to himself. Jess was probably right. Wilson did like having his daughter around. Carter felt a great sadness envelop him. Millie had ceased to 'be around' since Sophie had taken off for France with Rodney, and Millie had gone to boarding school. When she wasn't at school she only spent part of her holidays with him, the rest in France. Even when she was with him, work got in the way and he would take her over to Monica's place.

In retrospect, he had bitterly regretted the spat with Millie over her presence outside the incident room. But he was still worried about Millie's resolve to join the police, because her motivation seemed to be her admiration for Jess Campbell. At least he had not yet had to worry about a problem boyfriend. In that way, Barry Wilson's dismay at the prospect of Jade throwing in her lot with Alfie Darrow outweighed his. That did not mean Barry was entitled to put Alfie back in another hospital bed as soon as he got out of the one he was currently occupying. Stubbs had been told to call on Barry in the morning, and firmly explain the situation.

171

It turned out not to be the only cloud on the horizon. Carter had barely reached home, and was rooting about in the freezer for something for his supper, when his phone rang. He fished it out of his pocket and looked to see the identity of the caller. He sighed. It wasn't entirely unexpected. He just hadn't expected it this evening. He put the phone to his ear.

'Hi, Sophie!' he said. 'Are you at Monica's?'

'How do you know?' the familiar accusing voice sounded in his ear.

'I'm a detective, remember?'

'How could I forget?' asked his ex-wife. 'Well, yes, I am. I'm staying for a couple of days and I think it would be a good idea if we met. We need to talk about Millie.'

She was right, of course. She quite often was right.

'I'll try and get away a little early tomorrow and pick you up. We can have dinner at the Royal Oak in Weston St Ambrose.' He tried to inject some enthusiasm into his voice, but it wasn't easy.

'The Royal Oak is crummy,' said Sophie. 'Can't you think of anywhere better?'

'Think of it as a business meeting,' Ian advised her unkindly. To soften the brusqueness of his tone, he added, 'The restaurant is under new management. I've heard good things of the upgraded menu.'

'Upgraded? Not before time. It needed improvement!' snapped Sophie. 'I haven't forgotten the salmon.' She closed the call.

Carter stared at the silent phone, perplexed. Salmon? What salmon? When had he and Sophie last eaten at the Royal Oak? He couldn't remember the occasion, but it must have been when Millie was a toddler. However, Sophie had always had a good memory: especially for grievances.

Chapter 12

'He's not yet up to being interviewed, Inspector Campbell,' said the nurse firmly.

Jess had made it a priority to go to the hospital early the following morning. But the usual delays meant it was late morning before she'd arrived. A trolley rattled past her, pushed by an aproned woman. It had plates of food on it. The tin lids covering them didn't prevent the leakage of a smell of boiled vegetables. It pervaded the air.

'How badly injured is he?' she asked the nurse.

'Actually, he was lucky. No fracture of the skull. It's not as bad as it looks. But he is very bruised and sore; and he's pretty distressed. He's also rather confused. He keeps talking about a clock.'

'*A clock?* In what context?' exclaimed Jess.

'He claims he was attacked by a clock.'

'A clock used as a weapon?' asked Jess cautiously.

'No, it was a grandfather clock . . . and it attacked him.'

Great, thought Jess. *Alfie never did make a lot of sense and now he's making no sense at all!*

'I don't want to interview him,' she reassured the nurse. 'I just want to satisfy myself as to his general condition and get an idea of when he might be available to be interviewed.'

'You'll need to talk to the doctor. I'll see if one is available.'

Alfie was safe from the vengeful Barry Wilson while he was

here. No one would get past that nurse. Jess wondered how long she would have to wait for someone with the authority to let her see the patient. Fortunately, it wasn't long.

'Let's go and take a look at the patient, shall we?' suggested the young doctor cheerfully. 'He might be making more sense now.'

Well, there was a chance. As a police detective, one had to believe that, even about Alfie. But there was always a first time. Against the odds, this might be it.

Jess was pleased to see that at least Alfie was out of bed; and seated in a chair beside it. She would hardly have recognised him if she hadn't known he was the patient. His head was extensively bandaged like that of an Egyptian mummy. What could be seen of his face was a mottled purple from which two blackened eyes glared at her. His nose was badly swollen, possibly broken, and he had a split lip. His memory of how he came by his injuries might be faulty, if he was claiming to have been attacked by a grandfather clock. But someone had beaten him up, Jess had seen that for herself when she and Bennison had found him. At least he recognised his visitor correctly, and didn't confuse her with a piece of furniture.

'Bloody hell!' he moaned. 'Inspector Campbell. You can't question me. I'm too sick. Ask him!' He pointed at the doctor.

'I just came to see how you are, Alfie,' she promised him. 'We can talk about what happened when you're a little better.'

'I broke into that cottage; I'll cough to that,' retorted Alfie. 'But I wasn't there to thieve anything.'

'We'll talk about that later, too.' The likelihood was that, when he was asked about it later, Alfie was likely to deny breaking into the cottage, and come up with another, and totally unbelievable, reason for his being found there unconscious. However, Alfie already had a story prepared.

174

He leaned forward, gripping the arms of his chair. 'You need to talk to my girlfriend. Go on, Jade Wilson, talk to her! She knows why I was there, in that cottage. I was looking for somewhere to meet where we wouldn't be disturbed. It's all her dad's fault. Barry Wilson, you know him?'

'You mean the landlord of the Waggoner's Halt?'

'Yes! Him, the old misery!' snapped Alfie. 'He don't like me. He doesn't want Jade to see me. Blame him, if you want to blame someone.' He put a hand to his head. 'Ouch!' he added.

'Steady on, old chap,' advised the doctor, adding to Jess, 'You really can't question him, at the moment.'

'See? He says so!' Alfie declared triumphantly, pointing at the doctor as he spoke.

'Plenty of time for that later,' Jess consoled him. Alfie uttered a growl. 'I just needed to see how you are.' She smiled kindly at him. 'You weren't really attacked by a grandfather clock, were you?'

'No, of course I wasn't! I'm not barmy. I just thought there was a clock like that, in the corner of the room. I couldn't really see what it was. It wasn't moving, just stayed there, tall and narrow, absolutely still. There wasn't much light; and in that corner it was really dark. When it moved, it scared me something awful, I can tell you. But I knew it wasn't a clock when it – he hit me!'

'Right, well, I hope you feel better soon.'

Alfie watched her leave with the doctor. His expression, framed by bandages, looked understandably depressed.

'Well, he is making progress,' the doctor told Jess encouragingly, when they were outside the ward. 'He did claim, when he first regained consciousness, that he'd been attacked by a grandfather clock. I heard him myself. Mind you, when they come in late at night, they're usually drunk, in a complete daze; and fighting off the furniture is the least of it. But he came in late yesterday morning. He wasn't drunk. He was found unconscious in an empty house, is that right?'

'More or less,' Jess said noncommittally. 'But I should tell you that he's correct in saying that his girlfriend's father is on the warpath. He should not be allowed anywhere near Darrow. I can't stress that enough. We have warned the father off. But he is very upset – and a man of action. His name is Barry Wilson, as Darrow said.'

'Right. One outraged papa. We'll keep an eye open for him.'

Alfie, however, had other protection. As Jess was leaving, she encountered a large, flamboyant figure with a mane of dyed black hair, through which gleamed gold hoop earrings. She was wearing a tartan cloak and leopard-print trainers. Like a galleon under full sail, Sandra Darrow, Alfie's mother, bore down on Jess.

'Oy!' she greeted her. 'I remember you! You're that Inspector Campbell. You've always had it in for my boy. All you coppers have. He's got the right to a solicitor! You can't interview him without his being legally represented.'

'I haven't been trying to interview Alfie, Mrs Darrow. I just came to see what sort of a state he was in.'

'What sort of a state do you expect him to be in?' demanded the outraged parent. 'How would you be, after you'd been hit with a grandfather clock?'

'He wasn't actually hit with a grandfather clock, Sandra. At least, that's not what he's saying now. He had mistaken his assailant for a clock—' Jess did not get to finish the sentence.

'You're as bad as he is,' declared Mrs Darrow.

She swept past Jess and continued on her path to locate her son. Staff and visitors parted before her like the waters of the Red Sea.

Not only the nurse shielded Alfie.

Let Barry Wilson try and get past Alfie's mum, thought Jess. *He'll stand no chance!*

Stubbs was indeed paying a call on Barry as Jess was speaking to Alfie. The meeting was taking place in the Waggoner's barn which had been hastily restored to its role of incident room.

'My girl has got no sense!' declared the landlord. 'None of them teenagers has. I ask you, taking up with a useless waste of space like Alfie? But if the little rat was beaten up, it wasn't by me. Nor by anyone in my family! I don't say he didn't deserve it. If I *had* come across him by chance, I might have punched his nose for him. But I didn't meet him. I didn't attack him. I certainly never was in that cottage. Look at me! Do I look like I could climb through a tiny window?'

Stubbs looked at Barry, large, outraged, red-faced and muscular. 'We're not suggesting you were in Rose Cottage last night. We are not – not at the moment, anyway – suggesting you have anything to do with the attack on Darrow. But someone did attack him and he's in the hospital. They'll probably release him fairly soon. So I'm here to make it clear that no one, and that includes you, is to have another go at him.'

'I didn't have a go at him in the first place!' roared Barry. 'Not that I wouldn't be justified in doing so. But all right! If I see him, I might tell him what I think of him, and order him to stay away from Jade, but I won't hit him.'

'Glad to hear it,' said Stubbs.

'You got daughters?' Barry squinted at him.

'Yes, they're both under ten.'

'Wait till they get older!' warned Barry.

'Well,' said Ian Carter to Jess, late that afternoon, when she'd finished her account of her visit to Alfie. 'Whatever happened in reality, someone else was in the cottage with young Darrow. Alfie can't identify him. Resembling a grandfather clock isn't a reliable description. We know the assailant hadn't broken in, so he had a key. Where did he get it?'

'Eleanor's kitchen?' suggested Jess. 'Quite possibly. Eleanor herself had forgotten about it, but years ago, Lucinda Harrison gave her a spare in case of emergencies. Jade and Alfie didn't know about that key, but someone else did.'

'Who else would know it was there? When did he sneak in and take it? Or are we being led off down the wrong track in thinking the intruder had Eleanor's key?'

Jess considered this. 'The key is missing. So, it's reasonably probable that someone has it. During the day the kitchen door isn't secured. Either Eleanor herself, or Jade, is on the premises, so they don't see the need for that. There is also the question of who was prowling round the cottage with a torch the evening Eleanor saw an intruder; someone who had blatantly ignored the notice warning it was a crime scene. I would have liked to ask Alfie if he was there that evening, at least. If we can cross him off the list, it would help. But the doctor and the nurse at the hospital were determined I shouldn't question the patient. And Mrs Darrow certainly wouldn't have let me harass her son.'

'Mmn . . .' Carter mused. 'Although Eleanor now claims she didn't return the key to Jeremy Harrison, we can't take that as accurate. It could simply be that she's forgotten she did. After all, she had completely forgotten she ever had the key at all, until you asked her about it. It may be a wild guess, but could the murderer, who we know took the time to remove Harrison's personal documents and computer, also have taken a key from a bunch Harrison had? He didn't take *all* Harrison's keys, and that's been nagging at my brain. But how about this? If the killer had taken *all* the keys, we'd know he had them. Because he left most of the keys, it might not occur to us that he'd taken just one.

'Or, another theory. Eleanor keeps spare keys hanging up in her kitchen, you say. It's the sort of thing country people do. Did Lucinda Harrison do the same thing? And did the killer take those? We wouldn't necessarily realise it because we found Jeremy's keys—' Carter broke off. 'Where did we find them?'

'In the pocket of his jacket, hanging up in the hallway.'

She and Ian both sat quietly for a moment, then Jess added, 'If the killer did that, then he planned to return. Let's say he did return, for whatever reason we don't yet know, and unluckily for Darrow it was the night he chose to effect entry through a lavatory window.'

There was a silence. 'OK,' continued Jess briskly at last. 'We don't know how, but let's assume the murderer has a key. Let's also stop worrying for a moment how it came into his possession. Let's work out a plausible reason *why* he returned to the scene of the crime. Was there something he didn't find the first time he was there; and wanted to find very badly? We know the killer conducted a search while Harrison lay dead on the floor. But, although he found and removed other items, there could have been something else he wanted; wanted it badly enough to risk returning. What could it be?'

'And,' added Ian quietly, 'because Alfie turned up and

179

interrupted him, we have to assume before he found it, will he try again?'

'He'd be a fool to return again,' said Jess.

'Murderers are not always very intelligent.' Ian smiled. 'If they were, we might not catch them. By the way, now that we've decided to keep open the incident room in the barn for a few days longer, Sergeant Bennison had reported a surge in activity. She's had a lot of visitors and, while none of them is worried about Alfie, whom they seem to think expendable, they are very alarmed at the thought that a violent assailant is still around the area. They want him found and quickly. No one so far, however, has been any help.'

'So, we are assuming that it's the same person, are we? The murderer of Jeremy Harrison and Alfie's assailant? We're talking as though that's the theory we're working on. Of course, if Alfie's attacker was not Harrison's killer, then that means yet another person might have a key.'

'I'm not assuming anything,' Carter told her mildly. 'If anything, I'm inclined to think that whoever attacked young Darrow was there for opportunistic reasons, like Darrow himself. The wretched youth disturbed a burglar. That could be anyone, and unconnected with the murder.'

'Not an "anyone",' objected Jess. 'It was someone with a key, as we've discussed, or so it seems likely.'

'All right, someone local to the area, then. Perhaps some new information will come in tomorrow. For goodness' sake! Someone must have seen something unusual, someone taking an interest.'

'Yes, but if he was local to the area, including Weston St Ambrose, then it could be someone no one has paid any attention to,' Jess argued. 'I've been looking through the statements made by the local people who've come to the incident room. One of them was a Mrs Beryl Garley.'

Ian frowned. 'Garley? Haven't we had dealings with Garleys before?'

'Yes, in a minor way. They are a local family. Beryl Garley told Bennison she used to clean for the late Lucinda Harrison. She had been upset and annoyed that Jeremy had preferred to use a cleaning company. In her opinion, he had been asking for trouble, letting strangers into the house, as she put it.'

'She thinks one of the cleaners killed Harrison?' he asked.

'No, rather that she felt he was careless about who he let in. He allowed someone he didn't know to enter.'

'And you share her opinion?' Ian raised his eyebrows.

'No, quite the opposite. I think he was killed by someone he knew. The cottage is lonely, the weather was cold and wet. It was late in the evening and dark. What kind of casual caller would come knocking at his door in those circumstances? And in the unlikely event that he did, would Harrison let him in? Even open the door? What do you think?'

Carter conceded, 'You could be right.'

Jess leaned forward and added energetically, 'Come on! At the Waggoner's Halt further down the road there were people, but no one in the area of Rose Cottage, except Harrison's assailant. All the signs, the empty whisky tumblers and the broken bottle, indicate that Harrison was entertaining a visitor. Beryl Garley is wrong. He wasn't killed by a stranger. Perhaps it was even someone he expected.' Jess hesitated. 'Perhaps we should reconsider all those highly respectable people living in the large, comfortable houses in the area.' She paused. 'And the murderer needn't have been a man, you know.'

Ian Carter frowned and considered the matter. Then he stood

up. 'It's a plausible theory. But enough is enough for today. Let's see what happens tomorrow. Time to go home. I don't know about you, but my evening is going to be a busy one.'

She raised her eyebrows. 'Oh? Got a date?'

'Not a romantic one. I am to have dinner with my ex-wife at the Royal Oak in Weston St Ambrose. She wants to discuss Millie's ambition to join the police.'

'Sophie is staying with Monica?' Jess was startled. 'Is, what's his name, Rodney, there too?'

'No, I am to be spared Rodney's company. This is to be all about my failure to be aware of Millie's plans.'

'You didn't know about Millie's plan until the other evening!' Jess protested.

'Sophie will say I should have known. Perhaps she's right.'

There were several things Jess might have said about Sophie's role in all this. Such as, if Sophie didn't spend most of her time across the Channel in France, leaving her daughter in the UK, Sophie herself might be more aware of the fact that Millie was growing up and getting ideas about her future. *Not my business!* she told herself firmly.

'And you say this place is under new management?' Sophie asked, casting a critical eye around the dining room of the Royal Oak. 'You could have fooled me. It looks exactly the same as the last I was here.'

'When was that?' inquired Ian, curious.

Sophie flushed. 'A few months ago. Rodney and I brought Tristan over, so that Rodney's mother could see him. Of course, she'd seen him when he was tiny, but he'd got so much bigger. We spent one night at Monica's. Didn't Monica tell you that?'

'Your aunt is ultra-discreet. She probably thought that you

would have communicated with me, if you had thought it necessary.'

'Well, it wasn't necessary.' Sophie snatched up a menu card and glared at it.

'Millie also didn't mention to me that you, Rodney and her baby brother had all been on a visit to the UK. Was our daughter also being ultra-discreet? Or could it be she didn't know her mother, stepfather and little brother had been in the country?'

He could hear the steely note that had entered his own voice.

Sophie turned beetroot-red, which answered the question before she spoke.

Concentrating on the menu card, she said, 'It was just a flying visit. Rodney had to get back and we had Tristan with us. There wasn't time to go up to the school, so I didn't mention it to Millie. I didn't want to upset her.'

'You know, Sophie,' Ian said slowly. 'You really are something else.'

That took her gaze off the menu. She leaned forward. 'Don't talk to me as though you were interviewing someone you'd arrested.'

He ignored that and told her, 'Pull that trick again, Sophie, and I shall seriously consider going back to the court and asking for sole custody.'

From scarlet she turned pale. 'You wouldn't dare!'

'Oh, I'd dare, all right. It didn't occur to you that Millie might find out, anyway, after the fact? That Monica might not intend to tell her, but then let a word or two slip? Millie is quick on the uptake. Didn't you consider how hurt she'd be to think her mother had been in England and not even phoned her at school?'

'Has she found out?' she asked, and he saw the alarm in her eyes.

'Not to my knowledge. That doesn't mean she hasn't suspected and simply hasn't said anything to me. Millie is discreet and also loyal.' He emphasised the last word.

Sophie ran the tip of her tongue nervously over her lower lip. 'And I'm not?' The words were spoken as a challenge.

When he didn't reply, she said in a quieter voice, 'Perhaps I should have told her. If it happens again, I'll let her know. But it's not easy, you know, living abroad and trying to keep tabs on what's going on here.'

'Your problem. You chose it. Just don't make it Millie's too. Will you find time to go and see her on this visit?'

Sophie had had time to redeploy her arguments. 'Yes, I'll be going to the school to see her. And yes, it is *my* problem, and I'll manage it without advice from you. How long have you known she wants to join the police when she finishes university?'

'I didn't learn until last week.'

'You didn't suggest it?'

'No. I understand she thought of it for herself and confided in a careers adviser who visited the school.'

'She admires that colleague of yours, Jessica Campbell,' Sophie said bitterly.

'Jess is an admirable person.'

'Are the two of you in a relationship? I mean, other than professional?' Sophie put her head on one side and raised her eyebrows.

She's cut her hair, thought Ian. *And it suits her.* Aloud, he said, 'We're very good friends, or I like to think so.'

'You know that's not what I mean.'

'I know what you mean. The answer is the same. Even if it were different, it shouldn't concern you.'

'It does if it's influencing Millie.'

'You're not blaming Jess because Millie's considering her career options?'

'No, I'm not. If there is any responsibility for this – career notion Millie has taken into her head, it lies with you.'

'That's hardly a new accusation from you,' Ian said coldly. 'Anything you didn't like in our marriage was always my fault; and it seems nothing has changed now we are no longer married. The idea that Millie might consider a career in the police force certainly didn't come from me. I was as surprised as you.'

'It's not what I wanted for my daughter,' said Sophie and looked, briefly, as if she might burst into tears.

'Leave Millie to make up her own mind, for goodness' sake! Life isn't all about what you want, Sophie.'

'It's never been possible to discuss anything with you,' Sophie burst out, in a louder tone than she had been using. The two people at the next table looked across. Then they looked back at each other and whispered something. It was probably along the lines of 'the couple over there are squabbling'. Sophie reddened and looked down at her menu.

He was reminded that he'd advised Sullivan and his wife to move to this hotel rather than risk another lonely night in the campervan. Were they still here, and witnessing this? He looked around the dining room again. They had spoken of returning to Oxford.

'Now what?' asked Sophie testily. 'You look as if you're searching for clues.'

'No, just wondering if some people are here – I recommended this as a place for them to stay.'

'You're keen on this hotel, aren't you?' Sophie snapped. 'Provincial, traditional and limited. I can see why it appeals to you.'

He had long ago learned to evade the obvious provocation Sophie could dish out. Argument or energetic response just fed her satisfaction. Best ignore it.

'We're not here to talk about us, are we?' Ian asked mildly. 'I understood we're here to discuss Millie.'

'We are discussing Millie!'

'We started out doing that. But now we seem to be discussing us, you and me. That's an old topic, long resolved. Have you and Rodney got problems, as it's generally phrased?'

'Oh, so I can't ask about you and Jess, but you can ask me about my marriage to Rodney, is that it?' Sophie's eyes blazed.

'I don't give a damn about the state of your marriage to Rodney, not unless it's affecting my daughter.'

'Rodney and I are fine, thanks!' Sophie paused. 'Millie and Rodney get along very well.'

'I'm pleased to hear it.'

Oh yes, the inner Carter was raging, *Rodney works largely from home. Rodney isn't a police officer who is constantly on call; and away dealing with violent criminals, terrorists and murderers. Rodney's associates are all like Rodney himself. Rodney can arrange his own diary for the most part. Rodney is living in a French manor house. I'm living in what my daughter clearly considers to be barely above student digs.*

He asked, 'Is Rodney looking after young Tristan while you're here with Monica?'

'A young cousin of his is staying with us at the moment. She's on her gap year and travelling, as they do. She loves looking after Tristan, so we've made a sort of au pair arrangement. Just temporarily.'

A whole clan of Rodneys, male and female versions, with a replacement generation ready to take over.

Aloud, he managed to ask politely, 'That's very convenient. So, does that mean this cousin is going to be staying with you for quite a chunk of her gap year?'

'Shouldn't think so. She'll get bored eventually and move on.'

Suddenly, Ian was ashamed of his inner anger and what, frankly, was jealousy. He'd chosen the career he'd wanted. Rodney had chosen his. Sophie hadn't wanted to share his lifestyle, and perhaps he shouldn't blame her. She'd chosen to share Rodney's, but now there were hints that wasn't working out so perfectly, either. He wanted to ask: *Are you bored, Sophie? Do you feel the need to move on?* But he didn't, because he suspected that, whether or not she'd admit it, there was some truth in that.

Suddenly he felt sorry for his ex-wife. She wasn't a bad person, or lacking in talent or intelligence. She was attractive. She had a lot going for her. She just hadn't found whatever it was she was looking for in life. He found himself wondering if he should have tried harder, during their marriage, to find out what that was. Perhaps he had been selfish. On the other hand, she was intelligent enough to know the score. *A policeman's lot is not a happy one.* Too right. But she'd been bright enough to know what she had been marrying into at the time.

Aloud, he said, 'I was a policeman when we married. You knew that was what I had decided to be.'

'Yes, I knew. I thought I could cope with that. Turned out, I wasn't cut out to be a policeman's wife.' Sophie smiled for the first time that evening. 'You must have realised that?'

'It was pretty obvious.' To his horror, he heard himself say, 'Sorry.'

He'd irritated her now, as he so often had in the past.

'For goodness' sake, it was nobody's fault, just one of those

187

things. We should have had frank conversations like this at the time. We didn't. Perhaps we're just older and wiser now.'

There was a silence. Around them people were now chatting, eating, drinking. But they had run out of things to say.

'Do we have to eat here?' Sophie sounded moody.

'No, but it's late to go and find somewhere else – and the waitress is coming to take our order.' Ian looked towards the figure advancing on them, notepad in hand.

'Oh, all right, then.' Sophie didn't trouble to look at the waitress who'd reached her side and was smiling down at her. 'I'll have the Greek salad and the chicken.'

'I'll have the soup,' said Carter and smiled up at the girl. 'And the salmon, please.'

He'd abased himself enough. Now he was allowed his little get-backs, surely?

While others dined, Wayne Garley was making his nightly patrol. There might be a murderer about, but Wayne had taken his own precautions with regard to encountering a hostile force. The truth was that, in his youth, Wayne had accompanied his father when the old fellow went out rabbiting; and from time to time seeking other prey. On one occasion, Wayne had never forgotten it because he had been young and impressionable at the time, they had bagged a wild boar. It had been too large and heavy to transport in one piece, so they had had to cut up the carcase. That had been a difficult job, one that had remained vivid in Wayne's memory. Difficult to disguise that they were transporting hairy joints, seeping blood too.

When they finally got it home, his mother had demanded, 'What am I supposed to do with all that?'

In due course, he had inherited his father's shotgun. He had also inherited his father's poacher's coat, a baggy garment with large pockets as part of the lining, and his father's gun. His father had never owned a licence for the gun and neither had Wayne. He had not inherited his dad's penchant for poaching (perhaps the episode with the boar had put him off), and the gun had been put away for years, unloaded. He hadn't, in any case, anything to load it with. He'd never used it but it had sentimental value. If the coppers knew he had it, of course, they'd make a fuss. All the more reason to keep quiet about it. But, as a precaution, he'd taken it out and carried the unloaded weapon with him, just in case, on his nightly tour of Weston St Ambrose. It would frighten anyone off.

He suspected that, when he'd caught up with old Eleanor the other evening, she'd guessed the origin of the coat. She'd been a farmer's wife. But she had said nothing; and he wasn't worried that she would. She was a local woman, after all, and the villagers, whatever their walk of life, didn't go spilling the beans to outsiders. This evening the only creature he'd encountered had been the fox. He caught a glimpse of it most nights. He was used to it and it was used to him. They respected one another's space. That's how you got along in the country.

He'd reached the Waggoner's Halt, the limit of his patrol. After a brief debate with himself as to whether he'd go in for a pint, Wayne decided against it. He'd had enough for one evening and his own fireside called to him. He turned to go back, starting by walking along the old Roman road, as it was said to be. Wayne tended to share Eleanor Holder's thought about that, though it was true that those old Romans got about a bit. He could save time by climbing over a gate to his right and cutting across the fields. It was as he jumped down into the field that his foot struck something and sent it sliding across the grass.

'What's that, then?' Wayne muttered. He searched in one of the capacious pockets of his dad's old coat and found a torch. Normally he didn't need it. He knew his way round here as well as the old fox. But he was curious to see what the object was that he'd dislodged. The narrow beam of the torch swept across the grass and something glinted as if in reply.

'Hullo, what have we here?' He stooped and picked up the object. 'Now then, who left that there?'

He switched off the torch and stood with the object lying on the palm of his hand. It glinted again in the moonlight.

'What's more,' Wayne asked himself, 'what am I going to do about it?'

He'd make up his mind after a mug of tea by his own fireside, or by Beryl's. No, not by his sister-in-law's. He'd make up his mind first and tell old Beryl afterwards. 'That's it!' decided Wayne.

He dropped his find into one of the poacher's pockets and resumed his tramp across the turf towards his cottage. He felt disturbed. Sometimes, you decided what you wanted to do, and got on and did it. For the most part, Wayne had always taken that as his guiding principle. But, sometimes, things got in the way, and you finished by doing something you would rather not do. Life could play tricks like that.

Chapter 13

All had been quiet at the incident room since it was re-established in the barn at the Waggoner's Halt. A petty ne'er-do-well like Alfie Darrow couldn't compete for interest with a murder, even if, so the rumour mill had it, some other intruder had beaten young Darrow to a pulp. Everyone assumed he had been bent on theft; and anyway the police knew about Alfie already. Tracy Bennison, to her relief, had been released from the duty of overseeing the barn. She accompanied Jess today with renewed enthusiasm. 'Glad to be actually doing something!' she had explained.

They were on their way to interview the luckless Alfie. He had been allowed to leave the hospital; with the doctor's instructions to rest at home.

'So that's what he's doing, taking it easy!' Sandra Darrow informed Jess and Tracy when they appeared at her front door. 'And I'm looking after him, right? You can see him, but you can't go bullying him. Whoever it was knocked him about nearly killed him. He's all over bruises. The poor little sod has had a very nasty experience. And don't you go saying he went into that place to burgle it. He's done a lot of daft things, but burgling ain't one of them.'

'We know he's been badly beaten,' Jess assured her. 'I saw him myself in the hospital.'

(*And I saw him on the floor in the cottage before the ambulance came, but I don't think Mrs Darrow knows that. I'm not too keen for her to find out. And don't tell me your son hasn't ever tried his hand at a bit of burglary, Sandra! Though he's more of a sneak thief, a snapper-up of unconsidered trifles.)*

'And that's another thing!' Sandra was working up a nice head of steam. 'Going to the hospital and bothering him when he didn't know what he was saying. He was talking about being attacked by a grandfather clock. The doctor told me. And you go barging into that hospital and question him when he was already talking a lot of nonsense? You had no right to do it!' Sandra now seemed physically to have increased in size (from an already generous start in the weight department), and filled the entrance to her house as effectively as any barrier.

'I didn't question him,' Jess protested. 'I was there to check out his condition and to find out if he was lucid. And a doctor was present.'

Mrs Darrow squinted at her. 'Lucid? What's that?'

'Whether he made sense,' supplied Bennison, who appeared to have had difficulty suppressing a grin.

Mrs Darrow turned her attention to the sergeant and looked her up and down.

'I don't know you!' she said suspiciously.

Bennison held up her warrant card. But Mrs Darrow dismissed it with a scornful sniff. 'Whoever you are, the same goes for you!' she snapped. 'He don't never make any sense; but that's no reason for you to take advantage of him. Right?' She drew in a deep breath. 'I'm allowing you both into my house on the condition you don't bully him; and if he tells me later that you have, the next time you come, you'd better come with a warrant or you won't neither of you set foot over my front doorstep. Is that clear?'

She was clad today in a sparkly jumper, black leggings clinging to her chubby thighs and calves, and wearing her trademark gold hooped earrings. She had scraped her black hair into a topknot secured by a scarf; and she had taken time with her make-up. Jess felt a sudden respect for her. Her life could not have been easy. Now she was entering middle age without any husband or partner visible, and her grown-up son was still causing her problems. But she was not the sort to give in to life's vicissitudes.

'He's lucky to have you!' said Tracy with sudden and unexpected tact. Perhaps she had formed the same impression of Mrs Darrow.

The redoubtable Sandra's manner thawed a little. 'Yus! He is. He don't appreciate it. I've told him so. Over and over again, I've said to him, "Where would you be without me?" I've been saying it to him since he was in primary school. He never listened, not then, not now. The school reckoned it was an attention thing. He doesn't pay any, because he hasn't got any.'

'Do you think we could have a word with him now, Mrs Darrow?' asked Jess politely, taking a leaf from the sergeant's book.

'All right, come on in,' agreed the lady grudgingly. 'It's better than having a couple of coppers standing on my doorstep for all the world to see. I mean, look at the pair of you! You're neither of you in uniform, but it don't make no difference. Dressed like you are, you gotta be detectives. Face it, no one else dresses as boring as that, 'cept coppers. Plain clothes, I suppose you'd call it. They're plain, all right. Here, mind where you put your feet! I don't want mud tramped all over my hall carpet.'

She led the way to a small back room and flung open the door to announce, 'The cops are here to talk to you, so stop playing that silly game on that gadget!'

'I've got a Christmas sweater at home,' hissed Bennison as they entered the room. 'It's got glittery bears all over it. Perhaps I should have worn that.'

'I wouldn't advise it. Not if you've got your eye on further promotion,' murmured Jess in reply.

'You don't need me, do you?' asked Sandra. 'Only I've got things to do. But you just remember what I said, right?'

She turned to her son. 'You tell them what they want to know, you hear me? But if they give you any grief, you let me know when I come back.' She turned back to the visitors. 'You coppers, you remember it too!'

With that order flung at the visitors, she at last left them to it. She closed the door smartly and moments later they heard another slam, of the front door.

'Blimey!' muttered Bennison, who had seen Alfie's injuries when she and Jess had found him, but seemed now to be impressed by the amount of bandaging around his head. 'He looks like one of those Egyptian things they find in the Pyramids: mummies.'

'I did warn you . . .' cautioned Jess in an undertone.

Alfie watched them approach, a mixture of resentment and alarm flickering in his eyes. They peered out between the bandages and were the only feature that could be clearly seen.

'Have you come to arrest me? You can't! I'm seriously injured.' His voice was muffled and indistinct as it came through swollen lips. He was also having trouble with sibilants. Jess suspected he might have lost a tooth.

'You were the loser in your fight with the clock.' She smiled at him. 'I understand, however, that you just need rest, and it's good that you're out of hospital and at home. You look very comfortable here, so we'll just sit down and chat for a bit. All right?'

'How can I be comfortable? You blind or something? I'm all over bruises,' he informed her. The last word sounded like *booshesh*. With a rising note of triumph in his voice, he added, 'And my memory is clouded, on account of the blows to the head. So, you two can sit and chat as much as you like. Don't expect me to join in.'

He added crossly, 'I didn't fight the clock. I may have said something when I first got to the hospital, and it came out all of a muddle. But the scrap was with a bloke, a pretty big bloke. Only it all happened very quickly; and the memory is all of a blur.' He put a hand to his head. 'I'm muddled.'

'How big? As big as Jade's father, Barry Wilson?' asked Bennison.

Alfie shook his head, immediately regretted the movement, and muttered, 'Ow!'

'Did he threaten you with a weapon?' Jess asked him keenly.

'He didn't need a weapon. He was strong, I told you. And he was really scary, like, he wasn't human.'

There was a silence. Then Jess said quietly, 'Alfie, tell us everything you remember about this man. He was strong. He didn't speak. It was dark. But you and he were wrestling in that room and you had your hands on him, trying to fight him off. Describe those moments, the sounds he made, what it was like to touch him.'

Alfie sat, huddled and head down. When he began to speak again, it was quietly and without his usual protestations.

'He was tall and narrow, and kept himself very straight and stiff, like he was frozen. Not like a normal person would stand. That's why, when he stood so quiet in the shadows, I thought he was a tall clock, one of them very old ones that are worth a lot of money. Of course, once he moved, I knew he wasn't a clock. But he still wasn't really like a human. He didn't speak, only grunted and sort of growled. He was really strong . . . and he was hairy . . . I mean, he had clothes on, but his face was hairy. It wasn't like fighting with a bloke, more like fighting off an animal, a really big dog, or a bear. I was . . . terrified, that's the word, isn't it?' He looked up at them.

Jess said quietly, 'Yes, that's the word.'

'I really wasn't there to pinch anything,' Alfie went on miserably. 'I was only looking for somewhere to meet Jade without her dad knowing. If I could have got out of there, I'd have run a mile, run all the way back to this house and locked the door. Nothing could ever make me go back to that cottage again. And you can't make me!' He drew himself up, wincing as his bruised muscles protested. 'How could it be wrong for me to be there? The bloke who owned the cottage is dead, murdered. Nobody knows who owns it now. Probably no one. Anyone can go in there.'

'The previous owner had left a will. Lawyers will sort out the details. The death of Harrison does not mean you could make use of his home as you liked. It is, in any case, a crime scene. There's a poster outside, reminding the public to keep out.'

This argument did not impress Alfie, who looked down at his knees. After a moment's thought, he looked up at the two officers. 'I saw a film once about a *poltergeist*.' He pronounced the word carefully. It still sounded like 'poltergeisht'. 'Do you reckon it could have been that, an evil spirit? Those poltergeists are pretty violent. They throw things around. Or could it be the ghost of that bloke who was murdered? Jade thinks that might be it. He can't rest, until you find out who killed him.'

'No, Alfie,' Jess told him firmly. 'You were attacked by a human being, and one who was very angry, from what you tell me of him, because he hadn't expected you to turn up. But definitely not a ghost, or evil spirit – or an animal.'

'And clever enough not to speak even one word,' added Bennison.

'We'll go now, Alfie.' Jess rose to her feet and Bennison followed suit. Alfie looked immediately relieved, but it would be short-lived. 'We will be charging you with breaking and entering, Alfie, at a later date when you are feeling better. You do understand that?'

'He was already inside!' squawked Alfie. 'He broke in first.'

'That doesn't mean you could follow him,' Bennison told him.

Alfie considered this. 'I only broke the glass in that little window round the back because I couldn't open it any other way.' He put a hand to his head. 'I can't talk to you any more. My head hurts.'

'He isn't very bright, is he?' remarked Bennison as they left the house. 'I can't help feeling a bit sorry for him.'

'He feels sorry enough for himself,' retorted Jess sharply. 'And he's not so dim he can't argue his corner.'

As they left the village, they drove past the Black Horse pub. Despite the cold weather, a group of dedicated smokers had gathered outside the door on the pavement, puffing away content-edly and talking. Among them, Jess recognised Sandra Darrow. So that was why Sandra had been all dressed up and had taken such care with her make-up. This was, for her, the equivalent of lunching with friends.

'I know that one!' said Bennison suddenly.

'Which one? Where?' Jess looked around them.

'Standing with that group. It's Beryl Garley. She came to the incident room. As far as I could make out, it was just to tell us she'd cleaned for the victim's late aunt. She was nursing a grudge, because Harrison had dispensed with her services when he inherited the cottage. She had a funny little dog with her. Yes, there it is! Tied up to that bench.'

Bennison pointed at a bench of the type often found in parks, but this one stood outside the pub, against the wall. The smokers had all ignored it. Sammy, however, was tied to it. He was alternately watching the road and casting impatient glances at his owner.

'Well, she's local. I suppose those are her friends.' Jess's gaze scanned the group and caught sight of another familiar face, Wayne Garley. He looked discomfited at the sight of her.

Mrs Garley had now also spotted the two police officers. She said something and the whole group of smokers turned and stared at them, apart from Wayne, who slipped casually back into the pub. Sandra Darrow, however, fixed a hostile glare on them and began to harangue the crowd.

'What's the odds she'd blaming us for persecuting her injured boy?' Jess said quietly.

'We're not going to be attacked by an angry mob, are we?' Bennison asked.

'Shouldn't think so. We've given them something to talk about.'

They drove away, watched by all the members of the crowd of smokers.

'I reckon,' announced one of them, as the car disappeared, 'that they won't find who done it.'

'That doesn't give them the right to try and blame my son!' declared Sandra militantly. 'I know he's been in a bit of trouble before, but nothing serious. They came to my house to bother him, even though he's injured.'

'Ah,' declared another of the smokers sagely. 'Once you get on the wrong side of the police, they don't forget you.'

'It's not the fault of Alfie if the police have got a down on him,' insisted Sandra. 'He's not a bad boy, he's just got problems.'

'Who hasn't?' asked someone glumly.

In the car, as they rattled out of the village, Bennison spoke up suddenly. 'Those people outside the pub, they remind me of when I was a kid. I told you, my family lived in a tower block.'

'Yes, how do the Weston St Ambrose villagers remind you? I would have thought they were quite different to inner-city dwellers.'

'Not so much,' replied Bennison, 'not now I've seen them like that, hanging about together. The kids in our block did that. They'd all gather outside the entrance in a gang. It didn't mean they were all friends, not properly friends. They just all lived in the same place and, well, I suppose they all faced much the same future. So they stuck together.'

'And some of them gave you and your family grief, you said.'

'Until old Monty stepped in. Even before that, it wasn't the younger mob that made trouble for us. It was the teens, trying to prove themselves, you know? Looking at that lot by the pub, well, they all know one another, don't they? They've all lived here all their lives. Even if they don't have a lot in common, one to one, they all stick together faced with outsiders. Everyone needs to belong to a gang of some sort, to know someone has your back. The villagers here, the old families, don't like outsiders. If you haven't lived here all your life, they never really let you in. That's why I reckon we've been wasting our time at the incident room. If they knew anything, they wouldn't tell us. It's an "us and them" sort of thing.'

Bennison paused. 'Just my opinion,' she said. 'I'll concentrate on my driving.'

But Jess was looking thoughtful. 'You could be right, Tracy.'

'I've been offered a lift down to Weston,' said Jade. 'So I'm going to see my boyfriend.'

She was dressed for visiting, in her own style. She'd been generous with the eye make-up. Her multicoloured hair was twisted into a knot on top of her head and secured there with a large tortoiseshell spring clip. Between her head and her thin legs, cased in mock snakeskin cowboy boots, the rest of her body was wrapped in a peacock-blue quilted coat, matching one half of her hair.

'He's at home now, is he?' asked Eleanor. 'How is he?'

'He's at his mum's house. I suppose he's doing all right. I'll tell you when I get back, right?'

'Yes, of course.' Eleanor was suddenly moved to add, 'You look very nice, Jade.'

'Nice' wasn't perhaps really the word. Striking, yes. But Jade's normally belligerent expression was suddenly erased by a brilliant smile.

Then she turned and ran away towards the gate on to Long Lane where a car was parked. Eleanor didn't recognise it. She watched as Jade scrambled into the front passenger seat and the vehicle roared away. *Poor kid*, she thought, *she has no life, stuck at that pub with a grouchy old thug of a father. And the boyfriend is one of the Darrow clan. Always bad news, the Darrows. And the wretched little ne'er-do-well broke into Lulu's cottage.*

She could not help but still think of it as Lulu's home, as she always had. Jerry Harrison's time at the place had been but a brief interlude. A sort of hiccup. Life was full of hiccups, when you considered it; things that seemed permanent but were not, could never be, because time and tide stop for no man. You grip at what seems safe mooring, but it isn't, only a respite. Truth was, whilst she would not have wished Harrison murdered, she was also relieved that he was no longer there. The sight of him had always reminded her not only of her personal sorrow at the loss of her old friend but also as a reproach, because she had failed Lulu. She should have spoken up at the inquest.

'And said what?' she inquired of the pugs, who rolled their shiny glass-marble eyes up at her warily, sensing her bottled-up anger. 'All right, not you . . .' she added soothingly.

It was a busy morning and she missed Jade's help. *I won't be able to run the kennels for ever*, she thought. *Jade won't stay around much longer. She's young. There's nothing for the young here. Perhaps that's on her father's mind, too, and it's one reason why he's so grumpy. Perhaps, when all this horrid murder business is settled, I'll retire. I don't know what will happen to Lulu's place but if it comes on the market, I might buy it, sell up this place. Time's winged chariot, and all the rest of it.*

All this was very downbeat, and she needed cheering up. A cup of coffee should do it, and perhaps a nip of something. She set off towards the back door.

Then, midway between the shed and the back door, and out of the blue, she thought of one thing she could have told the coroner years ago. Lulu wasn't an idiot and she was prudent. When you live alone, you have to be. She had always had her mobile phone in her pocket, in case of a fall, or some other emergency. Even walking round in her dressing gown, she had the phone in her pocket.

Now Eleanor could hear the coroner's voice in her ear as he summed up. *Even if Mrs Harrison had been conscious for a short while, she could not have been able to reach the phone and summon help.*

'Yes, she bally well could!' snapped Eleanor aloud, alarming the pugs again. 'She would have had her mobile in her dressing-gown pocket.'

She hadn't said it at the time; and now she couldn't believe she'd been so remiss. It was such an obvious thing. She felt like jumping up and down on the spot with rage and frustration, right there, in the middle of the yard in front of the shed where she stored items connected with the kennels; and had her deep-freezer to hold her own iron rations. Thought of the freezer distracted her, made her think about supper that night. She'd get something out now, and take it over to the kitchen, leaving it on the table to defrost. She walked into the shed and began to search through the sealed packs. Outside, the pugs had begun to bark. They knew she was outdoors but they couldn't see her. Jade had shut them all in the outside pen before leaving, and, frustrated at not being able to join their owner, they were letting her know they were all there; and didn't like being ignored. They would be all right for a bit. She'd make that coffee. That's right. Don't brood on life's missed opportunities. Do something practical. It would be even colder by tonight. Eleanor selected a curry dish and set off back to the kitchen door.

She knew, as soon as she got there, that she had a visitor. The door, which she had closed on coming out into the yard, was slightly ajar. The pugs had been trying to attract her attention for a reason. Whoever the caller was, they should have taken more care about closing the door.

'Mary was right!' Eleanor muttered. 'I should be more careful. I can't rely on Jade to think about security.' She was also annoyed, because in weather like this, one needed to keep the house as warm as possible. She pushed the door open and walked into the kitchen.

The caller was standing by the larder door, a woman, tall, strongly built, blond and good-looking. *What*, Eleanor thought, *my mother would've termed. 'handsome' rather than conventionally beautiful. But striking, all the same.*

The visitor turned as Eleanor entered. For a moment she looked startled, but then that turned to guilty, as well it might. She spoke quickly, cutting off anything Eleanor might have asked.

'I'm sorry. I should not have come in. I did knock.'

Eleanor held up the frozen curry. 'I was looking in my freezer. It's in the outside store.'

The visitor looked even more embarrassed. 'Yes. The little dogs began to bark, so I thought you might realise someone else was here, a stranger.' She gestured at the open larder door. 'I wasn't going to take anything.'

'No,' Eleanor agreed. 'You were hoping to put something back. Have you returned it already, the key?'

'Yes. You had missed it?'

'To be honest, I had forgotten I even had it. Until that woman detective came and asked me if I had a key.'

The visitor looked downcast. 'Oh, so I really am too late. The police know.'

Eleanor shrugged. 'You're not the only one who is too late. I did nothing when I should have done something, years ago, when Lulu died. You had better sit down. I'll put the coffee on.'

Now she did close the back door but, even as she did so, thought that perhaps this was one occasion when it would be better to leave it ajar, in case she needed to escape.

The woman moved to the kitchen table and sat on one of the chairs. She gave a brief, embarrassed smile. *She's nervous,* thought

Eleanor. *And so she should be! But she isn't aggressive, thank good-ness. Or, at least, not yet.*

The visitor spoke, her tone rueful. 'Things are happening in the wrong order. I should first have explained who I am.'

'No need,' replied Eleanor. 'I know who you are.' She switched on the percolator. To do so, she had to turn her back to the visitor and once again it occurred to her, as she did so, that perhaps she shouldn't. But, when she turned back, the caller hadn't moved from her station at the table.

'He thought you had probably recognised him. That woman who cleaned for his aunt, she saw him once, and he knew from her face she'd remembered him, though she said nothing. We don't think she told anyone. We would surely have heard about it, eventually, if she had. But villages all over the world are small, closed worlds, aren't they?'

'Perhaps,' Eleanor acknowledged. 'I've never been a great trav-eller. Lucinda and I were alike in that way, content to stay put.'

The visitor looked embarrassed again. 'Yes, there is nothing wrong with that.'

'I wasn't suggesting there was.' Eleanor's tone had sharpened.

The visitor flushed and waited a few minutes while Eleanor busied herself taking down coffee mugs and hunting for biscuits. When she found some, they looked uninspiring. 'Best I can do!' she said briskly. 'I don't make cake.'

'Nor do I,' said the woman at the table. Then, unexpectedly, she asked, 'Lucinda, did she make cake?'

'She made an excellent sponge. She had been brought up by a mother who thought that a necessary accomplishment.'

'My mother sent me out to chop wood for the stove,' the visitor said ruefully.

Then she asked, 'So, can I tell you the rest of it?'

Eleanor considered her answer. 'I don't think I want to know the rest of it. Knowledge can be a burden.'

And it can be a torment, she added mentally. The percolator began to burp and the aroma of the coffee filled the air. Aloud, she added, 'Besides, I'm not the person you should tell. But it's entirely up to you. I'm the last person to give advice.'

Ian Carter looked up as Jess came into his office and asked, 'What's on your mind?'

'Is it that obvious?' she asked ruefully.

He put down the papers he was holding and smiled. 'You've got that ultra-thoughtful look on your face.'

'OK, it's like this.' Jess set about explaining her line of thought, beginning, 'I've been reading the statements made in the incident room.'

'They didn't tell us anything of any use,' said Carter. 'Waste of time and manpower all round.'

'Easy to miss something, though,' Jess suggested. 'Needles in haystacks and all the rest of it.'

He leaned back in his chair and studied her face. Then, he gave a sudden grin. 'You look smug,' he said.

'Oh, thanks!'

'I didn't mean to insult you. But you are about to surprise me, I fancy. So, tell me, what is this particular needle?'

'The statement of Mrs Beryl Garley.'

Ian looked startled. 'Are you still thinking about that? We've talked about this.'

'And we need to talk again. It's something Tracy Bennison said this morning, after we spoke to Alfie, and were walking back to the car. that's got me thinking. Beryl Garley insisted, when she originally spoke to Bennison, that Jeremy Harrison

205

was murdered because he made the mistake of letting strangers into his house. It's possible she was talking of the professional cleaning company that had supplanted her. She was still sulking about that. On the other hand, she wasn't accusing any of them. Only that Jeremy Harrison died, she reckoned, because he'd let strangers into the house.

'Bennison was talking about close communities. We'd passed the pub, the Black Horse, and Alfie's mother and her cronies were all outside having a smoke.'

Jess leaned forward. 'I think Beryl was putting up a different kind of smokescreen when she spoke to Tracy in the incident room. Harrison *didn't* let a stranger into the house. He let in someone he knew. He might not have been pleased to see him, who knows? It was a filthy night and he could hardly leave the caller standing about on the doorstep. So, he let him in. You remarked on it yourself, how he'd sat drinking with his visitor. That's not a stranger. It's an acquaintance of some sort.'

'Someone he trusted? We've come across that scenario before.'

'At any rate, it was someone he'd not seen for a while. Perhaps someone he didn't really trust,. We don't know. But it was a very cold night and raining. He really had to allow the person to come indoors.'

'Go on,' Ian said.

Jess continued.

When she'd finished, he asked, 'Are you suggesting the murderer might be a local man?'

'Not local, or not exactly. More, it might be someone who has connections, quite close links, with Weston St Ambrose.'

'Um,' Ian said doubtfully. 'Have you spoken to Eleanor Holder about any of this? I've a shrewd suspicion that she could tell us if you are on the right track.'

'I'm sure she could,' agreed Jess. 'But she's also what she prob-ably thinks of as discreet. She's certainly biased. Most of us can plead guilty to being that in some form or another. Our outlook is formed by personal experience.'

He smiled. 'Thus, all police officers tend to think the worst of a situation?'

'I like to think we try not to. But we are naturally suspicious, in light of experience.'

Ian leaned back, put his hands behind his head and said nothing for a couple of minutes. Jess, though obviously impatient at his silence, managed to wait.

At last, he said, 'Let's be clear about this. Are you accusing Mrs Holder of wilfully withholding evidence?'

Now it was Jess's turn to hesitate, before replying, 'I'm sure she wouldn't see it like that. Suppose we look at it from her angle? She was very close to her old chum, Lucinda Harrison. She didn't like and certainly didn't trust Jeremy Harrison. That skews her thinking to the point that she approaches everything that's happened at Rose Cottage, from when Lucinda died there to this recent murder, from the perspective of her old friend's fatal tumble down the stairs.'

Carter objected in a mild way, 'Are you about to suggest Mrs Holder might be behind Jeremy's death?'

'Oh, Ian!' Jess burst out in a most unprofessional way. 'Of course not.'

'Just thought I'd ask,' he replied. 'I like to be clear about these things.'

Jess drew a deep breath. 'OK, I'll make it as clear as I can. The single most important thing is, Eleanor is convinced Lucinda Harrison's death was contrived. That much she did tell me. I'm pretty sure she believes Jeremy was behind it. She knows she can't prove it; and that has been quietly weighing on her mind for years now. When I went to talk to her about Jeremy, what did she want to tell me? About Lucinda's death. Frankly, I think it had become an obsession with her.'

'And you passed on her views on that to me. So, I ask the same question. Has any evidence turned up since the inquest on her death, anything the coroner didn't know at the time?'

'No. Of course, we both realise she may be quite wrong. But try telling her that! If you really believe someone to whom you were close, saw probably every day, has come to harm through any kind of foul play, hard evidence doesn't come into it. The guilt is shared. The perpetrator of the deed is guilty. But Eleanor, too, feels guilty. I'm sure of it. She feels she let her old friend down because she has failed to – to put things right.'

Carter uttered a sound very like 'harrumph!'

Jess pressed on. 'The truth is that Eleanor didn't let Lucinda Harrison down in any way; and has nothing with which to reproach herself. But she's nursed her sense of guilt for years. Now it makes her see everything that's happened recently at Rose Cottage through a sort of prism.'

Ian looked at her thoughtfully. 'So, you think she believes she knows who contrived Lucinda's death, if that is what happened?'

'Oh, absolutely sure! She believes Jeremy Harrison was behind it. She can't prove it. But it colours her view of everything that's happened since.'

Ian asked quietly, 'And does she believe she knows who killed Jeremy?'

'I'm sure she has a theory.'

'In that case, any use going to talk to her again?' he asked.

'Not a bit. Eleanor is a lot like those little dogs she keeps. She doesn't like outsiders prowling round the old homestead. We have to consider what someone else has told us.' Jess hesitated. 'You're not going to like this much.'

'OK, let me hear the sibyl's warning!'

'Alfie Darrow broke into Rose Cottage and disturbed someone who had arrived before him. I believe he disturbed the murderer of Jeremy Harrison, who had returned for reasons we don't yet know. Alfie has had the fright of his life, and tends not to make a lot of sense at the best of times, even when he knows he's safe. But when Tracy and I went to talk to him about the attack, he told us something significant.'

'That he originally thought his attacker was a long-case clock?' Carter smiled wryly.

'No, that he felt as though he was fighting off an animal. It was hairy, among other things. Keep in mind it was quite dark.'

'So?' Carter prompted.

'Whom do we know who has a beard?'

After a moment, Carter asked very quietly, 'And Eleanor knows this?'

'I believe she does now. She may not have realised it at first. I'm inclined to give her the benefit of the doubt. If he had any sense, he'd have kept out of her way.'

'We can't question him on that basis alone. We need more.'

'Yes. And when we do know more, and we put it to Eleanor, she may well decide to speak. At the moment, we have to rely on Dave Nugent's expertise on the computer.'

Dave Nugent liked working in CID. Being out and about on a case was always interesting. But he was happiest sitting in front of the computer. Modern detection, he liked to tell anyone whom he could persuade to listen, had been immeasurably facilitated by the latest technology. It meant you could track down a fact it might otherwise take precious time to locate by more traditional means. It was now difficult to imagine how CID had ever managed before they could go online. You had to admire those old-time coppers. His grandfather, who had been a detective in those far-off days, occasionally pointed at any nearby computer and inquired what happened when one of those things went wrong – or there was a power cut. In the unlikely event of a glitch, Nugent told his grandfather, there were procedures for dealing with any emergency. This reply, sadly, did not seem to satisfy the old fellow. Worse, Grandad seemed to find Dave's reassurances amusing. And he also had to put up with the old chap's warnings that he was risking his eyesight. But you had to allow for Grandad's age and understandable fondness for a disappeared past.

Apart from his grandfather, and anyone else who appeared not to understand the finer points of modern policing, Dave had already reminded nearly everybody on the team, although he got told, sometimes politely, occasionally not, that they already knew, thanks.

As a result, he didn't get the opportunity to spread the word that often nowadays. Thus, he was pleasantly surprised when Inspector Campbell appeared in front of his desk and said, 'Records, Dave!'

Nugent's heart soared and his hands moved as if of their own accord to hover over the keyboard. 'What sort, ma'am?'

'First and foremost, I'd like the coroner's final report on the death of Lucinda Harrison, of Rose Cottage, Weston St Ambrose. I would also like any other records regarding Mrs Harrison. Incidentally, Harrison was her maiden name. She resumed it after her divorce. I need to know her married name.'

'Not a problem, ma'am,' said Nugent happily.

Later that day, he set off for the inspector's office with the results of his trawl through various records. *This is modern policing!* thought Dave triumphantly to himself. *This is how it's done.* Not everyone had to go out tramping round crime scenes and talking to a bunch of locals.

It was therefore ironic that, before he reached the inspector's office, curiosity caused Nugent to veer off course, attracted by a loud voice at reception, demanding to see 'the bloke in charge'. The member of the public speaking, as Dave saw when he arrived at the desk, was a weather-tanned, wiry figure, a countryman by the look of him. Nugent was sure he had seen him before.

'Carter, his name is,' declared the visitor. 'I want to speak to him.'

A prickle ran up Nugent's spine. 'Can I help?' he asked.

The visitor turned to him and looked him up and down.

'I've come in from Weston St Ambrose,' he said. 'My name is Garley. I've found a knife.'

Minutes later he was sitting in Carter's office. Jess had been called in too.

'I remember you,' she said. 'You found the drowned girl's body, wedged under a private landing stage, on a previous occasion when there was a murder at Weston St Ambrose.'

'Only because I was delivering a load of firewood at the time. We don't have murders all the time in Weston!' retorted the visitor indignantly. 'And normally, I don't go running to the police with tittle-tattle.'

'You certainly don't, Mr Garley. I don't think you gave a state-ment at the incident room when we were out there lately,' Jess said to him.

'I had no statement to give. But since there's been trouble about, I've been walking around the area of an evening, just checking.' He paused. 'I've been walking up to the Waggoner's for a pint, though it's not where I normally drink. On my way back last night, I changed my route. I walked down the old Roman road, intending to cut across the fields back to the village. It meant climbing over a stile. I jumped down on the field side and my boot kicked something away, something that had been lying in the grass, like it had been tossed over the hedge. I had a little torch with me, though I don't use it, not generally, I know my way around the whole area. Moonlight is good enough for me. But I was curious to see what it was, so I shone down the torch, and there was this knife, like someone had thrown it over the hedge.'

He took out a grimy handkerchief from his pocket and shook it out on to Carter's desk. A small but sharp and pointed-bladed knife clattered down.

'There you go,' he said. 'What do you think of that?'

'Good grief!' exclaimed Carter. 'Where exactly did you find this, Mr Garley? Can you show us?'

'Of course, I can show you,' was the dour reply. 'Like I said, it was in a field by the old Roman road. Now, I don't go giving statements. But when I find something like that, I know to hand it in, all right?'

When Wayne had left and the knife had been sent over to fingerprints, Carter said to Jess 'What I think – or hope, anyway, is that we have the murder weapon.'

'And with luck, there will be at least a partial print on it,' Jess added.

There was a tap at Carter's door and Nugent reappeared. 'Sorry to disturb you, sir, but I thought you'd want to know.'

'Know what?' asked Carter sharply.

Nugent shifted his gaze to Jess. 'You gave me a list of things to check out on the computer, in Records, ma'am. The thing is,

I found the record of Mrs Harrison's first marriage, as you requested. Harrison was her maiden name, as you said. The name of the man she married was Andrew Sullivan.'

'We need to impound that campervan!' Carter exclaimed. 'We need to do it straight away. Sullivan and his present wife were living in it at the Roman site when I first met them. However tidy and superficially clean they kept it; their fingerprints must be all over it. If there is even a partial print on that knife that matches . . . But if they realise we have the knife, then they'll either get the interior of that campervan valeted to showroom standard or they'll somehow arrange for it to catch fire. Also, Rose Cottage was subject to fingerprinting at the time of Jeremy Harrison's murder. Again, if there is even the smallest match . . .' He turned to Jess. 'Inspector Campbell! I do believe it's all coming together nicely at last.'

Fingerprints were being discussed elsewhere that evening, in a far more informal setting.

'They get fingerprints off all sorts, don't they, these days?' Beryl Garley said thoughtfully, later that evening. She leaned forward to prod the logs burning in her open grate. Her cottage was old and she had never had any form of central heating installed. Partly this was down to the cost of having it done. But mostly, it was because she didn't see the need of it. As the logs spluttered, Sammy, curled on the rug before the hearth, raised his head to make sure none of the sparks were coming his way. They weren't; and he settled down again.

'I grew up in this cottage and we never had central heating,' Beryl said now, sidetracked from her original line of thought. 'Not necessary. We were never cold when we were young and I've never been cold here.'

'I had to take the knife in to the cops,' Wayne told her, bringing the conversation back to the matter of his visit to the police. His present call on his former sister-in-law was to tell her all about it. He was seated on the other side of the fireplace, with a glass of Beryl's blackberry wine in his hand. 'I would never have gone gossiping with the coppers in Barry's barn. But when I found a knife, well, it might not be the murder weapon, and I hope it isn't. But I had to take it in.'

'Of course, you did, Wayne,' said Beryl. He looked relieved and she continued, 'Like you said, it could belong to anyone who dropped it there. Tinkers, maybe. The police might get someone else's fingerprints off it and it won't matter.'

Her visitor brightened briefly at this suggestion. But then he fell back into despondency. 'I shouldn't have decided to cut across that field. I'd never have found it, if I hadn't.'

'Some things are meant,' declared Beryl philosophically. 'You were meant to find it, that's what I think.'

'They should have got rid of it properly,' complained Wayne. 'Careless, just tossing it over a hedge!'

'Perhaps,' agreed Beryl. 'Likely they were in a bit of a panic.' She sipped from her own glass of blackberry wine. 'But don't worry about it. It can't be helped.' She held up her glass and peered at its contents. 'If I do say it myself, I think this year's batch of the blackberry turned out rather well. But it may be the last I make. There aren't the blackberry bushes around these days, not like there were.'

Chapter 14

'I'm afraid the building hasn't a lift,' apologised the earnest young woman who sat behind a desk in the spacious hallway. She had been busy at a computer and tore her attention from her work with a sigh of regret. Jess hoped their arrival had not disturbed the flow of academic concentration too badly. 'You'll have to toil up the stairs. Dr Sullivan's flat is right at the top. It was created out of the attic space. I understand he is expecting you.'

Carter smiled and said, 'Thank you. I'm sure we'll manage the stairs.'

'Oh, I didn't mean to suggest you couldn't!' she assured them hastily. 'Some of our visitors have trouble because they're a bit elderly. But you should be all right.' She smiled at them brightly, and returned her attention to her computer.

'I suppose that's an encouragement of sorts,' Ian remarked to Jess as they started up the first flight of stairs.

It was a bright cold morning but at least it wasn't raining when they arrived at the Institute at eleven that morning. They had made an early start from Gloucester and, on arrival in Oxford, had stopped to pay a prearranged courtesy call on Thames Valley police.

When they had made their way to the Institute, they found it to be housed in a tall, redbrick, mid-Victorian building that might once have been a spacious private house. A later wing had been added to the right of the façade, resulting in a rabbit warren of rooms inside, as they discovered during their ascent. Everywhere was very quiet, that sort of contained, academic silence that betokened the occupants were busy about their own particular interests. The staircase itself had a magnificent carved banister and, on the way up, doors appeared at unexpected levels. One was labelled Bathroom.

'A bit awkward,' observed Jess in the hushed voice the surroundings seemed to require. 'I mean, having to come down the main stairs, in full view of any strangers who might be visiting, wearing a dressing gown and carrying your sponge bag!'

'I think you'll find,' murmured Ian in reply, 'that the plumbing for something like a modern bathroom was installed at a later date than the house was built. Originally, an unfortunate servant would have had to toil up some back staircase with a ewer of hot water.'

Despite their low voices, their arrival had been heard or, more likely, the young woman downstairs had phoned to let Sullivan know they were on their way up. He stood in the open doorway of the attic flat and invited them in with a gesture of his arm that Jess thought slightly stagey.

'My wife will join us shortly, should you need to talk to her,' he informed them. 'She's over at the Bodleian, doing some research.'

In startling contrast to the rest of the house, the flat was decorated and furnished in Scandinavian fashion. The windows afforded a magnificent view of the Oxford skyline. *I suppose,* Ian Carter thought, *it goes with the job at the Institute here. Very nice.*

'May I offer you both coffee?' Sullivan asked courteously.

'Thank you, but we'd rather get down to business, if you don't mind,' Ian told him,

'Ah yes, business,' Sullivan replied with a wry smile. He gestured at them to take seats. 'I suppose this is to do with the death of Jeremy Harrison. I understand the police have taken possession of my campervan.' He frowned briefly. 'I hope we'll get it back.'

'It's what we've come to talk to you about,' Jess replied. 'This isn't a formal interview under caution, but you are, of course, entitled to have a solicitor present.'

'Are you likely to charge me with something?' Sullivan raised his eyebrows.

'Eventually, we may. We shall also require your fingerprints and those of your wife, for the purposes of elimination.'

Sullivan made no comment on this. But he did give a sarcastic little grimace. Jess pressed on. 'Do you want to call a solicitor, to be present at this meeting before we go any further? Or we can go to the nearest police station and a duty solicitor can be provided.'

Sullivan frowned disapprovingly at the thought of a duty solicitor, and shook his head. 'Not at the present time. But if I think you are becoming, well, intrusive, I may change my mind on that. Carry on for now.'

For a moment Jess felt she was in a tutorial; and had been picked out by the professor in charge of it to contribute a constructive comment or two. She pushed away the thought. 'It's come to our attention that, before your present marriage, you were married to the late Lucinda Harrison. She had lived at Rose Cottage before her death. Then her nephew, Jeremy, inherited it from her.'

Sullivan leaned back and steepled his fingers. 'You've done your homework, Inspector Campbell. You're quite correct. I was, for a short while, married to Lulu. And Jerry Harrison, conniving little trickster that he was, did inherit it from her.'

His tone was still polite and even. But Jess thought that, just for a moment, at the mention of Jeremy Harrison, there was a glint of something else in his eyes. It was as if a stage curtain had suddenly been twitched aside and back again. She thought that this academic scholar now in his later years, and much respected in his field, was probably not a man to cross.

Ian asked quietly, 'And you believe he was in some way responsible for your first wife's death?'

'Ah,' Sullivan wagged a monitory forefinger at him. 'Now, there you are jumping the gun, Superintendent! I suspect you have been talking to dear Eleanor Holder, my first wife's old school pal and lifelong chum. I know that's what she thinks. She told Marianna, my present wife, she thought Jerry might have engineered the fatal fall. Marianna had gone to the kennels to return the spare key to Rose Cottage. It was quick of you – the police – to work out Eleanor might hold an emergency key, and have forgotten about it. Marianna went to return it, if possible, without bumping into Eleanor. We counted on her either being out exercising the pugs; or being busy about the kennels. But Eleanor walked in on her, in the kitchen, before she could do it. They had a long chat. They got on really well, I believe.'

'And you don't agree?' Ian asked him. 'You never had any suspicion that Jeremy might have been involved in your first wife's fatal fall?'

'I have no idea whether he was responsible or not. I'm prepared to believe he would have been perfectly capable of it. But that's a horse of a different colour, as the old saying goes. Personally, I have no evidence to support such an explanation.'

Jess, unable to keep her voice neutral and aware her personal curiosity seeped through, asked, 'So, why did you go to see Harrison that evening? You did call on him that night, didn't you?'

'I don't deny it. Why should I? He owed me,' Sullivan said simply.

'Money?'

'Nothing so sordid!' Sullivan sounded reproachful. 'Something with much more of an emotional hold on me. He had deprived me of my family home, Rose Cottage. I wanted my property back.'

'*Your* home?' Jess could not help but sound startled.

'Morally, yes. So, you see, the situation was quite different to the suggestion you have just made: that I might have believed he brought about my first wife's unlucky, fatal accident. I had no evidence for that. Still don't! I didn't go there that night to accuse him of it. On the other hand, I knew he was living in what should be my house. So I told him it was time he returned it to me. Oh, in case you're wondering, I was prepared to pay him a fair market price for it. But he'd enjoyed it long enough without being in any way morally entitled to it. It was time to put the situation right.'

He had succeeded in momentarily silencing both his questioners. He smiled and continued, 'You'd like me to explain. But first, may I ask if either of you is married?'

Jess shook her head. Ian Carter said, 'I'm divorced.'

'Ah!' Sullivan turned his attention to him. 'Then perhaps you might agree with me that no one understands a marriage except the two people in it? Outsiders may think they do. But generally speaking, they don't, not really.'

After a moment's hesitation, Ian replied, 'Let's say I go along with that. Up to a point, anyway.'

'So, let me tell you about my first marriage. Lulu was the sister of a schoolfriend of mine, that's how we first met. She came with her parents to the school to watch, of all things, a rugby match.

I was pounding down the pitch, and some opponent tackled me, not far from the visiting spectators. Down I went and lay there, covered in mud and winded. Then I looked up and saw this stunning girl, standing just a few feet away, looking down at me and very worried. I think she called something out, probably asking if I was all right. I couldn't hear her; but I was instantly smitten, hook, line and sinker. That was it, really.'

Sullivan fell silent for a moment and neither of his listeners wanted to interrupt him. Eventually he continued, 'She was beautiful, and I later discovered it was not just in appearance. She was a beautiful person. I went off to study archaeology, and at the first opportunity, after I graduated, we were married. She was still very young when I married her; and I wasn't much older. Marry in haste, repent at leisure, eh?' Sullivan smiled at them again, but it was a sad grimace. 'My parents were delighted. They loved her, too, and welcomed her as a daughter-in-law.

'My father had been what they call "something in the City" and had made a fair amount of money. We lived in London, that was our main family home. But he had wanted us to have some-where healthier to go for holidays, weekend breaks, that sort of thing. So he bought an almost derelict pair of adjoining cottages just outside Weston St Ambrose, and had them converted into a single dwelling, Rose Cottage. My mother gave it that name.

'The location was a lot quieter then. Those big houses, that seem now to be lived in by wealthy retirees, hadn't been built. Greentrees, where Eleanor Holder runs the kennels, was there. But Eleanor didn't live in it then. Later, she and her husband farmed in the area. The Waggoner's Halt was also there, of course, but it was just a country pub. It didn't have the restaurant it's got now. Sandwiches and crisps were all they offered back then.'

Sullivan smiled reminiscently. 'Everything changes, doesn't it?

Later on, of course, after I'd grown up and left home, and my parents were themselves much older, spending every summer there didn't have the same attraction for them. They fancied warmer climates. They started holidaying abroad. Then I married Lucinda. It must have seemed the obvious solution to them. They had a charming cottage they no longer used. But there was a pair of newly-weds, on the lookout for a home. They probably hoped that in time it might prove the sort of family holiday home it had been for them. Lulu and I would take their grandchildren there.' He gave a wry smile. 'But Lulu and I didn't get as far as having children.

'Anyway, they gave it to me and my new wife as a wedding gift, to be our first home. Lulu was over the moon. She adored the place. She told me she never wanted to be anywhere else.'

Sullivan grimaced. 'And that was the problem. She really did not want to be anywhere else. I, however, started travelling the world on archaeological digs. She didn't want to come with me. She wasn't like – Agatha Christie, was it? The crime writer who married an archaeologist and travelled with him, happy to spend her time in the middle of deserts in a tent, washing bits of pottery and other stuff?'

'Agatha Christie,' confirmed Jess in a quiet voice.

'I was still young and, in many ways, stupid. I knew about ancient artefacts, but that was it. I wanted her to come with me to the various digs. When she wouldn't, well, I admit, I was resentful. I started playing around a bit, other women. Perhaps I thought, idiotically, that if she heard about it, she'd change her mind and join me. She didn't. In the end, we decided we'd made a mistake and we parted. I knew how much she loved the cottage and how she would hate to be forced to leave it, if we sold up and split the proceeds as part of the divorce settlement. I was, in any case, spending much of my time out of the country. Therefore I told her I was more than happy to let her keep the cottage, provided she agreed not to sell it without consulting me first. In case I wanted to buy it back, you understand. She was very grateful and went a bit further. She promised that she would put a clause in her will, bequeathing me the cottage if she predeceased me. Lulu wasn't the sort of person who would make a promise like that lightly. She meant it. We split up, and each went our own ways.'

Sullivan stopped speaking and fell into reverie. Eventually, Jess prompted him. 'And Jeremy Harrison? Where and when did he come into it? Was he the son of your old school pal?'

Sullivan started and stared at her. 'What? Sorry, no, he wasn't. Perhaps, if he had been Mike's son, he would have been an altogether different kind of chap. But he wasn't. He was the son of another of Lulu's brothers, a much older one. His parents were killed in a car crash not long after we married. As a result I didn't get to know them. The family members all turned up for our wedding, as families do. It was the first time I'd laid eyes on him. I remember this morose, taciturn youngster. He had very little to say for himself and I got the distinct impression he didn't like me and didn't want to put himself out pretending. Fine, I remember thinking. I don't like the look of you much, either, but after this, our paths probably won't cross again, so it won't matter. Boy! Was I wrong,' concluded Sullivan and fell into introspection again.

Ian had opened his mouth to prompt him, but Sullivan suddenly looked up and spoke again. 'Funny thing, you know,' he said. 'I ran into him a few years later in the Middle East. I was working on a new and very promising excavation. He was out there working at some oilfield. Expatriates living in those circumstances tend to form a club. The oilmen there had formed one and I, and some other colleagues working at the dig, were invited along one evening. I walked in and there he was: Jerry Harrison, as sour-looking as ever. You couldn't mistake him! He was sitting alone, and I got the feeling that was normal. I suppose you might say he didn't have the knack of making friends. Personally, I don't think he cared. He was one of life's natural loners. It didn't worry him.'

Remembering what Eleanor had said to her, Jess murmured, *'The cat that walked by himself.'*

Sullivan looked mildly surprised but nodded. 'Quite right, Inspector Campbell. Glad to hear you know your Kipling! He was pretty shocked to see me, I could tell. He muttered a few words as we shook hands. I asked him if he'd any news of Lulu. We had divorced by then, but I was curious to know how she was. He said yes, he'd visited her and she was very well, living at the cottage. An old friend of hers, Eleanor Holder, had moved to live nearby. I was pleased about that. I was a little worried about Lulu, all on her own in a very quiet spot. If Eleanor was near at hand, that was good news. I had no idea, of course, no idea at all what the blighter was up to.'

'What was he up to?' asked Jess.

'He had set about ingratiating himself, that's what!' barked Sullivan. 'I blame myself for not realising it straight away. But, well, he was Lulu's nephew and it seemed normal enough that he might visit his aunt, even stay with her, whenever he was back in the UK. I didn't worry about it.

'Besides, my own circumstances had changed. I had recently remarried, to Marianna, a colleague whom you've met. So I had other things to think about and, I confess, I rather put Lulu to the back of my mind. I thought she was all right. I was wrong.

Suddenly, I got a letter telling me she had died as the result of a fall; and would you believe it? Not long before her death she had changed her will. She had left Rose Cottage to Jerry outright, with no provisos. It gave me a hell of a shock. Right! I promised myself. You needn't think I'm not going to make a fuss about that, because I am. There was no way she would have gone back on her promise to return the property to me in her will, unless someone had worked hard on persuading her.

'But work got in the way and so did my travels. Then, a few years later, I was offered and accepted the position here as the director of the Institute. The decision was taken for the Institute to organise a dig at the neglected Roman site outside Weston St Ambrose. I must stress that the decision was not mine alone. The board took it. But I took my chance and, while Marianna and I were in the area, looking around and planning what we would do when summer came and a team could work there, I decided to call on Jerry. I wanted to tell him I knew he'd somehow talked Lulu out of leaving the cottage to me. I wanted it back. I would tell him so, to his face, the sneaky blighter.'

Sullivan gave a humourless grin. 'He opened the door that night and saw me, on the doorstep, rain dripping off the porch on to me. He looked surprised, horrified, scared and disbelieving, all at the same time.' The speaker gave a dry chuckle. 'The visit was worth it, just to see that. Dickens probably had an expression like that in mind when he wrote of Scrooge seeing the first of his Christmas ghost visitors. I thought old Jerry was going to faint. Perhaps that was why he wasn't quick enough to shut the door in my face, and I walked in before he could pull himself together.'

'But you had armed yourself with a knife,' Ian suggested. 'You meant to threaten him? Perhaps not to kill him, but to frighten him.'

Sullivan held up his hand and said, 'No, there you are quite wrong. That – the bit about arming myself – is incorrect. *I* had brought no knife. Please, believe me. I did not go there armed and ready to kill, much less intending to do him any physical harm. *He* had a knife, however. That was something I hadn't considered, that he'd be armed. I've thought about it since. He hadn't been expecting me, so he must have got hold of a weapon somehow, quickly and without my seeing him do it. There was a moment. He went to fetch a bottle of whisky; and I think he must somehow have managed to squirrel away a knife at the same time. He was scared of me because he had a guilty conscience. But I didn't attack him. *He* attacked *me*.'

'But you managed to get the knife off him and, what? Did you still only mean to frighten him? Is that what you are going to claim? You killed him by accident?' Carter asked.

'Of course!' Sullivan snapped. 'What advantage would it give me if I went there to kill him? That wouldn't get me Rose Cottage back!'

'Well, as it happens,' Jess told him, 'it might have given you an opportunity to do just that. In his will, he specified that the property and its contents should be sold at auction and the proceeds divided between various named charities. You could have attended the auction and bid openly for your former home.'

Sullivan looked thunderstruck. Eventually he managed to gasp, with such a complete loss of his former bullish self-assurance that it might almost have been comical, if the circumstances had not been so serious: 'You mean, I could simply have bought it back, once he was dead?'

'Yes, Mr Sullivan, that is the case. And if you knew that, it gives you a motive.'

'But I had no knowledge of the conditions of the fellow's will!

How could I?' He shook his head in bewilderment and suddenly looked a much older man.

Behind them, a woman spoke. Marianna had arrived on the scene and they had not realised it. They didn't know how long she had been listening; or whether her husband had known of her presence.

Now she burst out vigorously: 'Andrew didn't kill him, I did!'

Both Ian Carter and Jess spun round to face her. Carter was immediately reminded of his first sight of her and how he had thought her a modern-day Viking. Her hair was not worn in its usual ponytail today, but loose on her shoulders. Her blue eyes blazed. Her attitude was one of someone ready to repel any attack. He found himself thinking, although it was inappropriate for the moment, that she looked magnificent. But that did not in any way excuse or mitigate what she had done – or was now claiming to have done.

'I had no choice. He was trying to *kill* my husband!' she was declaring. 'They were fighting, rolling about on the floor. Neither of them realised I had arrived. I had been worried about Andrew and followed him to Rose Cottage. It wasn't the first time I'd done so. Andrew went down there once before, but that woman who keeps the little dogs was outside with some of her animals. She was watching the place. Andrew had seen her, too, and left with me. We didn't need – Andrew didn't need – a spectator.

'But on that second night, Harrison opened the door and let Andrew in. I was very worried how their meeting would go. Andrew was so determined to demand Harrison sell him the cottage. I didn't believe for a minute that Harrison would agree to that. I had tried to tell Andrew. But my husband believed he had right on his side. The English tend to believe in reasonable discussion.' Marianna shrugged.

'When they started to fight, I heard the racket they made. I could hardly not do so! It was a pity that woman with the dogs wasn't there because she might have realised something was wrong and called the police. As it was, I was the only one who could help. And I had to help, I had to do something.'

Marianna fairly seethed with remembered anger and frustration. 'What would you have done? Just stood there and listened? No, you would have been as desperate to get into the place as I was! But I couldn't open the front door. I hammered on it and shouted at the window. But they couldn't hear me and it was urgent that I get in there. I ran round to the back and by luck, the kitchen window was ajar. I scrambled through. They still didn't hear me; they were creating such a commotion. Clearly the fight was still going on in there; and I had no way of knowing who was getting the worse of it. Of course, my instinct was to help my husband. I ran towards it and found myself in the room and saw them, wrestling for possession of a small knife.' She leaned towards Carter. 'I had to get it from them.'

Carter found himself rewording this in his head as 'I ran towards the sound of battle!' That was what her ancestors would have done.

Marianna let out a yelp of frustration. 'It was useless! Neither of them was aware of my presence. He, Harrison, held the knife. But Andrew managed to get him to drop it. It skidded across the carpet and stopped at my feet. It was an odd sort of thing, with a bone handle. Not very big, but big enough to wound or even kill. Then Harrison saw me and let out a roar, like an animal. He threw himself across Andrew towards me, to recover the knife, before I could get it. But I was quicker. I snatched it up and I stabbed that awful man in the neck. The whole thing was very quick.

'I grew up in the countryside in Sweden, you know. My father was a schoolmaster. Where we lived was quite far north and forested. Very beautiful, but home to all kinds of wild animals. Wolves, bears, smaller creatures. If you went walking, it was as well to keep an eye open. Mostly, they avoid human contact. But if the situation arises, and they believe they are cornered, they won't hesitate. Thinking back, I suppose that is what Andrew had done, though unintentionally. He had cornered a bear. If a wild animal attacks, or even looks likely to do so, you don't hesitate, either, to do whatever you can to frighten it off. If you are lucky, you can frighten it enough. But I couldn't chase Harrison away from my husband. He left me no alternative. To save Andrew, I had to kill the attacker.'

She frowned reflectively. 'And he was just like a wild beast, that Harrison. He had the eyes of a forest creature. You know what I mean? I could see the fury in them, and the intent to kill. But I couldn't see past them into his brain. I could not have made any contact in any other way. Anything I might have said, he wouldn't have heard. He was completely . . .' Marianna paused and waved her hands, seeking a way to put what she meant into words. 'Fixed on making the kill. He had ceased to be human. I was the only one there who could stop it, save Andrew. What would you have expected me to do? Just stand and watch? Of course not!' She fell silent at last.

Jess spoke sharply. 'You had taken possession of the knife, deprived Harrison of his weapon. There were now two of you in the room, against Harrison's one. You could simply have left. The two of you could have just walked out of that cottage and Harrison could no longer have prevented you. You now held the knife, after all.'

Marianna turned her attention to her. 'I was not then thinking as clearly as you are now, Inspector Campbell. Nor do I believe that Harrison was. He might have attacked us as we tried to leave, with some other weapon he had snatched up. You didn't see him and the state he was in. I did. There was no time to think it through; and it was not the moment to take any further risks. I made my decision and took the only chance I might have.'

'So it was Harrison's own fault that you stabbed him?' Jess held her gaze. 'Do you know, Mrs Sullivan, how often I – and other police officers – have heard a criminal blame the victim in cases of violence? They say something like, "He or she was asking for it. He or she threatened me. I feared for *my* life . . ." They can't or won't take responsibility. In many cases they have lived with violence all their lives. But sometimes, just like you, Marianna, they are educated people. They should have known better. They should have had more personal discipline. But they didn't. Whatever had happened that evening, whatever scene you walked into in that room, once you picked up the knife, you – and no one else there – were in control.'

Marianna flushed; but for the moment had no reply.

'Oh, and by the way, we believe we have the knife,' Jess added.

Both Sullivans gaped at her.

'It appears to have been thrown over a hedge near the Roman villa site. A local walker found it; and brought it in. You will be required to give your fingerprints and we are fairly hopeful of finding at least a partial print on the knife handle.'

Marianna muttered, 'I should have thrown it in the river. I was panicking, I suppose. It was stupid of me.' She looked at them with a new respect. 'You are very thorough,' she said.

'We do our best,' Carter told her.

But Marianna's admiration was qualified. 'But I was foolish, and still panicking, when I threw it away! I should have disposed of it properly. Then no one would have found it and you would not have it. So you were lucky, too.'

This was true, thought Carter. *And, of all people, it was Wayne Garley who found it. He might well have not brought it to us. Against the odds, he did.*

'To move on from the fatal attack,' he resumed. 'While Harrison was sprawled lifeless on the floor, you removed his computer and personal documents,' Carter went on now, regaining his authority. 'That shows cool-headedness. You weren't panicking. It would have been understandable if you had both of you just run out of the cottage. But no. You had killed him and cold-bloodedly stood there by his body, and discussed what to do next, and made a decision to search. Why? What use would any of the documents be to you? It must have taken up time searching for everything; and someone else might have knocked at his front door at any time.'

'To confuse any investigation, that is why we took every personal document we could find, and the computer,' Marianna retorted. She turned her attention back to him and appeared relieved to have the chance to do so.

Carter realised with shock that she had read the earlier admiration that had been in his mind for the physical image she'd presented. I, too, should know better, he told himself sternly. She is a clever woman and she knows how to manipulate a situation. He said sharply, 'Go on!'

Marianna was calm now. 'It was my idea. I persuaded Andrew. He wanted us to get away from the place, but I told him we had plenty of time to search. Who else would come to interrupt us, on a night like that?'

'You were still taking a risk,' Carter told her. 'As for who else might have turned up? Well, you and your husband had already done that. Harrison had not expected you, or any other visitor, that night, had he, Dr Sullivan?' He turned to him. 'That is why you chose it.'

'I was more than willing to go along with it, search for his personal documents,' Sullivan hastened to put in. 'I admit I had another reason.'

'What was that?' asked Ian curiously.

'Quite simple, really,' Sullivan replied. 'He was dead, true enough. But I wanted to wipe all trace of him off the face of the earth. You probably think that stupid and vindictive. Saying it to you now probably sounds really petty; and I'm embarrassed to admit it. Besides which, it was a waste of time. Those kinds of records can be recovered without too much trouble from other sources, so destroying them wouldn't do that. After all, I suspect you had no trouble tracing my marriage to Lulu when you set about doing it. You did do that, didn't you? But it's how I felt at the time.'

Ian Carter drew a deep breath and exchanged a glance with Jess. Then he said, 'In view of what you have both told us, it would be improper to question you any further here. I must ask you both to accompany us back to Gloucester where you will be questioned separately and formally. The full interviews will be recorded. I repeat, you will both be entitled to have a solicitor present at that time, if you wish. In fact, I advise it.'

Chapter 15

Jess sat across the table from Sullivan in the interview room, with Tracy Bennison silent and watchful alongside her. She began, 'Perhaps we can now talk about the return visit you paid to Rose Cottage and the assault on Alfie Darrow.'

'Is that his name? Wretched little thief!' growled Sullivan. His controlled manner and calm speaking style suddenly snapped.

'Well, he claims he had broken into Rose Cottage for a different reason, not theft. His motivation, he claims, was romantic. He was looking for a place to meet his girlfriend.'

Sullivan let out a great shout of 'Hah! He wouldn't know the meaning of the word "romantic"!'

'Words can carry different meanings for different people,' Jess said diplomatically. 'I do agree, he *had* broken in. But neither did you, Dr Sullivan, have any right to be there.'

Sullivan said quietly, but in a tone of absolute conviction, 'If anyone had a right to be there, I did. It was my home for every holiday of my childhood and the place I took my new, first, wife. That double-dealing creep, Jerry, had stolen it from me. As I told you, I had an arrangement with Lulu that, if she predeceased me, her will would ensure it came back into my possession.'

Jess sighed. 'I do understand that you may feel that way. But it *wasn't* legally your home, was it? No matter how strongly you felt you had a moral right to it. It was Harrison's. Your former wife had left it to her nephew by marriage in her will. Her reasons for doing so must remain anyone's guess. But she did it. She had made a promise to you; but she had changed her mind. She was entitled to do that.'

'Jerry persuaded her to change it!' Sullivan insisted.

'You don't know that. You suspect it. You may be right. But you don't know it for a fact,' Jess pointed out.

Her reply irritated Sullivan. He leaned back in his chair, scowling, and crossed his arms. 'Do you really understand my feelings on the subject, Inspector Campbell? I do wonder about that. And remember, I knew Jerry Harrison. You didn't.'

Jess waited a few moments, before replying, 'I'm a police officer. My duty is to apply the law. The thing to bear in mind about the law is that it applies to everyone. Whatever your feelings about Rose Cottage, and however many emotional connections you cling to, they don't count.'

'What you are telling me is that that waste of space, Darrow, may be guided by the heart. Preposterous suggestion, if ever there was one. I, on the other hand, may not!'

Jess knew very well that it would be a mistake to lose her temper. But she heard herself snap, 'That is not what I am saying at all. And you know it!'

'Please don't tell me what I know, Inspector, or what I feel. Those are private matters and I don't intend to share them either with you, or with your Superintendent Carter.' Sullivan spoke quietly but there was steel in his voice.

Jess had not meant to glance at the one-way glass panel that allowed interested parties to watch what was happening in the interview room without being seen. But she did, despite herself. It was only briefly, but Sullivan noticed. He smiled.

Jess knew Ian Carter was watching, but wiped the awareness from her mind. She regained her composure and continued evenly:

'We realised you had not forced an entry on the occasion of your second visit; because you had acquired a key – stolen a key, more rightly – since the night of the fatal attack on Harrison. It wasn't taken off the victim's own keyring, was it? We'd found that. Nor was it among the items you and your wife had either destroyed, or removed and disposed of in some other way, when you realised Harrison was dead. You had "borrowed" it from a bunch of keys hanging up in Eleanor Holder's pantry. Later on, your wife attempted to return it, but was caught in the act by the householder. Possession of the key did not give you any right to be there. It was still – is still – the scene of a crime; and police notices outside around the property clearly state that. You were there quite illegally.'

'If you insist,' Sullivan agreed. He rearranged his posture, crossing his legs and folding his arms. 'It is a point of view and you have explained why you hold it. You are entitled to do so. That does not mean I have to agree.'

Jess found this casual attitude immensely irritating, but there was nothing she could do about it. *Ruddy man!* she thought. *I'm not a student at some tutorial he's conducting!*

'I had been trying to keep out of Eleanor's way,' Sullivan was saying. 'It seemed discretion might be best. It had been years since she'd seen me. I was not only much older and wrinkly; I'd grown a beard. But she might have recognised me. She's pretty sharp. No one else around there would have known me well enough. I was a boy when I stayed there with my parents; and a much younger man when I lived here with Lulu. I was away on field trips a lot, even then. So I was pretty confident on that score.'

Overconfident! thought Jess. *Beryl Garley, for one, identified you. I wonder if you realised that, or considered that any other of the older villagers might have remembered you, even after so many years?*

She managed not to say this aloud. But she couldn't help thinking that he probably didn't worry much about Beryl. When he came to Weston St Ambrose as a young boy, with his parents, Beryl, Wayne, all of the older villagers would have been young too. He'd probably struck up holiday friendships, roamed across the fields in their gangs, perhaps hunted for Roman tesserae on the site where, later, he would plan to excavate in earnest. And none of them had liked Jerry Harrison. Loyalties forged in childhood stand the test of time.

Sullivan had begun speaking again. 'But Eleanor was definitely a risk. Despite my efforts to keep away from her, it was difficult because she walks those dogs of hers every day, all over the area. I think she did get a really good look at me one day in the lane that runs past the site of the lost Roman villa. I don't know what she was doing down there, because she doesn't usually walk that way. Call it Fate. I admit it did bother me and, unwisely perhaps, I decided to call in and see her at Greentrees.

'She wasn't around when I went. That kennel maid she employs part-time was there, but she was busy cleaning out the dog pen. The kitchen door was unlocked. I suppose that was in case the kennel maid wanted to go in to the kitchen and make herself a cup of coffee – or use the facilities, as they say. I thought I'd wait for a little while to see if Eleanor came back. The larder door was open and I noticed that there were bunches of assorted keys hanging on hooks screwed into the back of it. They all looked pretty old keys. Some had discoloured labels, so I went to have a look. We archaeologists have curious minds. One of the keys was labelled "Rose Cottage". It was as if it called to me; and it occurred to me that she wouldn't miss it if I just borrowed it. I was curious to go back to the scene of my dust-up with Harrison and check round it. Also, to be honest, I wanted a few minutes alone in my old home, with my memories. I might not get another opportunity.' Sullivan briefly looked sad and broke eye contact. Then he concluded briskly, 'With that in mind I put the key in my pocket and left without seeing Eleanor.

'I hadn't counted on that wretched youth. I was in the cottage, just wandering around, and feeling quite emotional, I don't mind telling you. I hadn't put any light on or switched on a torch. I knew the place, you see, like the back of my hand. I was in the living room when I heard the break-in. I didn't know who it was, or whether the intruder might be armed. I just stood still and waited. You say he wasn't there to steal. I can tell you he was having a good look round. He was interested in the television, for a start. Then, he started to move round the room and within a moment or two, he'd have reached me. So I acted first. I thumped him a few times to teach him a lesson. I hope it did.'

'You could easily have killed him,' Bennison pointed out, breaking her silence.

'Well, I didn't!' argued Sullivan, sounding a little sulky. 'And don't tell me he would be a loss to society, or that he is the sole support of his aged mother, because I don't for a moment believe either of those things would be true.'

'He does live with his mother!' Bennison flung at him. 'And she is on her own!' She caught Jess's eye and subsided. Sullivan's solicitor looked up sharply, and scribbled another note on the pad before him on the table.

'I have to say,' Jess said to her when they had left the interview room, 'I don't think Sandra Darrow would like to be described as an "aged" mother.'

'Sorry to burst out like that, ma'am,' Bennison replied. 'Sullivan was just so – so irritating.'

'Yes, he is,' agreed Jess. 'Very irritating. But, no matter how annoying the accused may be, don't let him rile you.'

Bennison sighed. 'Am I ever going to be as good at this as you are?'

Surprised, Jess exclaimed, 'You're doing fine, Tracy!'

'I see they're sticking to their stories,' Ian Carter said.

'You believe their version of events? Both Sullivan's and his wife's?' Jess asked.

'Do you?' Ian raised his eyebrows.

'In a way, yes, I do,' Jess agreed reluctantly. 'Marianna's fingerprints are on the kitchen window frame and the draining board of the sink. She did climb in that way, as she said.'

Carter looked discontented. 'They, particularly Sullivan himself, have an explanation for everything.'

'Yes, Sullivan has an answer for everything. So does his wife. But it doesn't matter now what you or I think, does it? It will be down to judge and jury,' Jess pointed out. 'It's an unusual case in many ways. Both their stories might seem unlikely to some. But, on the other hand, there is a sort of logic underlying it all, holding their claims together. Sullivan maintains Harrison allowed him into the cottage after he had knocked at the door one dark and stormy night. Harrison later attacked him with a knife. I can believe that Harrison might do that. And his partial fingerprints are still on the knife handle. He must have been really scared when he opened the front door and there stood a man he must have secretly dreaded would walk back into his life one day. I wonder what he thought years ago, when he was sitting in that social club run by oilmen in the Middle East somewhere, and in walked Sullivan, who then proceeded to ask him for news of Lucinda. But he was in no danger from Sullivan then. Lulu was alive. The ownership of Rose Cottage was not in dispute.

'But it was altogether different when Sullivan walked into that lonely cottage, years later, determined to settle an old grudge. I can believe Harrison took an opportunity to arm himself with whatever was to hand, just to frighten off his visitor. But, when he tried to use it, Sullivan managed to get it from him. In the struggle, the knife dropped to the carpet. At that point, Marianna, by her own account, arrived. She feared for her husband's life, picked up the knife and struck out at Harrison with it, fatally wounding him. Self-defence all round. That's the story the defence will put forward.'

'Marianna was correct in saying she would have done better to throw the knife in the river,' Ian said. 'The water is high at this time of year and running at full spate. We could have sent in divers, but I don't suppose for a moment they would have found it. Luckily, she panicked and threw it over the hedge from the window of their vehicle on their way back from Rose Cottage.' He smiled. 'We're lucky Wayne Garley found it; and even luckier that he broke the habit of a lifetime and decided to bring it in to us.'

Jess nodded her agreement, adding, 'The Sullivans claim to have burned the documents they took; and committed the computer to a recycling centre after smashing up the hard drive with a hammer. You can't say they weren't thorough. Oh, and Sullivan withdrew that remark he made when we spoke to him in Oxford, about removing Harrison's personal documents and computer because he wanted to wipe all trace of the man off the face of the earth. His solicitor must have had a word with him about that.'

Ian grimaced. 'You can be sure he did. It would undermine

their defence. You know, if we accept their account of what happened that night, then it's a great pity Sullivan's wife didn't accompany him when he walked up to the front door of Rose Cottage. If Harrison had admitted two people, and not just the one caller, I don't think he would have tried to attack them both at the same time.'

'How many instances of murderous attacks, that have been the result of chance, do you recall?' Jess asked. 'If this or that had happened, instead of something else . . . We just have to deal with the aftermath of what did happen. It probably happened much in the way they described. But Harrison's death could still have been avoided. On the other hand, I suppose, if Marianna hadn't arrived on the scene, it could have been Sullivan's body the cleaners found on the carpet the following day.'

Ian nodded and, after a moment's thought, he added, 'One thing you'll be interested to learn. They have retained the services of a very distinguished counsel to represent them at the trial. Sir Montague Bing, no less, has come out of retirement and is reportedly champing at the bit to present the defence.'

'Good grief!' gasped Jess. 'That's going to cost them a pretty penny!'

'Oh, the old boy is keen to do it. It seems he is an old friend of Sullivan's family.'

The pugs were beginning to recognise Jess. They clustered round her feet on her arrival at the kennels, uttering a few token grumbles. But they seemed otherwise prepared to accept her presence. Their owner showed no surprise at Jess's arrival either.

'Ah . . .' she said with a sigh. 'I am, of course, pleased to see you. But I suspect this isn't a social call. I can guess why you've come.'

'And what would be your guess?' asked Jess.

'You've come to accuse me of withholding information, I dare say that's what you'd call it. You want to know if I had recognised Andrew Sullivan; and if I did, why I didn't think to tell you. I won't deny it. But not at first! I wasn't interested in them at all when they parked their campervan on the so-called Roman site. I thought they were wasting their time. I did, eventually, decide that the grey-bearded older man with the Swedish wife was the enthusiastic young archaeologist who had married my friend, all those years ago. Although I must stress that, at first, I wasn't sure. I hadn't seen him for years and time had taken its toll of both of us. Was that humourless academic, such a sobersides, really the dashing young rugby player who had swept Lulu off her feet? Then I got a closer look at him in the lane that runs past the site of the presumed Roman villa. I fancy he had been avoiding me. But when they drove past and I saw his face in profile, well, despite the beard, I began to think that, yes, that's the man. He had borrowed my spare key to Lulu's cottage, I later learned. But he sent his wife to return it.'

Eleanor frowned. 'I've never been quite able to believe in that Roman villa, you know. But he and his archaeologist wife obviously were prepared to believe in it. Or, at least, to undertake serious research and an excavation to establish its existence.'

She had led Jess into the house as she spoke and they were now sitting, as before, in the untidy but comfortable sitting room. Jade was summoned to remove the pugs. She took the opportunity to declare a beef of her own, standing with hands on hips and multicoloured hair a-tumble before the visitor.

'That history guy beat up my boyfriend, didn't he?' She glared at Jess. 'Don't you let him get away with it!'

She didn't wait for a reply but withdrew, in good order, surrounded by pugs.

'Poor Jade,' said Eleanor, and sighed. 'I was hoping she'd lose interest in that young man. Now, I suppose, she feels she has to speak up for him.' She turned her attention back to her visitor. 'I never did speak to Andrew while he was around the area. He sent his wife to return the key, as I said. She tried to slip in and do it while I was outside. But I walked in on her in the kitchen. We had a long chat, she and I, mostly about his encounter with young Darrow. She told me nothing of what had happened the night Jerry Harrison died.' Eleanor gave a dry smile. 'And I didn't ask. I didn't consider it my business. No, that's not true! The truth is that I didn't want to know. I rather liked her, you see. She's the practical sort, like me. Not a bit like Lulu.'

She paused, looking thoughtfully down at her hands. 'I should have told you, I know, that I thought I recognised Andrew when they drove past me in the lane. I'm sorry. But it was only a glimpse and after so many years . . . I really couldn't be sure. He'd been a fit young man when I last set eyes on him, remember. I'd heard there were a couple of archaeologists camping out at the so-called Roman villa site. I hadn't heard his name. There was no reason I thought Andrew might have returned. I really must stress that. The two of them, he and his present wife, didn't show themselves much. They stayed down there at the site, living in that van. You can't expect people to know who he was – or who he had been years ago. Do you think they were hiding? Sleeping in that campervan, I mean. They could so easily have booked into the Royal Oak in Weston St Ambrose. I believe that later they did so.'

Jess murmured, 'Yes, they did. Perhaps they thought the site more private. The Royal Oak is a local meeting place. People are in and out all the time.'

The reply, such as it was, seemed to energise Eleanor. 'Look!

He and Lulu were both so young when they married. Even while they lived at Rose Cottage together, he was away such a lot. People change. Memory gets muddled.' She looked up. 'He took an awful risk, didn't he? Coming back here? I wasn't the only one who thought he looked familiar, though much older. I think Beryl Garley, who used to clean for Lulu, may have twigged who he was. Something Mary Pickering said gave me that idea. But it wasn't enough to make me sure.'

'What did Mrs Pickering say?' Jess asked.

'Only that her cleaner, that's Beryl, didn't like the archaeologists being there, even sleeping there in that campervan of theirs. Mary put it down to the real locals not liking incomers of any sort and, if the archaeologists had decided to come back in the summer and excavate the site, there would have been a lot more strangers around.'

'Mrs Garley did come to the incident room,' Jess said, more to herself than to Eleanor. 'I think her intention was to muddy the trail. Even now, she won't admit to recognising him.'

Eleanor hesitated before she replied. 'Beryl couldn't have been sure; and certainly not sure enough to point a finger. That would be a serious thing to do, suggesting someone might be a suspect! Also . . .'

'There's another reason?' Jess asked.

Eleanor appeared even more embarrassed. 'Well, you see, perhaps you should bear in mind that Andrew's parents originally bought Rose Cottage, many years ago. The family, with the young Andrew, came down often. Local people got used to seeing them around, saw the boy grow up. In due course, Andrew brought Lulu to live there. That made them, in Beryl's view, sort of locals, too. Do you see?'

'Yes, I do understand that, Eleanor.' Jess hesitated. 'Do you also think that Beryl Garley found Lucinda's death suspicious and thought the nephew might have been involved?'

'Everyone did!' said Eleanor simply. 'And nobody liked Jerry, anyway.'

'It takes more than suspicion and dislike to lead to a police investigation,' Jess told her gently. 'It takes evidence.'

'Lulu would have had her mobile phone in her pocket. She could have called for help!' Eleanor said sharply.

'If she were conscious.'

'I know.' Eleanor nodded. 'We can't rewrite history, can we?'

'No. But it would have been helpful, Eleanor, if you had mentioned at once that you'd recognised, or thought you might have recognised, Andrew Sullivan.'

'I'm sorry. I really do apologise, but I only caught a glimpse of the man, you know, as they were driving past me. And at the time I was trying not to tumble into a wet ditch, with the pugs in tow.'

Eleanor gave herself a little shake and sat up straight. 'If anyone from that Institute does excavate at the site in the summer, I hope they find something! Then I'll have to eat my words and admit there really was once a Roman villa there.'

'In my opinion,' Jess said bitterly to Ian, 'the true villagers all knew who Andrew Sullivan was. But they wouldn't say. In their minds, they were protecting one of their own. In addition to that, they hadn't liked Jeremy Harrison one bit, and may even have suspected, as Eleanor does, that he had a hand in his aunt's death. Eleanor won't give up that theory, you know. She can't accept that evidence will never come to light to prove it. It's a very sad situation, because it eats away at her.'

'Cases we can't solve – or find enough evidence for to bring to court – lurk at the back of police detectives' minds, too. We learn to live with it. If Millie ends up in CID, she'll have to learn to live with the reality that not all cases can be solved, or be proved against a suspect.' Ian smiled sadly. 'Half of me, you know, is very proud she wants to join the force. The other half, well, that's not so happy. But then I've been telling myself that—' He broke off.

'That what?' asked Jess.

'That the hardest thing to admit is that you can't control your children for ever. Goodness knows, it's difficult enough to do when they're young.'

'Too much control isn't such a good thing, is it? They've got to learn to think for themselves. It seems to me that Millie does that pretty well.' Jess smiled. 'And if she does eventually follow in your footsteps into the police force as a career, then it's in part, at least, because she's proud to have you as a dad.'

Ian looked startled. 'I don't know that she admires me. If anything, she thinks I can't cope, not with daily life anyway. I get the impression that we are only a couple of years from her helping me to cross the road.'

'Rubbish!' was the robust retort. 'You're imagining it.'

He gave a wry smile. 'One thing I am certain of. If Millie does join the force, Sophie will never forgive me.'

After all, when had Sophie ever forgiven him for anything?

Chapter 16

Barry Wilson entered the small room behind the bar which served as a sitting room of sorts for himself and his daughter. To be fair, they seldom sat in it. His ex-wife, when she'd still been around, had bestowed the title of 'sitting room' on it. Perhaps she'd hoped to make this part of the pub more of a home. She'd quickly abandoned her attempt to do that and left, but the title lingered.

Barry himself occasionally referred to it as his office, on the grounds that he sat at its dusty table when he had any forms to fill in. Jade never sat here. If not working behind the bar, or helping out at the kennels, she took off on her own business and, of late, that appeared to involve Alfie Darrow. Glancing round the cramped room with its mish-mash of furniture unwanted elsewhere, he judged it critically in a way he hadn't done for a long time. He had to admit it was hardly cosy. That could be because they didn't use it much; or because to make it more of a home space, a homemaker would be needed. Someone who would do a bit of tidying and dusting, run a vacuum cleaner round . . . That ruled him out and Jade wouldn't step up to the mark. She didn't even help him keep the bar area tidy; and the cook's wife already cleaned the restaurant and would adamantly refuse to tidy elsewhere. Quite rightly, of course. He didn't blame her for that. He could have asked his daughter to do a bit more. But, to own the truth, he feared she'd rebel and leave. She didn't mind looking after the bar, because that gave her the chance to talk to people. With a shock, he realised that he had never considered she might be lonely.

Nor had his former wife ever been very interested in cleaning and polishing, he had to admit. They'd never really got along. He'd needed a wife to help set up the pub and expand the business, so he'd married a local girl. His thinking at the time had been that a wife who had family in the area would be happy to stay around. His reasoning had been wrong.

She'd also left their daughter behind with him, and he found that hard to accept. You'd think a mother wouldn't do that. Not a proper mother. Now, he realised that the only way she could leave and make a fresh start somewhere was if she left alone. Jade had always been a problem. But she was his daughter and he cared about her. One day the Waggoner's Halt would be hers. In truth, Barry worried more about the pub than he did about anything else. As a young man he'd earned the money to buy it in a lucrative, if only marginally legal, way as a prizefighter in matches organised among the traveller community.

Even with her discontent and moodiness, it had not occurred to him until fairly recently that Jade might not want to take on the Waggoner's, any more than her mother had done. And then there was the problem of young Darrow. The thought of that useless little lout behind the bar and with his fingers in the till . . . It made Barry's blood boil. He'd sell the place first to prevent such a thing happening.

A clatter on the stairs announced the arrival of Jade herself, wearing her padded coat, teamed with a knitted hat pulled over her ears. It was a funny sort of hat, in Barry's view. It had little woollen ears, pointed like a cat's, attached to it.

'You off to visit young Darrow again?' he asked.

'I might be!' said Jade defensively.

'Really keen on him, are you?' asked Barry.

Jade thought about it before replying. 'Not as keen as I was,' she admitted. 'It was such a stupid thing to do, break into the cottage. He thought he'd get me to go there with him. But I don't think I would've done. It'd have been too creepy.'

'Right,' said Barry. He suddenly felt more cheerful. 'I know you've got your head screwed on the right way. You look out for yourself, girl!'

'I will!' said Jade. 'You don't have to worry, Dad.'

Millie was still very much on Ian's conscience. It hadn't been much of a half-term stay with him. He phoned her the following weekend.

'I hope you weren't bored when you came down here recently?' he asked her. 'I'm sorry I had to leave you with Monica so much.'

'I like Monica. Anyway, it was interesting, watching an investigation taking place, even if,' Millie's tone hardened, 'even if you chased me away from the incident room. That was a public area and I was part of the public.'

'All right, I'm sorry about that!' Ian surrendered. Sometimes it was the only thing to do when a dispute couldn't be settled without more bad feeling being raised. 'But you hadn't told me you were thinking of joining the police.'

'I was waiting for a good moment,' retorted his child crisply.

He could have told her there was never a good moment for that kind of life-defining discussion. He tried diplomacy instead. 'Did talking to Jess help?'

'Oh, yes, quite a lot.'

'Did she warn you that a lot of the things you see or learn are very unpleasant?'

'Oh, yes. Murders and so on. But you get used to it, I suppose? You have. Jess has.'

Carter heard himself say, 'Getting used to it isn't the same as becoming indifferent to it. You must never let that happen. Whoever is lying dead, was alive once. No one deserves to have life snatched away ahead of due time, and violently.'

'Of course not.' There was a pause. 'I have thought about it all, Dad. Anyway, this time the murderers were those archaeologists we met in the pizza restaurant. It makes you think.'

'That's all I ask you to do, love, think about it. And I know you will. You've got your head screwed on the right way. Whatever you decide, you know I'll support your decision. And your mum will come round to it, too, once she's got used to the idea – and if it is what you finally decide to do.'

'Sure, Dad. I know you will. Mum, too. It just came as a bit of a surprise to her. She doesn't really like surprises. She likes to know what's going on.'

Ian thought, *Perhaps that was what was wrong in our marriage. Poor Sophie never really knew what was going on in my life. I'd ring home and cancel dinner, or stay out until the early hours if there was an emergency . . .*

There was a pause, then Millie added unexpectedly, 'And you don't have to worry about Mum and Rodney. I know Mum gets a bit worked up about things sometimes, like my choosing the police for a career, but she gets over it pretty quickly. It's the same with the second thoughts she's been having about living in France. She'll get over that, too.'

'She's told you about that, about whether she wants to stay in France?' asked Ian, surprised. *Not just told Monica, then,* he thought.

'Not exactly . . .' Millie hesitated. 'I worked it out for myself. But they're all right in France. And, Dad?'

'Yes, sweetheart?'

'I'm all right too, you know. You don't have to worry about me, either.'

Chapter 17

The case of the murder at Rose Cottage was long over as far as the investigation went. Fingerprint experts had done a good job and retrieved two sets of prints from the handle of the knife Wayne Garley had found. One set was indeed Marianna's. The other set, to their surprise, had been that of the victim, Jeremy Harrison.

'Well, that backs up Marianna's version of the events at Rose Cottage that evening. It would seem the knife belonged to Harrison and he had produced it, either in defence or attack,' Carter said.

'Sir Montague Bing will make the most of it, anyway, when arguing for the defence,' Jess predicted. 'Perhaps, after all, Marianna was lucky the knife was found. It backs up her story.'

The case, as far as the investigation went, was done with. But it wasn't the only death that had taken place at Rose Cottage, and Jess did not like loose ends. Eleanor Holder had been so insistent in her belief there had been foul play.

Jess also felt there were still unanswered questions connected with the death of Lucinda Harrison. Nothing solid enough to warrant reopening the case, but still . . . It would be nice to be able to assure Eleanor that another look had been taken at the evidence presented to the coroner all those years ago, and possibly set Eleanor's mind at rest. That was one of the reasons she'd requested Nugent to find the coroner's report on Lucinda's death.

The case had not troubled the coroner greatly. It was very sad, he had opined. But there was no reason to suspect foul play. Jess was inclined to agree with him. Only the evidence of the postman who had found Lucinda's body caught her interest.

Mrs Harrison had been an early riser; he told the court. Weston St Ambrose was the first place he visited on his country round; he was always there a little after breakfast-time. By then, Mrs Harrison would be dressed and about the place, perhaps washing up her breakfast dishes in the kitchen, or out and about in her garden. He had therefore not been surprised to find the front door ajar when he'd driven up in his van that morning and got out with the package he had to deliver. She received a fair number of packages of various sorts. He'd called out at the door and fully expected to see her appear almost immediately. When she didn't, he had taken a quick look round the garden. It was reasonable to think she'd opened the door to go out. But she had been nowhere in the garden, so he returned to the front door.

'Elderly folk living alone,' he'd explained to the coroner. 'Sometimes the milkman and the postman are the only early callers at the house.' So he had ventured to give the door a little push. 'I could leave the package where she could see it.' But what he had seen was poor Mrs Harrison, sprawled on the hall floor at the foot of the stairs, still in her nightwear and dressing gown. 'And dead, poor lady. I'm not a doctor but even I could tell. She was already pretty cold. I rang the emergency services and the police anyhow. They told me to wait there until they arrived. My round ran late the whole of the rest of the day. I left the package on the hall table.'

'I'm sorry, Eleanor,' she told Mrs Holder now. 'There is no reason to suspect foul play.'

This time, on her arrival, Eleanor had produced the sherry

bottle and glasses at once. 'Your visit isn't official this time, is it?' she asked as she poured them both generous measures. 'I mean, it's nothing to do with your recent inquiries?'

Jess confirmed this and told her what had brought her. Eleanor listened in silence; then sat for a while sipping her sherry and thinking it over.

'Thank you for taking another look at the coroner's decision,' she told Jess eventually. 'I fully accept that the police can't do anything more; especially not now that – well – that Jerry's dead, too.'

She sighed. 'But I am sorry Andrew was led to do what he did – with the help of his wife. It was foolish of him to go to see Jerry that evening. It was bound to end badly. But, well, Lulu had been his first love and it was only the archaeology that brought the marriage to a halt. The lack of shared interest; not a lack of affection. I'm sure he loves his second wife. But there's a corner of his heart that had always belonged to Lulu. There is never really closure, is there?'

'Personally,' Jess told her, 'I believe you were not the only person to recognise him. The villagers who remembered him and his parents holidaying together at Rose Cottage . . . Well, they may have had their suspicions.'

'Weston St Ambrose people, the real natives born here, they have long memories,' Eleanor agreed. 'And I wasn't the only person to have my suspicions about the manner of Lulu's death. At any rate, none of them ever liked poor old Jerry. I call him "poor old" now. But they say you shouldn't speak ill of the departed. Death is a great leveller, isn't it?'

The day was over. Most people were preparing to retire to their beds. But not all. The night always has a population of its own.

Some of it was human, out and about on private business, not all of it quite legitimate. Then there was the animal world that operated at night. The dog fox, for example. But tonight was different. Reynard was uneasy. He had been following his usual foraging path and had reached the edge of the garden of Rose Cottage. Here he stopped, raised his pointed muzzle and scented the air. For wildlife, the air carried messages, and tonight the fox read 'danger' in it. The danger could not yet be seen or heard, but it was out there, approaching. The fox turned back without a moment's hesitation. He bounded back the way he had come, ears attuned to any new sound, seeking a refuge: somewhere the threat out there could not reach the creatures of the night.

Within Rose Cottage, the fire had been set in two places: in the sitting room and in the kitchen. The first flames had begun to creep along the skirting boards, giving voice in angry little cackles, as if gremlins had arrived and were arguing. Little red and yellow tongues leaped up, licking at the walls. Then the carpet began to smoulder and burn. The flames wrapped themselves around the legs of the table and chairs before moving on to other furniture. The chintz armchair covers gradually turned brown, and withered away in patches as they smouldered. The paperback books intended for visitors to read on rainy days were quickly consumed. Then, suddenly, the flames were leaping up everywhere, cackling like dancing witches, displacing the bickering gremlins.

In a very little time the burning areas had spread, reaching out and joining forces to form proper bonfires. These fires began to roar and throw long yellow, red and orange arms into the air, joining in the crazy dance. Heat caused the window glass to shatter. The orange fingers stretched out into the night. Rose Cottage burned.

At the Waggoner's Halt, Barry Wilson had called 'Time!' three-quarters of an hour earlier, and the last customers had set off back to their homes. He and Jade had gathered up the glassware and Jade was noisily loading up the dishwasher. The machine was a relatively recent acquisition made after Jade had gone on strike and refused outright to wash any more glasses by hand. Barry saw the dishwasher as an interloper and resented it deeply. But he recognised that this had been a battle he couldn't win. He carried the empties to the metal tank that stood there. It took him a couple of journeys. They crashed down into the interior, making a racket that blocked the ears and senses to all else.

Besides which, Barry felt tired. Feeling weary was a relatively new thing at the end of the day. Yes, he'd always been ready to clear the bar and shut the door when the last patron had left. But there had always been that sense of satisfaction the pub continued to do well. He still felt that. Yet, undeniably, something had changed. He couldn't remember feeling so tired, just a year or so ago, at the end of the working day.

'You're getting older, Baz!' Steve, the chef, would say. 'We all are.'

I could retire, Barry thought. *But I don't want to, not just yet. What would I do? The pub, let's face it, is my life.* He looked across to the barn. He was glad the police had packed up their incident room and left. He ought to feel pleased that the shadow of unsolved murder had passed away from the Waggoner's Halt. He was pleased, but still, something lingered, a sense of business left unfinished.

A footstep behind him caused him to look round and he saw the chef.

'Maggie and I are leaving now, Baz,' said the chef. He'd always called Barry 'Baz' since childhood. There were cousins, after all.

'Sure,' said Barry. 'Goodnight, Steve.'

Steve turned away and, a few minutes later, Barry heard his

car drive away. *For as long as Steve and his wife wanted to carry on running the restaurant,* he thought, *I'll carry on with the bar side of the business. Keep it in the family, that was the thing.* But he couldn't do that, not once he retired. Jade wanted to get away from the whole Weston St Ambrose area. He couldn't stop her going eventually. Just so long as that clueless little blighter, Alfie Darrow, was out of her life once she left. However, since that business at Rose Cottage, he sensed that Jade's eyes had been opened to Alfie's many faults and general uselessness. He was now optimistic that, once Alfie had recovered from his injuries, Jade would give him the elbow.

'Where are you tonight, then, Foxy?' he murmured aloud before he turned back to the pub. Before he left, Steve often threw the odd scrap of food out for the fox's supper. Barry paused at the back entrance to the Waggoner's Halt. He looked over his shoulder. There was something different about tonight, but he didn't know what it was. It wasn't raining but a stiff breeze had sprung up. Tired, that's what he was. They were all tired. It wasn't surprising, considering all that had been going on lately. He wouldn't have any trouble getting to sleep tonight. He'd be away as soon as his head touched the pillow.

Barry was right about that. But what he hadn't expected was how soon he'd be awakened by fists hammering on his bedroom door. Someone was shouting. It was Jade. He sat up and called out, 'What is it?'

'There's a fire!' she shouted.

Barry leaped out of bed. 'Bloody hell! Where? Have you called the fire brigade?'

He couldn't smell smoke or hear any flames crackling. But a dusky rose glow bathed the room. The door opened with a crash and his daughter erupted into the room in her pyjamas.

'Look out of the window, Dad!' she yelled.

Barry didn't need to be told. Something was clearly wrong. He ran to the window and pulled aside the curtains. The sky outside was red and the cerise glow bathed everything. A distant crackle was audible. He pushed open the casement window. The crackle grew louder immediately and became a roar. There was smoke now, too, and enough sparks for a firework display filling the air. It was accompanied by an acrid smell and it billowed up, snatched by the wind, and was blown in the direction of the pub. It got into Barry's throat and he began to cough. He pulled the window shut to keep it out.

'Yes, I did call nine-nine-nine!' Jade snapped in answer to his question. 'It was the first thing I did. I'm not daft! But they said it had already been reported and the fire brigade was on its way.'

Barry stared out at the scene. It was as if it were daylight out there. He could see every bush and tree, the old barn, the trestle tables in the yard.

'It's Rose Cottage!' he gasped. 'It must be. Nothing else in that spot is large enough to make that big a fire.' As he ceased speaking, a distant crash was audible, and the flames, released, reached up into the air.

'Roof's gone,' said Barry to his daughter, his voice suddenly sober. 'It's fallen in. Get dressed, girl, quickly! If the sparks blow this way, they'll catch the roof of the barn. We need to get the hose out and start dousing the thatch.'

A distant clamour was added to the commotion. The fire engine was arriving.

Eleanor awoke because all the pugs were giving voice. She sat up in bed and, for a second or two, did not know where she was or what was happening. Everything was red, as if someone had gone round the room with a tin of paint. Then she realised there was a fire; and the source of it was Lulu's cottage. She dressed hurriedly then ran downstairs and out into the yard. It was as light as day out there. She needed to reassure the pugs, and hurried towards the kennels. The dogs were in a frenzy now and couldn't be silenced. 'It's all right, boys!' she called out to them, as placatingly as she could. It made no difference.

There was someone else in the yard, behind her, someone calling her name, a man's voice. She turned and recognised Philip Pickering.

'I'm sorry, Eleanor,' he gasped. 'It's Lulu's cottage!'

He's been running, she thought. *He's run from his house up here. Mary's probably told him to check on me.*

'Yes!' she gasped. 'How did it start?'

But he couldn't know that, she thought as she asked the question. *Of course he couldn't.*

He answered it, even so, in a manner of speaking. 'No idea! But the fire brigade is on its way. Listen, Eleanor, Mary asks if you'd like to come down to our house and wait there with us? Harry and Caroline are already there.'

'I can't!' Eleanor told him. 'I mustn't leave the pugs. As long as they know I'm here somewhere, it will reassure them. They'll know immediately if I leave the premises. Otherwise, I would come back with you, Philip. Just to stay here and know that Lulu's home is burning down, it's awful . . .'

She had read of people wringing their hands in distress, but had never done it herself, was not even sure quite what it looked like. But now she found herself flapping her hands around in a distraught fashion. She grasped them together to control them.

'Look here, my dear,' said Philip gently. 'You shouldn't be on your own. How about I go back and fetch the others? Then we can all sit up here with you until – well, until things quieten down. It probably won't be until morning. I'll bring a bottle of whisky. Oh, Billy will have come along, too.'

'Yes, yes, thank you,' Eleanor gasped gratefully. 'I'll go indoors and light the fire—' She broke off. 'Light a fire,' she repeated in a hoarse whisper. 'Oh, Philip, who on earth could have done this? It couldn't happen by chance!'

'Hold up, my dear,' urged Philip. 'Look, I don't have to go back. I've got my mobile phone here. I'll call Mary and tell her the plan. Then everybody can walk up here.'

A discordant jangle split the air. The fire brigade was arriving.

'They made good time!' said Philip approvingly.

Down the road, in Weston St Ambrose itself, the news had also spread. People watched from their bedroom windows or, in some cases, had even emerged from their front doors in their dressing gowns, to stare as the fire engine raced past.

Monica Farrell, in her cottage opposite the church, heard the clamour and, after a quick look from the window to make sure the source of the fire wasn't nearby, pulled on her dressing gown and went down to her kitchen to make herself a hot drink. She couldn't just go back to bed and fall asleep. She didn't know where the fire was, but guessed it might be one of the houses in Long Lane. But why should one of them catch fire? They were modern, relatively newly built (by comparison with the old cottages in Weston's main street), and probably all had some form of central heating, not open fires. The cat flap in the kitchen door rattled and one of the cats squeezed through. He gazed at her; his eyes filled with alarm.

'Oh, Tigger, there you are!' Monica exclaimed.

Tigger, so named for his striped coat and in tribute to the

stories of A. A. Milne, uttered a mew and ran past her into the sitting room. Monica followed him and found all four cats assembled there. They prowled restlessly around, jumping up on the chairs and off again.

She sat down with her cup and now she, their leader, was there, the cats, with the exception of Tigger, settled in favoured spots around the room. Tigger jumped up on to the window ledge and squeezed himself between the drawn curtains and the windowpane so that he could see what was happening, should there be any more activity.

Not everyone had bothered to watch for the fire engine, nor reacted as it reached Weston St Ambrose and made its noisy way through the village and down Long Lane. Wayne Garley sat in his sister-in-law's cottage, in his accustomed chair by one side of the small fire in the grate. It had now burned down to glowing embers; but still the little room was warm and cosy. His father's baggy old poacher's coat hung on a hook in the kitchen, emitting an acrid scent. Beryl was on her hands and knees in front of the open door of her sideboard and hunting about inside. Bottles rattled and chinked as they collided. Beryl eventually emerged backwards holding one of them. With an effort, she got to her feet and turned towards her guest.

'Blackberry's all finished,' she said. 'But this is the gooseberry. I think that's turned out all right.'

'Fair enough,' said Wayne.

Beryl poured them each a glass and took her own seat opposite her guest. Sammy was in his accustomed place in front of the fire, keeping an eye on the crackling wood logs as he usually did.

'Think the fire brigade will be able to save the old cottage?'

'Not a chance,' replied Wayne comfortably. 'The whole place is full of stuff that burns easy. The roof will go. The only part of the whole cottage that will survive is likely to be the stone outer walls. When those old buildings go up in flames, they go lock, stock and barrel.'

'It always was an unlucky house,' observed Beryl. 'After all, no one knows what caused poor Mrs Harrison to plummet down those stairs. Then her nephew moved in there and he was stabbed; and left bleeding to death on the carpet. Not that anyone is likely to grieve over him. Miserable sort of bloke. It's best that the old place is gone. Do you think anyone will rebuild it?'

Wayne considered the problem, lips pursed. 'Shouldn't think so. Leastways, not to be as it was. Most likely, someone will buy it for the land, pull down what's left of the walls and build a brand-new place from scratch.'

'Oh, then, job well done,' observed Beryl. She raised her glass of gooseberry wine in salutation. 'Cheers, Wayne!'

'Cheers, Beryl, old girl!' he returned the salutation.

Some had yet to learn that Rose Cottage had gone up in flames. Ian Carter and Jess Campbell were sitting over a meal at an Indian restaurant in Cheltenham.

'I couldn't face going back to the hotel in Weston St Ambrose,' Ian had told her, when suggesting the outing. 'Not for a good while. I don't think I want to go anywhere near that whole village for as long as I can think of excuses for staying away. And we ate out Italian when Millie was here. So, I thought, if I booked a table somewhere else . . .'

'I'd love to join you,' said Jess promptly. She grinned at him. 'You were going to suggest that, weren't you? I'm not jumping to conclusions?'

'Of course, I meant for the two of us to eat out together,' he told her.